"A delicious, twisty tale, it features food, friends, fiends, and a mysterious antique cookbook that binds them all. Kate Carlisle's most delectable installment yet. Don't miss it!"

—Julie Hyzy, *New York Times* bestselling author of the White House Chef mystery series and the Manor House mystery series

"Saucy, sassy, and smart—a fun read with a great sense of humor and a soupçon of suspense. Enjoy!"

—Nancy Atherton, *New York Times* bestselling author of the Aunt Dimity mystery series

"A cursed book, a dead mentor, and a snarky rival send book restorer Brooklyn Wainwright on a chase for clues— and fine food and wine—in Kate Carlisle's fun and funny delightful debut."

—Lorna Barrett, *New York Times* bestselling author of the Booktown mystery series

"A fun, fast-paced mystery that is laugh-out-loud funny. Even better, it keeps you guessing to the very end. Sure to be one of the very best books of the year! Welcome Kate Carlisle, a fabulous new voice in the mystery market."

—Susan Mallery, *New York Times* bestselling author of *Evening Stars*

"Suspenseful, intelligent mysteries with a sense of humor. . . . Kate Carlisle never fails to make me laugh, even as she has me turning the pages to see what's going to happen next."

—Miranda James, *New York Times* bestselling author of the Cat in the Stacks mystery series

continued . . .

"*A Cookbook Conspiracy* is another superb entry—and this one is succulent as well—in Kate Carlisle's witty, wacky, and wonderful bibliophile series . . . highly entertaining."

> —Carolyn Hart, *New York Times* bestselling author of the Death on Demand mystery series

"A terrific read for those who are interested in the book arts and enjoy a counterculture foray and ensemble casts. Great fun all around!"

> —*Library Journal* (Starred Review)

"Carlisle's story is captivating, and she peoples it with a cast of eccentrics. Books seldom kill, of course, but this one could murder an early bedtime."

> —*Richmond Times-Dispatch*

"Well plotted. . . . Carlisle keeps the suspense high."

> —*Publishers Weekly*

"Kate Carlisle weaves an intriguing tale with a fascinating peek into the behind-the-scenes world of rare books. Great fun, and educational too." —*Suspense Magazine*

TITLES BY KATE CARLISLE

BIBLIOPHILE MYSTERIES

Homicide in Hardcover
If Books Could Kill
The Lies That Bind
Murder Under Cover
Pages of Sin
(an enovella)
One Book in the Grave
Peril in Paperback
A Cookbook Conspiracy
The Book Stops Here
Ripped from the Pages
Books of a Feather
Once upon a Spine
Buried in Books
The Book Supremacy

FIXER-UPPER MYSTERIES

A High-End Finish
This Old Homicide
Crowned and Moldering
Deck the Hallways
Eaves of Destruction
A Wrench in the Works

A HIGH-END FINISH

A Fixer-Upper Mystery

Kate Carlisle

BERKLEY PRIME CRIME
New York

BERKLEY PRIME CRIME
Published by Berkley
An imprint of Penguin Random House LLC
375 Hudson Street, New York, New York 10014

Copyright © 2014 by Kathleen Beaver
Excerpt from *This Old Homicide* by Kate Carlisle © 2014 by Kathleen Beaver
Penguin Random House supports copyright. Copyright fuels creativity, encourages
diverse voices, promotes free speech, and creates a vibrant culture. Thank you for buying
an authorized edition of this book and for complying with copyright laws by not
reproducing, scanning, or distributing any part of it in any form without permission.
You are supporting writers and allowing Penguin Random House to continue to
publish books for every reader.

BERKLEY is a registered trademark and BERKLEY PRIME CRIME and the B colophon
are trademarks of Penguin Random House LLC.

Hallmark Movies & Mysteries is a trademark of Crown Media.

ISBN: 9780451469199

First Edition: November 2014

Printed in the United States of America
5   7   9   10   8   6

This is for my brother, Bill, whose colorful descriptions of his life as a painter of Victorian buildings in San Francisco I have audaciously stolen for this book. Love you, Bill.

ACKNOWLEDGMENTS

With this new mystery series, I would like to thank a few people who helped me bring it to life.

Many thanks to the brilliant Susan Mallery, Christine Rimmer, and Theresa Southwick for helping me construct the wonderful world of Lighthouse Cove.

I owe so much to Maureen Child for her gentle prodding and companionship on our journey up the creek.

I wouldn't make it through a month without my mystery pals, Hannah Dennison and Daryl Wood Gerber, and their constant support, humor, and intel.

I'm completely indebted to Jenel Looney for her amazing creativity, passion, and talent.

As always, I am grateful to my agent, Christina Hogrebe of the Jane Rotrosen Agency, for her unfailing guidance and enthusiasm.

I'm honored and thankful to work with my wonderfully insightful editor, Ellen Edwards, and the fantastic team at New American Library/Penguin.

It was particularly helpful to grow up with a general contractor for a father, so I give special thanks to my dad for those fascinating trips to the dump. Who knew I would be able to use such uplifting experiences in a book someday?

And finally, a big fat thank-you to my family, especially my husband, Don, whose good looks, patience, and bartending skills make every day worthwhile.

CAST OF CHARACTERS

Shannon Hammer—contractor in Lighthouse Cove, California

Jack Hammer—Shannon's father

Uncle Pete Hammer—Shannon's uncle, winemaker and owner of the Town Square Wine Bar

Chloe Hammer—Shannon's sister

Jane Hennessey—Shannon's best friend and owner of Hennessey House, the newest small hotel in town

Lizzie and Hal Logan—Shannon's friends and owners of Paper Moon book and paper store; their kids are Taz (11) and Marisa (13)

Emily Rose—Shannon's friend and owner of the Scottish Rose Tea Shoppe

Marigold Starling—Shannon's friend and owner, with her aunt Daisy, of Crafts and Quilts

Eric Jensen—the chief of police

Mac Sullivan—a famous crime novelist

Tommy Gallagher—police officer and Shannon's high school boyfriend

Whitney Reid Gallagher—Tommy's wife and Shannon's worst enemy from high school

Jennifer Bailey—Whitney's best friend

Penelope "Penny" Wells—the new bank loan officer

Wendell Jarvick—Shannon's short-term tenant

Jerry Saxton—a real estate agent and Shannon's blind date

Joyce and Stan Boyer—Shannon's homeowner clients

Luisa Capello—a high school friend

Cindy—head waitress at the Cozy Cove Diner

Rocky—cook and owner of the Cozy Cove Diner

Augustus "Gus" Peratti—Shannon's auto mechanic

Wade Chambers—Shannon's head foreman

Carla Harrison—Shannon's second foreman (husband, Chase, and daughter, Keely)

Todd, Billy, Sean, Johnny, Douglas—Shannon's crew

Jesse Hennessey—Shannon's next-door neighbor and Jane's uncle

Mrs. Coleen Higgins—the neighbor across the street

Chapter One

"You could've warned me that installing drywall would be hell on my manicure."

I looked down from my perch at the top of the ladder and saw my best friend, Jane Hennessey, scowling at her hands. They were smeared with sticky joint compound. She had flakes of drywall stuck to her shirt and there were flecks of blue paint highlighting her blond hair.

"I did warn you, remember? I told you to wear gloves." *And a hat,* I thought to myself, but didn't bother to mention it aloud. I wondered, though, where in the world that blue paint in her hair had come from.

"The gloves you gave me are so big and awkward, it's hard to work in them."

"I'm sorry, princess," I said, hiding a smile. "Why don't you go rest and I'll finish up here?"

She laughed. "And have you rubbing my nose in the fact that I'm hopeless at manual labor? No way."

"I would never do that." But I laughed, too, because of course I *would* do that, and I'd expect her to do the same for me. We had known each other since kindergarten and had become best friends when we realized that the two of us were taller than all of the boys in our class. These days, I was still pretty tall at five foot eight, but Jane was two inches taller than me and as svelte as a supermodel.

Despite her delicate hands and my teasing, she had never been a stranger to hard work. This might have been her first experience with hanging drywall, but there was no way she would give up before the job was finished. This place was her home as well as her business, so I knew she wanted to be involved in every aspect of the renovation.

Jane had inherited the old mansion—formerly a brothel— three years ago, after her grandmother died. The imposing structure was a glorious example of the Victorian Queen Anne style, with an elaborate round tower rising three stories at the front corner; steeply gabled rooftops; four balconies; bay windows; six fluted chimneys; and a wide-planked, spindled porch, which spanned the front and wrapped around one long side of the house.

But except for the common rooms on the ground floor and Jane's grandmother's suite on the second floor, the rest of the house had been dangerously moldy, musty, and drafty when we first started to work on it. During our first inspection, we'd found rodents living inside one wall, a nest of bees swarming in the attic, and termites infesting the wood on the western side of the house. The plaster in some rooms was cracked or simply gone. To put it mildly, the place was falling apart. Through much of the initial demolition work, we'd had to wear full-face respirators to protect ourselves from the mold, asbestos, and toxic dust, among other substances.

The rooms that hadn't been devastated by the ravages of time had been ruined by something almost worse: bad taste.

Jane's grandfather had had a peculiar fondness for 1970s-era wood paneling and had used it to hide much of the richly detailed Victorian-era wallpaper throughout the house. The gorgeous mahogany bay windows in the dining room had been covered over with a high-gloss pale pink paint. And in the bedroom where we were currently working, the decorative redbrick chimney had been disguised with fake yellow plastic flagstone paneling. Plastic!

No wonder Jane's grandmother had divorced the man.

Luckily for Jane, though, she had a best friend in the construction biz. Namely, me. I'm Shannon Hammer and I own Hammer Construction, a company that specializes in Victorian-home restoration and renovation right here in my hometown of Lighthouse Cove. I took over the company five years ago when my father, Jack, suffered a mild heart attack and decided to retire.

I had agreed to help Jane refurbish the mansion with the aim of turning it into Hennessey House, an elegant small hotel. It was the perfect solution for Jane, who had studied hotel management and had been running the Inn on Main Street for the past five years. I enlisted some of my guys to help us out, too, whenever their presence wasn't demanded at one of my other job sites. After three long years, we were getting close to finishing all fourteen guest suites. The extensive repair and intricate repainting of the exterior of the house had been completed last week. The day after that, Jane had met with a landscaper to start taming the wildly overgrown gardens that circled the large house. When she wasn't busy working on the property itself, she was tweaking Hennessey House's new Web site.

In two months, she would officially open for business and the place was already sold out. Everyone in Lighthouse Cove was excited for her.

"Okay," Jane said, rubbing her hands clean with a wet towel. "What's next?"

"Once the mud you're applying is dried and sanded," I said, "we'll be ready to paint this room." I climbed down from the ladder and picked up the pole sander to smooth out a section of dried mud on the opposite wall. "And before you know it, we'll be done."

"Hallelujah." There was true relief in Jane's voice and I couldn't blame her for it. When she'd insisted on helping me get this last room completed, I'd warned her that while installing and finishing drywall wasn't terribly hard, it was frankly a big pain in the butt and seriously time-consuming. I admit I'd skimmed over the details about the damage it could do to one's nails, but I figured that was a given.

Many homeowners I'd worked with thought that hanging drywall was a simple matter of screwing some four-by-eight sheets of the hard wallboard to some studs and voilà! You had a wall. If only that were true, but no. You had to measure and cut the drywall to fit the walls and ceiling. This wasn't easy, for at least three reasons.

First, because you had to cut the boards evenly, so that involved clamps and rulers and math.

Second, because drywall boards were heavy and awkward for a person to maneuver around a room.

And third, because drywall had to be cut twice. I could explain why, but it still might not make sense.

And then you needed to figure out exactly how far apart the wood studs were and make marks on the drywall sheets accordingly. This way, you'd be sure you were screwing the sheets into the wood and not into semi-empty air. This involved more math and measuring. With newer homes, the wall studs were typically sixteen inches apart, but with old Victorians like this one, you just never knew.

I could go on and on about the joys of hanging drywall. No wonder I lived alone.

But here was the really fun part: once the drywall sheets were screwed to the studs, you had to cover up the seams, or joints, with joint compound. Joint compound was a muddy concoction known more simply as—wait for it—mud. You spread the mud along the seams and over the screw holes and then sanded it down to make the wall smooth and flat enough to paint.

Once you had a layer of still-wet mud over the seam, you ran a strip of special tape over it. Then you covered that tape with another thin layer of mud and left it to dry, sometimes overnight. The next day you would apply another, wider layer of mud, smooth it out, and let it dry. After one more layer of mud was applied and dried, the sanding began.

For someone unfamiliar with the process, it probably seemed like a great, big waste of time. But, trust me, if you missed a step or cut corners, you could screw up the wall and be forced to start over.

It was enough to make a grown contractor cry.

I preferred to do things right the first time. And, luckily, during those long, waiting-for-the-mud-to-dry periods, there was plenty of other work to do.

"This is going to look great," Jane said, stepping back and taking in the room.

I almost laughed as I glanced around. We were staring at four walls covered in plain old drywall with wide white swaths of dried mud running every which way. A paint-spattered tarp lay over the old hardwood floor. Our tattered work shirts were equally spattered. My heavy tool chest, miscellaneous pieces of equipment and power tools, several buckets, and a stepladder were gathered together in one corner. It looked like a typical unfinished construction site to me, but I knew what she meant. I said, "It'll be beautiful once the walls are painted and the ceiling is spackled and the moldings are added and the floor is finished."

An hour and a half later, Jane and I were covered in fine white dust from all the sanding we'd done, but we were finished for the day. After removing our masks and goggles and shaking the worst of the dust off outside, we washed up in Jane's laundry room sink.

"Oh, shoot, it's getting late," Jane said, drying her hands on an old dish towel. "I almost forgot you had a date tonight." She glanced at me. "I hope you plan on showering when you get home. You look like a raccoon."

"Thanks. And please don't call it a date."

"Oh, come on. You'll have a good time."

I gave her a look. "Really?"

She chuckled. "No, probably not. But at least you'll be able to enjoy a good meal. And Lizzie will be off your back for another few months."

"Promise?"

"Well, no."

I frowned. "I don't know why she's picking on me when you're the one who dreams of having a great romance."

"Because I've already been her guinea pig once this year," Jane said dryly. "I threatened to put spiders in her shoes if she ever tried to set me up again."

Our friend Lizzie was blissfully married, with a darling husband and two great kids. Lately it had become an obsession of hers to arrange blind dates in the hopes of getting her friends married off and happy, whether they wanted to be happy or not. Of course I wanted to be happy, meet a nice guy, and settle down, but the very idea of going on a blind date to accomplish that goal made me shudder with dread.

Lizzie's persistence had worn me down, though, and I had finally relented. Tonight I would meet Jerry Saxton for dinner at one of my favorite seafood restaurants on Lighthouse Pier. Dinner—that's all it was. I refused to call it a blind date (even though that's exactly what it was). I'd never met Jerry, but Lizzie had insisted he was a great guy, nice-looking, and successful, with a good sense of humor.

As I dried my hands, I mentally shrugged off most of my concerns because, as Jane said, at least I would enjoy a good dinner and maybe even have a few laughs.

But on the four-block drive home, I thought back to another one of Jane's comments earlier that day. She had wondered aloud why a man with all those so-called wonderful qualities needed to be set up on a blind date. It was a good question. Maybe he was wondering the same thing about me. I sighed as I pulled into my driveway, knowing it wouldn't do any good to dwell on those questions right now. In less than two hours, I would discover exactly why Jerry Saxton had agreed to go out with me.

I greeted and fed my dog, Robbie—named for Rob Roy, because Robbie is an adorable, smart West Highland terrier—and my cat, Tiger. My father had given me Tiger as a kitten a few years ago, picking her out of a litter because the color of her fur was so similar to my hair color. I named her Tiger because of her dark orange stripes and because she was oh so fierce.

I managed to shower and dry my impossibly thick, curly hair in record time. Getting dressed took a few extra minutes because I was undecided about what to wear. Nice pants and a jacket? A dress and high heels? Jeans and a sweater? The weather was mild for October on the Northern California coast, but the wind was always unpredictable, especially by the water. A chilly breeze could kick up in a matter of seconds.

I thought of the wide, worn wooden slats of the pier and shoved my high heels back into the closet. I could just see myself getting a heel stuck and wobbling like a goose in front of the whole town.

"Boots, no heels," I muttered. I slipped on my best black pants and a pretty teal blouse that brought out the green in my eyes. My short black leather jacket completed the outfit, along with earrings and a pair of black ankle boots. If Jerry was shorter than five foot ten, he would thank me for eschewing the high heels.

The easiest way to get to the pier three blocks away

from my house was to walk. As I passed my next-door neighbor Jesse's house, he came scooting out the door and down his front walkway to greet me. Jesse Hennessey was a good old guy, a former Navy man now in his seventies. I'd known him practically since I was born because he was not only my neighbor, but also Jane's great-uncle. I always made time to chat with him.

"I've got five dollars on you, kiddo," he said, his voice raspy from years of drinking, smoking, and brawling.

I frowned for a second, but then it clicked and made perfect sense. "Are you telling me there's a betting pool going on? Over me?"

"Sure is," he said, and cackled. "It's not every night that young Shannon Hammer goes out on a blind date. Everyone in town wants in on this action."

I shouldn't have been surprised, but I was. And a little creeped out, too. There wasn't much I could do about it now, though. We walked together toward Main Street. "I'm going to regret asking, but what's the bet?"

He snickered. "Either you go home with the guy or you wind up kicking him in the, uh, you know, the family jewels. It's even odds, I might add."

"That's . . . horrible." I had to press my lips together to keep from laughing. Jesse was known for his salty language. I was pretty sure it was just for shock value, especially when it came to me and Jane.

I tried for a serious look. "I'm going to have a perfectly nice time tonight, Jesse, so I wouldn't bet money on either of those outcomes. They're beyond long shots."

"But that's why there's so much cash riding on this." He rubbed his hands gleefully.

"You're all crazy—you know that?"

"Yeah, I know. But what the hell? If nobody wins, the money'll just roll over into the next big pot."

I was almost afraid to ask the next question. "So, which way did you bet?"

"I figure you'll kick him in the nards." He grinned. "Don't disappoint me."

I laughed. Couldn't help it. I knew he meant it as a compliment, but, honestly, here I was, heading for the first blind date I'd ever been on and I was the subject of a betting pool down at the pub. This was life in my small town, and the pub was the epicenter of it all. That's where the betting always started.

And now that we were speaking of bets, I was willing to *bet* that my father and uncle were right in the middle of the action. Which was just *wrong* of them in so many ways. And right in a few others, I had to admit.

We reached Main Street and I gave Jesse a tight smile. "Wish me luck."

"You don't need luck, kiddo. You look beautiful." He gave me two thumbs-up and strolled back to his house while I walked briskly down Main Street and past the town square until the street dead-ended at Lighthouse Pier.

"That was fun," I said, as Jerry and I walked down the stairs from the pier to the boardwalk for a stroll. "But you didn't have to pay for dinner."

"It was my pleasure," he said. "I had fun, too."

We walked along without talking for a full minute, taking in the charming shops and cafés and the colorful hodgepodge of humanity. I was surprised that I felt so comfortable. Jerry had been a gentleman all through dinner: easy to talk to, a good listener, friendly, and interesting. He asked me questions about my life, laughed at my stories, and entertained me with funny ones of his own, too.

He was a successful real estate agent who brokered deals up and down the north coast. His home was in Pentland, two towns north of Lighthouse Cove, which explained why we had never met until that night. He was obviously successful in business and I could see why. He was charming and smooth and very good-looking, tall and muscular with a sly smile and twinkling blue eyes. His attention was on me throughout the meal, and I appreciated that I didn't once catch him looking over my shoulder to see if someone more appealing had entered the room.

We shared a good, crisp sauvignon blanc along with the deep-fried popcorn shrimp appetizer. I ordered fish and he had lobster.

We'd been seated next to the wall of windows and the view of the sunset was spectacular. Because the sky was still light and the weather remained mild, we decided to take a walk after dinner.

After strolling a few blocks along the boardwalk, Jerry stopped and pointed across the sandy expanse to the waves crashing down by the shore. "How do you feel about walking in the sand?"

"I feel good about it."

"Let's go."

Laughing, we stepped onto the sand and headed down to the shoreline. When we reached the edge of the wet sand, we stopped to gaze out at the water.

"I love this time of evening," I said, staring west toward the Sandpiper Islands, seven miles off the coast. "The islands are still silhouetted by the last rays of the sunset. It's nice, isn't it?"

"Yeah." Jerry shoved his hands into his pockets. "I've been told that a clipper ship sank out there somewhere a few hundred years ago."

"That's right," I said. "Plenty of divers have gone down to investigate."

He nodded. "I've sold houses to some of those would-be treasure hunters so I'm all for keeping the legend alive."

"It's more than a legend," I said. "It's all true. Every few years, a gold doubloon will wash up on shore and everyone goes crazy. There's a shop on Main Street with one of them in the window. They'll happily sell it to you for a few hundred thousand dollars."

"I'll pass," he said, chuckling.

We watched the last streams of coral-and-pink clouds fade in the evening sky before heading back toward the boardwalk and the pier.

"I still can't believe you've spent your entire life here," Jerry said. "Didn't you ever get the urge to move?"

"I went away to college," I said, "and a few years later, I moved to San Francisco. I was only there for about a year, and then my dad had a heart attack so I returned to take over the family business. I'm glad I had the chance to live in the city, but I'm happier back here."

"I can't believe you're happier here. I love San Francisco."

"This is home," I said. "I missed the beach and the

trees and my friends. My work. The town square has everything. I love it all."

Halfway back to the boardwalk, Jerry stopped and turned to check the darkening horizon. "I confess I'm still not used to living in such a small town."

"I've frankly never thought of Lighthouse Cove as small," I said, following his gaze. "Pentland's a little bigger, isn't it?"

"Yeah, but believe me, it's small."

"I guess if I'd lived in a big city most of my life and then moved here, it would take some getting used to. But I know this place and I enjoy it. Even when the gossip is all about me."

He leaned closer and I could feel his breath on my cheek. "Why, Shannon, have you been stirring up gossip?"

"Nothing too outrageous." I laughed lightly and took a small step backward.

"Outrageous, huh? Tell me all about it." He moved in again and I inched back. "I want to hear all about Shannon's outrageousness."

"It's time to head back to the boardwalk," I said, ignoring his request. "It's getting pretty dark out here."

"I like the dark." He raised his eyebrows. "You're not scared, are you?"

"No," I said, trying for a laugh, though I had to admit that Jerry was getting a little too close too fast. "I just think it's time to call it a night."

"But we're just getting started." He drew me close and kissed me. It should've been a romantic move, but it didn't do anything for me. I wasn't getting any kind of an affectionate *Hey, I like you* feeling from him, so the whole move felt kind of cheesy. Besides, the walk in the sand had reminded every one of my muscles that I'd worked a long day.

"Sorry, but it's getting late," I said lightly, pulling away. "I've had a great time, but this walk made me realize how tired I am, so I'm going to say good night. Thanks again for a nice evening." I started toward the boardwalk, but the sand made it slow going.

"Wait. No way." He grabbed my arm and turned me around to face him. My purse went flying. "What are you trying to pull?"

I leaned away from him. "I'm not pulling anything." I got a look at his face and saw the furrowed brow, the bared teeth. Someone had flipped a switch and Jerry had gone from good guy to big jerk. "We had a fun evening. It was nice to meet you, and now I'm going home."

"That's not how it works." His expression darkened and he grabbed my arms.

I felt the first inkling of fear and tugged my arms away. "Good night, Jerry."

"I don't think so," he said.

I tried to run, but the sand was like a trap and I was no match for his longer, stronger legs. He caught me and hauled me against him, my back to his front.

Disgusted, I pointed up at the pier where people were still dining and strolling and staring out at the ocean. "Look, there are a bunch of people who can see what you're doing, so just leave me alone. I'll walk away and we can forget this ever happened."

"I say we give 'em something to talk about." He whirled me around and jerked me into his arms. There was nothing tender about the move and it was alarming to see how quickly he pinned me against him. I was strong from years of construction work, but I was no match for his innate male strength.

"This is ridiculous," I said. "Let me go." I pushed on his chest, struggling for some space. But his arms wouldn't give an inch and I couldn't maneuver myself away from him.

"Yeah, that's more like it," Jerry murmured as he pressed himself against me.

"No, it's not," I insisted, wishing I had something heavy to smack him with. This would teach me to go on a blind date without a set of tools. All I had in my purse was the pair of needle-nose pliers I'd used to fix my sunglasses earlier. Not exactly the best bludgeoning tool to discourage an aggressive jackass.

He nuzzled my neck and made a moaning sound, oblivious to my struggles.

"Stop it!" I shouted to get his attention as I arched away from him.

But he wasn't about to stop. Instead he reached up and tried to grope me, but I managed to twist and wriggle out of his way. He tried again and I elbowed his hand away.

"Don't be such a prude," he snapped.

"I'm not. I'm just not interested." The irony was that I would've gladly kissed him a few minutes ago, but now I was disgusted by him. And just a little bit scared, although the watchful crowd on the pier was a good sign that nothing too awful could happen. I hoped.

Shifting quickly, he yanked my jacket off my shoulders and moved in to try to kiss me again. Now my arms were pinned so I couldn't shove him away. I had to contort my head and neck in every direction to avoid his mouth. My head butted against his and it must have shocked him, because he let down his guard for a second.

"What the hell's your problem?" he sputtered, rubbing his forehead where I'd struck him.

"I told you to stop." I used the moment of distraction to shrug my jacket off completely.

He grabbed my arms again and shook me hard. "I paid for dinner, babe. I expect you to show some gratitude." He tugged me close again.

"I'll give you the money back!" Up on the pier I could see people pointing and staring at us so I yelled out, "Help!"

He laughed. "Like they can hear us over the waves." With a grin, he slid his fingers around the neck of my blouse, and I slapped his hands away. We struggled. I tried shoving him again, but he didn't budge.

"Come on, babe, stop playing games."

"I'm not playing games." In that split second while he was moving in close again, I did what my construction guys had always instructed me to do in a situation like this. I slammed my knee up into his crotch.

Unfortunately, he was too close and too damn tall, so I only managed to clunk my knee into his.

"Oww! What the hell?" He reached down to rub his knee and it gave me another chance to strike. This time I kicked his shin as hard as I could and was happy I'd decided to wear boots.

"Damn it!" He pushed me away.

"I'll aim higher next time!" I said. I didn't add that I would need a stepladder to do any proper damage to the big lug. His height had been a good quality at the beginning of the evening. Not so much now.

I kept my focus on him as I cautiously bent to pick up my purse. He wasn't ready to call it quits, though, and I watched him plant both feet in the sand to balance himself, waiting for his moment to attack.

I knew I couldn't run around him, so I would just have to fight it out here and hope that someone on the pier would help. Jerry took two creeping steps toward me and I swung my purse at his head. He caught it and laughed, tossing it onto the sand.

He thought he had me now and leered in triumph.

That's when I stomped down on his instep. He yowled like a wounded animal and hopped around until he lost his balance and fell backward.

I grabbed my jacket and started to dash off—until I felt cold air hit my skin. I looked down to see my teal blouse rippling in the breeze. He had torn it off my shoulder!

I turned back and yelled, "You big jerk!" I was so angry. He'd ripped my clothing! What a Neanderthal! I knew it was wrong, knew I should just keep moving, but I wanted to give him a swift smack across his big stupid head. *Just walk away,* I thought.

I started to move, but stopped when I heard another sound.

Applause?

Looking up at the pier, I saw two men rushing down the stairs toward me. The rest of the people standing at the railing were clapping and laughing and whistling. I even recognized a few of them when they waved at me. What did they think was going on here?

Jerry raised his head and glared at me. "You'll be sorry for that."

"Oh yeah?" I felt safer now that we were about to have company, so instead of slapping at him like I wanted to, I reached inside my purse and pulled out the only weapon I had on me. My pink needle-nose pliers. I leaned over and snipped them in front of his face a few times.

He recoiled. "Get that thing away from me!"

"Just a warning," I said with deadly calm, furious with myself for ever believing that he might've been a nice guy.

His lip curled in disgust. "You're a freak."

"You're a bully," I said, just as the two men from the pier reached us and tried to lift Jerry up.

Jerry growled at them and waved them away so they dropped him instantly. He was either embarrassed or in pain. I didn't care which one it was.

"You're a loser!" he shouted.

"Loser?" I cried in disbelief. "I'm a loser? You're a vicious twit!"

"Prude." He spewed the word.

"Idiot." I leaned in close enough for him to hear me above the crashing waves. "I'll kill you if you ever come near me again."

I murmured my thanks to the two men as I walked away.

"You okay?" one of them asked me.

"Just great." I limped across the sand to the fading

sound of hoots and whistles and cheers. *Only in Lighthouse Cove,* I thought, and realized that some of those people up there might've been in the betting pool at the pub.

Was that the reason an audience had gathered to watch? Had they been waiting to see if we would kiss and go home together? Had the applause come from the winners of the bet?

I wondered if my neighbor Jesse was part of the crowd.

I hoped he was happy since I had just helped him win the pool. Okay, maybe I hadn't struck Jerry in the *family jewels*, exactly, but I'd come as close as I ever wanted to get to Jerry Saxton again.

Chapter Two

I didn't sleep well that night. It wasn't because I felt guilty. Far from it. Jerry had deserved everything he got. Including the kicks and my flimsy death threat. I mean, it's not like I would ever follow through, for goodness' sake. But it felt good to put some fear of God into the man.

But no, the reason I couldn't sleep was because half the town had been out there to witness the fight, which meant that people would be talking about me for weeks. I didn't care as much about them overhearing the death threat, since any other woman would have said the same thing.

But I hated being taken for such a fool by that big creep. To think I'd actually started to like him. It made me feel like a complete idiot.

And here was a question for the ages: Why did Jerry want to kiss me in the first place? I could tell he didn't feel romantic toward me. Had he honestly thought he deserved "payment" for one lousy dinner? I didn't get that mentality. One of these days I would ask a man I trusted to explain it to me.

But back to the subject of my small town and the fact that in a single instant I had become fodder for the gossip mill. Everyone in town knew I hadn't been out on a regular date with a man in years. Obviously, that was what had spurred the creation of the pub's betting pool. So now, if there was someone living under a rock somewhere, even he or she would hear all the gory details soon enough.

One thing is for sure, I thought as I climbed out of bed. *I will never go out on a blind date again.* At least I had some remnant left of the good judgment I was once famous for.

Normally I was willing to put up with the usual goodnatured teasing from the locals. But in this case I wasn't ready to face people yet. As I washed my face and brushed my teeth, I decided I would avoid my usual haunts for a few days until everyone found something more interesting than me to chatter about.

I would have to cancel my breakfast with Dad at the Cozy Cove Diner. I couldn't face being grilled by him just yet. Instead maybe I would swing by the Scottish Rose Tea Shoppe on the town square. My good friend Emily owned the shop and would be sympathetic to my need for a friendly face and some privacy. Right now I could use some quiet solidarity. The only downside was that I would have to make do with English breakfast tea rather than coffee. But fine, I would do it and blame that pompous jerk Jerry Saxton. What a nightmare he'd turned out to be. *One of these days,* I thought, *that man is going to push some woman too far.*

Exhausted after a long night of head-spinning replays of that ugly scene by the pier, I decided to go for a run. I threw on my sweats and sneakers and jogged down to the beach for some exercise. Not only would it clear my head, but it would also keep me in shape. In my line of work, it was important to stay strong and agile. My work was labor-intensive and I didn't ever want to have to shirk any of the physical tasks I made the guys on my crew perform.

The sun was just peeking over the eastern hills when I reached the boardwalk. Others were already out on this brisk, clear morning, running with their dogs or walking to the rhythm of whatever music was blasting into their ears through their tiny earbuds. It was an unwritten rule at this early hour of the morning that nobody had to speak to anyone else if she didn't want to, but I did give a brief, friendly nod to a few of the locals I passed.

At the low concrete seawall that separated the board-walk from the sand, I hesitated. A chill skittered across my shoulders as I gazed at the wooden stairs that ran down from the pier. I hated that I was having any reaction to this spot at all. And I refused to let thoughts of that jerk kill my run or my enjoyment of the morning. This was *my* beach and no way was Jerry Saxton going to ruin it for me.

I hopped over the seawall and plowed my way through the stretch of sand to the water's edge. As I started my slow run south, I concentrated on my breathing instead of the disturbing image of Jerry Saxton grabbing me.

Pacing myself, I passed all the familiar landmarks: the paddle tennis courts where I'd strained a ligament in my knee four years ago; the rocky breakwater where my high school boyfriend, Tommy Gallagher, had first kissed me; the penny arcade where Tommy had won the fake diamond ring I still kept tucked away in my jewelry case; the T-shirt shop where Jane and I got our first real jobs when we were sixteen; the fire pit where Tommy had tearfully broken up with me.

Obviously, there was a time when my entire life revolved around Tommy Gallagher. Those days were long gone, thank goodness, though there was some comfort in knowing that the two of us were still friends.

The sound of my own breathing and the pounding of my shoes against the hard-packed ground drove me on. I followed the slow curve of blond sand that marked the beginning of the Golden Strand, where some of the town's most prominent citizens lived in beautiful Victorian-style mansions built by my father.

The Strand was also the gathering spot for our resident tai chi master to lead his followers, along with any willing tourists and locals, in his early-morning rituals. Many of the tourists who flocked to Lighthouse Cove came to experience the healing serenity our happy little town was famous for. We boasted more New Age healers per capita than any other town in the state, although their number was rapidly being surpassed by winemakers opening wine bars.

As I ran, I found my rhythm and was able to relax enough to expand my focus. The ocean smelled briny this morning. The pink-and-coral shades of sunrise were muted against the stark blue backdrop of the dawn sky. Bold seagulls paraded in the wet earth, dispersing mere seconds before I invaded their sandy territory.

I reached the old Fun Zone Pier a mile south, slapped one of the wood pilings for good measure, and turned toward home. My heart hammered in my chest. The sweat and exertion kept at bay the memory of last night's events. I mindlessly calculated how many calories I'd burned so far, as if it mattered.

Three-quarters of a mile later, I slowed down and began to jog around in circles, moving slower and slower to bring down my heart rate. I stopped running altogether and watched the waves dwindle and roll onto shore, almost touching my feet as I cooled down. Stretching my arms up above my head, I bent over leisurely until my hands grazed the smooth wet ground. Tiny air bubbles rose where sand crabs had burrowed beneath the surface. I smiled at the sudden desire to plunge my hands into the wet sand and dig some up.

The image transported me back to the summer when I was sixteen years old. Tommy and I had been spending the day down at Barnacle Beach and, just for fun, I had filled a Styrofoam cup with a few dozen tiny sand crabs and had run back to the blanket to show Tommy. Rich girl Whitney Reid and her snooty friend Jennifer Bailey were sunning themselves nearby and I overheard one of them say, "Is she going to start a crab farm?"

The other girl snorted. "I swear she's dumber than a bag of rocks."

Tommy had pretended not to hear, but I was pretty sure everyone on the beach that day could hear the two girls talking about me. Tossing them a dirty look, I walked away with as much dignity as I could muster, down to the water's edge, where I released the tiny creatures. I should've dumped the cupful of crabs onto the girls' backs, but I wasn't mean enough to do it.

I could still recall the feeling of impotent fury as my

teenage self dashed into the water to cool off. First of all, I wasn't dumb! I was one the smartest girls in our class. But I couldn't exactly shout out that fact to the rest of the beach crowd.

And second, I was just showing Tommy some sand crabs, for goodness' sake. It's not like I wanted to keep them for pets. Hell, maybe I was dumb, because I couldn't figure out why those girls had to be so mean all the time. I'd begun to feel like I was the personal target for Whitney's venom and I didn't know what to do about it.

Whitney was a member of the privileged crowd whose wealthy parents had been coming to Lighthouse Cove on vacation for years. Enchanted by the beauty of the majestic redwood trees, the windswept cliffs, and the wild Pacific Ocean, many families had moved here permanently to take advantage of the good schools, idyllic lifestyle, picturesque harbor, historic Victorian architecture, charming shops and restaurants, and burgeoning wine industry.

My friends and I had always reached out to welcome any new kids to town, but Whitney and her pals had never accepted the gesture. Looking back now, I could see how important it must have been for them to maintain the great imaginary divide that existed between the wealthy new residents and the working-class townies. I just wasn't sure why.

The rich kids would have been horrified to learn that my father had his own very full bank account, too, after years as a builder of mansions for the rich and powerful. He didn't like to show it off, though, preferring instead to remain the hardworking, easygoing man he'd always been.

My little sister, Chloe, had hated being called a townie, and as soon as she graduated high school she'd escaped small-town hell to follow her dream of making it big in Hollywood.

I'd had a dream, too, of marrying Tommy and living happily ever after in Lighthouse Cove. But that dream was crushed when he announced at the fire pit one night that the horrible Whitney Reid was pregnant and he was going to marry her. Sure enough, the two were wed within the month. In three quick years they produced three kids, an apparently brilliant feat that Whitney continued to flaunt in my face to this day.

Tommy, however, was simply too nice to be an enemy and he and I had remained good friends after all this time, much to Whitney's eternal annoyance.

A seagull shrieked at me, shaking me out of my melancholy reminiscences. Thank goodness. As I slowly stood upright again, stretched and rolled my shoulders a few times, I wondered why my mind had dragged itself back to those bad old days. Maybe it was the ugly altercation with Jerry that had brought all that unhappy boyfriend stuff to the surface.

Evidently I had more than a few issues to work through this morning. One jog on the beach wouldn't quite fix them.

A tinkling bell announced my arrival at the Scottish Rose Tea Shoppe on Main Street. Emily Rose came out of the kitchen, looking fabulous in a cheery apple-embossed apron over black pants and sweater. Slim and sophisticated, she wore her straight dark hair wrapped up in an elegant twist, giving her the look of a beautiful young Audrey Hepburn. She was smart, too, with a wry sense of humor and a kind heart. Even though she was in her early forties, almost twelve years older than I, she was one of my dearest friends.

"Oh, Shannon, love," she cried, taking both of my hands in hers. "I heard what that horrible man did to you. Let me get you some tea."

I smiled at her idea of an all-purpose remedy. "Sounds perfect. And maybe a currant scone to go?"

"To go? No, no, you don't," she insisted, her Scottish brogue coming through. "You'll stay and sit and enjoy yourself. The girls are all here for you, so go join them. Wait." She grabbed a clean dish towel and handed it to me. "You're glowing a bit."

"You mean sweating?" I laughed and used the towel to pat down my still-damp face and neck. "Thanks."

She pushed me toward the cozy back room, which was used for private parties. "I'll bring some treats to you in a jiffy."

Her words sank in. "The girls are all here?"

She glanced over her shoulder at me. "I rang them up when I saw you jog by earlier. I knew you'd have to come back this way eventually, so if you hadn't stopped in we were planning to lasso you."

I could listen to her talk all day long, even though it was occasionally necessary to ask her for a translation.

The tension in my neck loosened slightly as I realized my friends were circling the wagons on my behalf. I entered the back room and Lizzie sprang from her chair and grabbed me in a tight hug. "I'm so sorry! I'm so sorry! It's all my fault."

"It wasn't your fault," I murmured, patting her back to comfort her. She laid her head on my shoulder, or tried to, anyway. She was barely five foot one, but every inch of her was perky and vibrant. Her dark hair was cut in a short, sassy style with long bangs that emphasized her big eyes. She chose to wear monochromatic colors because she thought it made her appear taller. I loved her; I truly did. But I wouldn't be going on another of her blind dates again.

"I feel so guilty." She sniffled. "You could've really been hurt."

She had no idea how right she was about that.

"Let her catch her breath, Lizzie," Jane said.

"I will, I will. I'm just so upset about this and, oh, God, wait until Hal finds out. He'll track Jerry down and punch his lights out."

"Tell him not to bother for my sake," I said. "I already took care of it."

"And good for you! Did you really kick him in the . . . you-know-what?"

"No, but I kicked him in the shin. I was wearing my ankle boots, so I caused him some pain. I wish I'd worn my steel-toed work boots, though. I could've really done some damage."

"The ankle boots I talked you into buying?" she said, brightening. "So I sort of helped you out, right?"

"Nice try, Lizzie," Jane said.

Lizzie's smile fell. "They all agree it's my fault." She still held on to my waist, but she was so petite that her arm barely fit across my back. "And they're right. I'll never forgive myself."

"So you'll stop setting us up on blind dates?" I said, teasing her as I took my place at the table.

Her mouth snapped closed and she glanced around at each of us.

"Oh, Lizzie," Jane said, shaking her head. "You're incorrigible."

"I just want you all to be happy," she said in her own defense.

"Let's change the subject," I suggested brightly, and grabbed the teapot. I poured hot tea into my cup and then added a dollop of milk, as Emily had instructed me on numerous occasions.

"Don't listen to those ninnies who insist on milk first, then tea," she liked to say.

On the walls of the tea shop she'd hung colorful frames with prettily printed instructions on everything having to do with tea. How one held one's cup, for instance, and the proper way one stirred the hot liquid with one's spoon. Placed prominently in the center of the wall was the etiquette of adding milk to tea, along with the reasons why the rules had changed from the days when the way you added milk to your tea could determine your very status in society.

Back in the olden days, the teacups were of such poor quality that they were liable to crack when hot tea was poured into them. Therefore, milk was added first. These days, the quality of the cups was no longer an issue.

Additionally, there were so many types of tea on the market today that it was important to look at the tea in the cup to determine how dark and strong it was. Only then could you gauge the proper amount of milk to add in order to suit your own taste.

Emily, despite her delicate looks and kindhearted smile, was a hardheaded Scotswoman through and through. She was very strict about such things, and there was no way I would ever argue with her. The same couldn't be said for some of her other customers, though. I wouldn't have been surprised to learn that wars had been fought over this very sticky issue.

I took my first sip and sighed with pleasure. It wasn't coffee, but it was strong and good and I was happy to be here with my closest friends. I set the empty teapot at the side of the table. "What's going on with the rest of you? Marigold? How are you?"

"I'm dandy. Thanks," Marigold said, reaching across the table to squeeze my hand. "We're more worried about you, though, so don't try to wiggle off the topic."

I exchanged glances with the other girls. Marigold had a natural reserve that made her opinions seem all the more vital since she only voiced them occasionally. She was close to my age of thirty, but she hadn't grown up around here. She had been raised in rural Pennsylvania in an Amish community. When she was twenty, she left her family and quit the life to join her free-spirited aunt Daisy out here in Lighthouse Cove.

The first thing Daisy had done to honor her niece's courageous decision was to suggest that she change her staid Amish name of Mary to the more quirky and pretty name of Marigold. Together they owned the beautiful Crafts and Quilts shop a few doors down on the square. Many of the exquisite goods in the shop were handmade by Marigold's Amish family and friends back home in Pennsylvania. It was her way of staying in touch and supporting her people, even though she had eschewed their lifestyle.

Today she wore an artsy sweater made of chunky, colorful strands of different types of yarn and fabric. Her long, thick strawberry blond hair was woven into a braid straight down her back and tied with a bit of filmy blue ribbon. She sold the sweaters and fabrics and ribbons in her shop, along with other types of clothing and quilts, and all sorts of carved wooden toys, boxes, and knick-knacks. Wearing her own inventory was the best advertisement she could make.

"Tell us what happened," Marigold urged.

"All right, all right," I said with a sigh, and rubbed my stomach. "I'll tell you everything once I've had something to eat."

"Perfect timing," Emily said, carrying a heavily laden tray to our table. She unloaded a fresh pot of tea and a three-tiered tray of yummy-looking miniature pastries and sandwiches.

"Can you join us?" I asked.

She picked up the empty teapot and glanced toward the doorway that led to the main tearoom. "Julia's working today, so I might manage to pop in and out."

"Good."

"Relax and enjoy," she urged, patting my arm. "I'll be back."

"Thanks, Emily." I smiled as she walked back into the main room. She was 100 percent Scotswoman, and yet to look around her shop, you would think she was a raving royalist. The shelves near the front of the store were filled with all sorts of interesting Scottish items, such as haggis in a can and spiced eggs. But scattered throughout the charming rooms were also plenty of English delicacies along with displays of English bone-china cups and dishes that sported pictures of the queen, Prince William and his duchess, and the royal grandbaby. A flat-screen TV monitor in the corner of the main room silently screened BBC News all day long.

Emily had arrived in Lighthouse Cove fifteen years ago with her boyfriend, an American fisherman who had gone into business with one of our local fishermen. Her boyfriend died in a tragic boating accident a few years later, just days before Emily was scheduled to open her tea shop.

Her friends were afraid that his untimely death would cause her to leave and go back to Scotland. But the tea shop had sustained her through her bereavement and now she had a thriving business and a good life here.

I had consumed three little triangular sandwiches, two tiny almond scones, and my fourth pastry (in my defense, they were all *teensy*) when Jane turned to me. "You've eaten enough, so take a breath and tell us what happened."

"I can talk and eat," I muttered, slightly miffed that she'd called me out for stuffing my face. With a sigh, I pushed my plate away and told them everything about my evening with Jerry. Starting with the friendly dinner, I described the nice walk afterward on the beach and ended with details of Jerry's awkward assault. As an afterthought I mentioned the ridiculous applause coming from the looky-loos standing on the pier. When I was finished, the girls were silent.

I took the opportunity to pop another mini cheese Danish into my mouth.

Jane looked grief stricken. "He could've hurt you badly. You're lucky you didn't end up in the hospital."

I agreed, but didn't say it out loud for fear of alarming

Lizzie any more than she already had been. "I'm fine now. I should've gone to the police last night and I still intend to, but—"

"You must," Lizzie insisted. "I'll go with you."

I gazed around the table. "I really appreciate you all being here for me."

"We love you," Marigold said fervently, then frowned. "I would've hugged you earlier, but you've clearly been out jogging. So, you know, there's sweat."

"Yeah, that's my excuse, too," Jane said, laughing. "Lizzie had no choice. She was forced to hug you because she's guilt ridden."

"I am!" Lizzie wailed, then made a show of brushing off her clothing. "But she really does work up a sweat."

Everyone laughed, including me. Emily came back to pour more tea and sit for a few minutes. I gave her a brief recap of what had happened the night before.

There was a break and Marigold spoke. "I know another woman who went out with that man."

We all stared at her.

"Well?" I said. "What happened?"

She pressed her lips together. "I don't believe it went smoothly."

"Why didn't you tell me?" Lizzie said.

Marigold blinked at her. "You never asked."

"Do we know her?" I asked.

"No. She visits twice a year to shop and go wine tasting."

I leaned forward. "I would really like to talk to her."

"I don't know her too well," Marigold explained, "but she's a good customer. She comes in early autumn and late spring every year and always orders a new quilt. The last time she was in the store, she seemed more nervous than I've ever seen her. I asked if she was all right and she ignored the question, but then asked me if I knew someone named Jerry Saxton. I told her I'd never heard of him, so she didn't go into much detail, and I didn't want to pry."

No, Marigold wouldn't pry, I thought. But I wished she had, just a little.

"I was concerned," she continued, "because she wouldn't take off her dark glasses. I could see a bruise on the side of her face and she looked terribly pale and downcast. At the time I considered going to the police, but then I must've gotten busy and forgot all about it."

Marigold sipped her tea and glanced around the table. "To be honest, her behavior and the bruise might have nothing to do with Jerry, but given Shannon's experience, I thought I ought to mention it."

We all contemplated that silently for a few minutes, and a short while later the party broke up. It was just as well, because Marigold's story had depressed us all.

I spent the rest of the day avoiding people while trying to forget the blind date from hell. I did some touch-up sanding at Jane's place, then ran by two of my construction sites to check on the progress. At both stops, I was encouraged to hear my guys' outrage over the ugly incident on the beach. I assured them all that I was fine and that yes, I'd delivered a good, swift kick to Jerry Saxton, just as they'd all instructed me to do at one time or another.

Apparently the rumor mill had already spread the news that I had kicked Jerry exactly where my neighbor

Jesse had bet I would. I didn't have the heart to mention to the guys that my kick had missed its mark by a few important inches. It would've disappointed them.

On the way home, I stopped at the bank to get some money. I was a silent partner in several of my friends' businesses and had promised to drop off some cash to one of them to expand the holiday inventory. I didn't like leaving a paper trail—which sounded shifty but really wasn't—so I always gave them the dollars instead of writing a check.

While I was waiting in line, a well-dressed, friendly-looking woman with a short cap of blond hair walked up to me. "You're Shannon Hammer, aren't you?"

"Yes?"

"I'm Penelope Wells, the bank's new loan agent. But call me Penny, please."

"Nice to meet you, Penny." I hesitated, then said, "I'm just here to withdraw some cash."

She grinned. "I know you're not here to see me. I just wanted to introduce myself because I'm looking for a contractor to renovate the kitchen in the house I just bought. You were highly recommended by several people."

I beamed at her. "That's so nice to hear." We arranged to meet at her house the following day around noon. After exchanging business cards, we shook hands and she went back to her office.

Saturday at noon, I arrived at Penny Wells's charming one-story Victorian just as she pulled up in a sporty little Miata. She was on her lunch hour, so she gave me a fast tour of her kitchen and explained what she had in mind for the redo. I took lots of notes and we flipped through some kitchen-design books for ideas on ways to finish the room. I checked for load-bearing walls and inspected the attic for any surprises, like termites or holes in the insulation or weird wiring.

"It's an old house, but it's in good shape," I said when I got back to the kitchen. Pointing at the books, I asked, "Did you see anything you like in there?"

"Oh, tons of things. Can I keep these for a while?"

"Sure. Just put yellow stickies on the pages you want to show me. I assume you're going to interview a few more contractors?"

"No," she said, shrugging. "I want you."

"Oh." I was pleasantly taken aback. "Okay, great. But if you change your mind, it's fine. Always good to get a second opinion."

"Your reputation precedes you. Both in construction and in personal-defense skills." She chuckled. "They're calling you the Emasculator down at the Cozy Cove Diner."

My mouth fell open. "Oh no. But I didn't—"

"I think it's great," she interrupted with a laugh, but it faded quickly. "That jerk deserved what you gave him and a lot more."

"You know him?"

Her lips were pinched together. "We've had a few interactions. My bank handles some of the home financing for his buyers."

There was something in her eyes that told me maybe she'd had an encounter with Jerry, too. Boy, the guy really got around.

"I see," I said. "Well, I hope he's nicer in business than he is in his personal dealings."

"He's very charming. But it's all an act."

I sighed. "I can't believe they're calling me the Emasculator. It sounds like the name of some perverted superhero."

She chuckled. "It suits you."

"Thanks a lot." I started to laugh.

"So, you're hired. When do we start?"

"I appreciate the vote of confidence. I'll write up an estimate and get it to you in the next few days. Once you're ready to go, I'll start looking for materials and my guys can move forward on the demo."

"Perfect. I've got to get back to work." She grabbed her purse and briefcase. We walked outside, shook hands, and parted ways.

I was proud of myself for making it through the rest of the day without once thinking about my role as the Emasculator. Especially since a part of me really liked the nickname. I mean, I hadn't allowed Jerry to hurt me too badly. I'd stood up and defended myself, and that felt good. Still, living in a small town where people thrived on rumors and chitchat, I'd do best to keep a low profile. I worked hard the rest of the day and didn't talk to anyone but my guys.

Early Sunday morning I was able to spend a few hours in my garden, weeding and pruning and babying my plants. Robbie and Tiger joined me outside, playing and sniffing and weaving up and down the narrow walkways between the raised beds of vegetables and flowers. When they grew tired of all that fun, they slept in the sun up on the patio.

The garden had been created by my mother, Ella, who was a botany professor and renowned horticulturist. She had expanded the garden until it filled every inch of our large backyard, right up to the fence where she experimented with espaliered apple and peach trees.

She taught us how to start a worm farm and grow string beans on a kid-sized teepee. I still remembered the sound of her laughter as she tried to teach my sister and me the Latin names of plants. She died when I was ten years old, and after that the garden became overgrown and weed infested.

It wasn't until I broke up with Tommy years later that I rediscovered some of the joy she'd inspired in me. It had started as a way to keep busy so I wouldn't go crazy, but I spent hours every day that summer cleaning, weeding, cultivating, and expanding the flower beds and adding herbs and more vegetables around the perimeter. Gardening became my solace. I cleaned out the old equipment shed and turned it into a garden room, where I would hang herb cuttings and dry flowers. I made potpourri and experimented with tinctures. I canned green beans and tomatoes in thick jars with basil and rosemary sprigs. I steeped herbs in oils and vinegars and gave them away as gifts.

I worked like a dog every day and went to bed exhausted every night. I did whatever it took to avoid staring at the sudden gaping hole that was my life. My mother's garden saved my sanity.

To tell the truth, it hadn't taken me long to get over Tommy's betrayal because, hey, karma was a bitch named

Whitney and he was stuck with her. Besides, once I went off to college and met other guys, I realized I could no longer blame Tommy for much of anything. No, my problems with men were all my own fault. I wasn't quite sure why, but I'd done something horrible to irritate the dating gods.

For example, I met my first college boyfriend in American history class. Alan was so cute. We talked all the time and connected on every level. He loved my friends and always gave the best advice on what to wear to parties and school events. There was only one problem. The morning after our first night together, Alan confessed that he was gay. Not the most flattering thing a girl wants to hear.

And then the year I lived in San Francisco, I met another really great guy. He picked me up in a gorgeous vintage Corvette and we drove across the bridge to Sausalito for dinner. Halfway through our date, he was arrested for stealing the car.

I could now add Jerry Saxton to my list of disasters. As an acknowledged magnet for dating nightmares, why was I so surprised when my evening with Jerry Saxton had turned out so badly?

Meanwhile, I had managed to steer clear of Tommy and Whitney for those few years. But once I'd moved back to town and taken over Dad's company, I realized I would be running into Tommy everywhere I went. Not just randomly around Lighthouse Cove, but all the time. Tommy had joined the police department, which shared a parking lot with City Hall. Part of my job as a general contractor was to file building permits and check on various statutes and zoning information to make sure my company was always in compliance with the local codes and regulations. And I did all of that at City Hall.

So one of the first things I did when I took over the business was track down Tommy and inform him that we were going to remain friends whether he liked it or not. He didn't realize we'd ever stopped, but that was Tommy for you.

After that talk with Tommy, I was able to relax and move along with my life. But lately I felt like I was waiting for something to happen. I just didn't know what. I would look at my friends and wonder if they were happy. Was I happy? I found myself guarding my heart and wondered, *From whom?* Maybe that was why I had finally agreed to go out with Jerry. I needed to shake things up. Unfortunately, given my past experiences, I should've known better.

So, now I was stuck back in that loop of waiting for something to happen and not knowing what. And for someone as proactive as I was, that feeling could drive me a little crazy.

So, I worked. In the garden. At my construction sites. With my friends. I ran on the beach and worked out at the gym. I bundled flowers and dried herb cuttings to give to neighbors and my friends, who used them to decorate their town square shops.

It all helped, but I still couldn't get rid of that antsy, unsettled feeling. It was like a dream where you knew something important was about to happen but you weren't sure if you were wearing the right outfit. Okay, bad analogy. Let's just say it was all very weird.

And the ugly confrontation with Jerry Saxton hadn't exactly improved my mood.

When that edgy feeling got really bad, I would go swimming or take a long drive, or I'd go shopping, usually at the hardware store. Everyone felt better when they had a new tool to play with, right? But I was afraid a new power drill wouldn't fix things this time.

Sunday afternoon, I spent two hours cleaning and preparing one of the guest apartments over my garage for the tenant who would arrive the next day.

A few years ago, I had decided I could make a little extra money by cleaning out the big old storage room over our four-car garage and turning it into rental space. I hired one of my guys and we refurbished it, creating two good-sized guest suites, both with bathrooms and kitchenettes. I reinforced the stairway and repainted the fanciful wrought-iron railing. Outside each door I arranged a patio chair and side table for reading or dozing in the sun.

When I was finished, I took pictures and posted them on the town's Web site with some details and room rates. Each suite had an ocean view out the bay window and was furnished with a small dining table and chairs, a king-sized bed, and two nightstands, plus a love seat and a comfortable lounge chair for reading or watching TV. There was space for a compact desk and matching chair, too, and I threw in free Wi-Fi to attract business travelers.

These days, I was able to keep both spaces rented for five months out of the year. The rent money went into my emergency fund, which I accessed only for emergencies. Duh.

I wasn't really happy about the tenant who would be

arriving the next day, but I'd had no choice in accepting him. Wendell Jarvick showed up for two weeks each fall and did nothing but whine the whole time. Everyone in town knew and hated him because he complained about his meals, his bed, the insects, the sand, the ocean, the crowds, the weather—everything. Some of the towns-people swore he brought the bugs with him.

One of Wendell's biggest complaints was that he could never get the same hotel room two years in a row. There was a reason for that, but no one was about to explain it to him. The fact was, we had all conspired to spread the pain so no one person or establishment would have to put up with the obnoxious man for two years running.

This year, it was my turn. Wendell would arrive to-morrow and stay for two weeks, much to my dismay. And probably his, too.

I had just finishing polishing the table surfaces when my cell phone rang. It was Stan Boyer, the new owner of a house I was renovating, a once-noble but now broken-down Victorian at South Cove, as we called the southern end of Alisal Cliffs, overlooking the beach.

"I just got a call from the neighbors," Stan said. "They were out walking their dog and heard water running over at our place. My wife and I are still in San Fran-cisco, so I'm hoping you might have time to drive by and check it out."

"I'll go right now." I didn't want more water damage on top of everything else that was wrong with that house. There was an old sump pump located in the dilapidated basement. I had a feeling that's where the problem might be. I glanced at my watch. I still had a few hours of daylight left. "I'll call and let you know if there's a problem."

I took a last look around the guest suite to make sure everything was ready for Wendell's arrival. Then I ran downstairs and into the house to grab my purse and an emergency tool kit, just in case.

It was getting chilly by the time I reached the Boyers' historic Victorian home. It had been built in 1870 in classic Second Empire style with its tall, narrow lines and high mansard roof. The style had never been one of my favorites, although I suppose it had its charms. It always reminded me of the Addams Family house or, worse, the house on the hill in the movie *Psycho*. What can I say? I was an impressionable kid when I first saw that movie.

It didn't help that the house had been built on a jagged rock cliff away from the other homes in the area, which gave it a dark, desolate feeling. But maybe that was just my imagination.

I climbed the front stairs cautiously, since two of the planks had rotted out. I stood at the front door for a few seconds and listened. Sure enough, water was running somewhere in the house. Maybe it was just a toilet and I could jiggle the handle and leave. But life was rarely that simple.

The basement stairs were accessed through a door off the kitchen. My workers and I kept the door locked because the deteriorating wood stairs were so dangerous. We had run ropes along the sides of the stairwell for the guys to grip when going up or down and we'd fashioned a ramp made of a long row of two-by-fours nailed together. But it was still a precarious descent.

I unlocked the door and heard the water rumble louder. *Definitely the sump pump,* I thought. I pulled the string that dangled above my head to turn on the light, but nothing happened.

"Damn bulb must've burned out," I muttered, and went out to the truck to get my flashlight. No way was I navigating down there without a light.

The flashlight threw wild shadows onto the walls of the narrow stairwell. I had to aim it downward to make sure I didn't take a tumble, especially since the ramp was so steep and not bolted down yet. I clung to the rope with one hand and held my breath as I tiptoed the rest of the way down.

The sump pump was at the far end of the cavernous room. I could hear the water gushing now. The drainage basin must've become obstructed somehow. I moved carefully across the room, avoiding the low-hanging beams and the heavy columns of wood that held up the house.

Even with my flashlight guiding the way, I almost tripped over something on the floor.

It was an arm.

My heart was pounding in double time and I trembled so hard I almost fell. There was a man lying facedown on the cold, broken foundation, his arms flung out from his body. My flashlight beam was wavering, but I managed to train it directly at the man's head.

I backed up and almost tripped against one of the new weight-bearing posts. I squeezed my eyes shut but I could still see the blood caked to his temple where someone had bludgeoned him with something like a baseball bat.

Chills crept down my spine as I recognized the face of the man whose blood had pooled on the floor beneath his cheek. It was Jerry Saxton, my blind date from the other night. He was dead.

Chapter Three

I sat at the top of the stairs outside on the front porch and watched the two police cruisers pull up in front of the Boyers' house. Only minutes ago, I'd raced out of the house and called the police faster than I'd ever done anything in my life.

Tommy Gallagher slammed the door of his cop car and strolled up the walkway. When he reached the base of the stairs he stopped with his hands on his hips and grinned up at me. "Hey, Shannon. Looking good."

I would've laughed if I wasn't still shaking. Tommy was the only guy I knew who would greet someone so cheerfully at a murder scene.

"Hi, Tommy."

The man was always in a good mood. *He has never been a raving genius,* I thought sentimentally, *but he is a good-hearted man.* And still cute, too, with a ready smile, twinkling eyes, sun-bleached hair, and a rangy build. I was glad we'd managed to stay friends despite his really bad taste in wives.

He turned to watch his boss approach. "Have you met our new police chief?"

"Not officially," I said. A new police chief was big news, so I'd certainly heard of him and seen him around town a few times. But up close, he was even more imposing than I'd thought before. He stood about six foot four, with dark blond hair brushed back from his forehead. His police-issue bomber jacket couldn't disguise the fact that he had muscles on his muscles.

And he was, well, adorable. Honestly, the guy looked like the movie-star version of some Nordic god. He probably practiced making angry faces in the mirror, just so he'd be taken seriously.

"Chief," Tommy said, "this is Shannon Hammer. She found the body. Shannon, say hello to Eric Jensen, chief of police."

I was right. Nordic. So here I was, a girl named Hammer, staring at a guy who looked like Thor. Coincidence? *Why hasn't Lizzie tried to set me up on a blind date with him?* I wondered, and quickly shook the thought away. *No more blind dates, remember?* Besides, Chief Jensen might be married. Except I hadn't heard about him moving here with a wife.

He stared back at me, unsmiling, his dark blue eyes studying me. It was the complete opposite of the cheery greeting I'd received from Tommy. "Ms. Hammer."

I nodded. "Chief Jensen."

"You Jack's daughter?"

"Yes."

"Nice guy," he said with a somber nod. "I've run into him at the pub a few times."

It was good to know he liked my father. So maybe he wouldn't throw me into a dank, windowless dungeon, which was the vibe I was getting from him at the moment.

"You found the deceased," he said.

Tripped over. Found. Same thing. "Yes. Down in the basement."

Chief Jensen rested one hand casually on the butt of his gun and glanced around. "Is this your home?"

"No." Because of his blunt questions, I was tempted to leave it at that, but I relented. "I'm renovating this house for the owners, Stan and Joyce Boyer. I'm a contractor. One of the neighbors reported hearing water running so I came out to investigate."

He nodded slowly, glanced around the front yard, then back at me. "Please wait out here." He started to walk up the stairs.

"Stop," I said.

He raised one eyebrow. "Beg your pardon?"

Yes, he was being uptight, but it sort of went with the territory, I guessed. I couldn't let him break his neck, after all. "That plank you're about to step on is rotten. You'll fall through if you put too much pressure on it."

He started to skip the step.

"Stay on the far left edge and you'll be okay."

He probably hated following my advice, but he wasn't stupid. He took the step, then halted. "Now what?"

"The next one's fine."

He climbed another step and waited until I said, "That one's good on the right side."

Following my directions, he made it all the way to the top and then stood on the porch staring down at me. His lips twitched as he asked, "Any other hazards I should know about? Minefields? Falling ceilings?"

"Not right away. Go straight down the hall to the kitchen. It's on your left. On the far side of the refrigerator is an interior door that leads to the basement. It's unlocked, but here's where it gets tricky. Watch your step going down, because there's no light and the stairs are gone so you'll have to negotiate a precarious ramp to get all the way down."

He nodded, glanced around some more, and finally jerked his chin toward the front door. "Come on. Show me."

"How can I resist such a kind invitation?" I muttered, and stood and brushed off my jeans.

Tommy chuckled and followed the two of us inside. We made it slowly down the ramp with only a few curse words muttered. I led the way across the cold room and stepped aside so the two cops could check out the body.

Tommy homed in with his flashlight. "Hey, isn't that Jerry Saxton?"

"Yes, it is," I said.

Tommy grinned at me. "Heard about your big fight on the beach the other night." With a nod of approval, he added, "Heard you got him good. That's my girl."

The chief glanced over his shoulder. "Got him good?"

"Yeah," Tommy said, with a little too much enthusiasm. "She kicked him in the family jewels and threatened to . . ."

My eyes goggled and Tommy's voice faded as he realized what he was saying. He inched away from me, knowing he was in big trouble.

Jensen gazed steadily at me. "Threatened to . . . what?"

"Nothing, Chief," Tommy said quickly.

The chief's gaze didn't waver from mine. "I've heard some of this story. So, you knew the deceased."

"No," I protested. "Well, not exactly. We went out on one date. That was enough. And, yes, I kicked him, but not in the . . . oh, never mind." I'd already realized that nobody wanted to hear the true story of what had happened that night on the beach.

He studied me in the glare of the flashlight for a long moment. "But you did threaten to kill him."

"Yes, because he attacked me viciously," I countered, hating the defensiveness in my voice. "It was just a figure of speech. I didn't kill him." Under my breath I added, "But I don't blame whoever did."

He glanced down at the body, then back at me. "You think he deserved to die?"

"I think he was a violent misogynist. It was only a matter of time." I moved toward the ramp. "I'll wait outside, if you don't mind."

I went back to the front porch and sat on the steps, trying to calculate my chances of staying out of jail. They weren't good, for at least three reasons. First, not only had I kicked Jerry the other night after he'd assaulted me, but I had threatened to kill him, as well. Loudly. In front of witnesses. On the upside, though, those same witnesses had seen him attack me first.

Second, I was the lucky one who had found his dead body. A coincidence, yes. Absolutely. But what were the odds of convincing Thor of that?

Let's be logical, I thought. *If I'd killed Jerry Saxton, why would I be dumb enough to report the body and then stick around until the police arrived?*

Excellent point, I said to myself. The police couldn't possibly accuse me of murder if they were being sensible about it.

On the other hand, they might come up with any number of contradictory scenarios. Maybe I had lured Jerry to the basement of this old house, tempting him with promises of an assignation. I'd been lying in wait, and when he arrived, I snuck up behind him, and coshed him over the head.

I definitely would've had to sneak up on Jerry, because there was no way he'd have let me get close to him again. But Chief Jensen didn't know that.

A third glaring mark against me was that I was the general contractor for the Boyers' rehab. I had complete access to this house. I had a reason to be here, but what was Jerry's excuse? Did he know the Boyers?

I heard footsteps and shifted around. Chief Jensen was backlit by the entry light shining through the open doorway. *Those are some big shoulders,* I thought. Then I noticed he was holding a heavy pipe wrench in one gloved hand.

"Is this yours, Ms. Hammer?"

I jumped up and stared at the wrench. It was pink. My dad had bought me a complete set of sturdy pink tools when I took over the company from him. That wrench was part of the set. I finally met Jensen's calm gaze. "What are you doing with that?"

"Found it at the bottom of the sump basin, under a few feet of really foul water. It was wrapped in this towel." He held up a soggy, dirty, disgusting towel. "That's what was clogging the drain."

I tried to swallow, but my throat had gone dry. "Is the wrench . . . Is that the murder weapon?"

"Is it yours?"

My stomach lurched. I was biting my lip so hard, I could taste blood. "I think so."

"Did you notice it was missing?"

"No. I leave a tool chest here, so I don't know if it was missing or not. I . . . I like to keep some of my tools on-site when I'm working on a long-term job. It's just easier, you know? I have so many tools and some are pink and some aren't, but . . ." I was babbling, so I shut up.

"I'm going to need you to come down to the police station right now."

It was hard to breathe. "Am I under arrest?"

"Not yet," he said, sounding reasonable. "We just need to ask you some questions."

That wasn't good. I'd seen enough TV crime shows to know that much. I nodded dumbly. "I think I'll call my dad."

While I talked to my dad on my cell phone, I wandered around to the back of the house, away from the big ears of the police.

"I'll meet you at the station," Dad said immediately. "We'll straighten this whole thing out."

"He thinks I'm guilty," I whispered.

"No, he doesn't, sweetheart," he assured me. "He's not a stupid man. Just tell him the truth and you'll be out of there in no time."

After ending the call, I gripped the old porch railing and stared out at the water. The waves were calmer along this part of the shore, due to the wide arc of land that swept around to the south to create the so-called cove that gave our town its name.

I smiled at Dad's promise to straighten this whole thing out. I knew he couldn't really do anything, but it was a relief that someone who loved me would be nearby in case something bad happened. As I walked back to the front of the house, my unsettling thoughts were interrupted by a quiet conversation I could hear taking place near the front door.

"Not a good idea, Tom." It was the police chief talking. "Just leave her truck here."

"It won't be safe out here overnight," Tommy said.

"She should've thought of that before . . ."

I didn't catch the last part of the chief's comment but I had a feeling it wasn't complimentary.

"I've known her my whole life, Chief. I'll follow her to the station. There won't be any problems." I appreciated Tommy's vote of confidence.

"You know her well enough to vouch for her?" the chief asked sharply.

Tommy hesitated, then said, "I would trust her with my life."

Hot tears sprang to my eyes, a rare occurrence. I'd always known Tommy was a good friend, but hearing him defend me to his boss, especially with everything that was going on, meant a lot.

It also meant something to know that the chief of police didn't trust me to drive my own car to the station. That made me so angry, I wanted to spit nails. But I would just have to live with his attitude. Thor was new in town. He didn't know me. Didn't know who to trust and who to suspect. I could only hope that he was good enough at his job to learn quickly.

I wiped my eyes and sniffled once, composing myself

before coming into view. Another patrol car had arrived and two more cops I recognized were scanning the yard in front of the house.

"Get your keys, Shannon," Tommy said casually. "I'll follow you to the station."

"Okay." I gave the chief a prickly look as I passed him. He raised that one eyebrow again, and even though I couldn't see him as I walked down the steps, I knew his gaze never steered away from me.

When I reached the walkway, I turned to look up at him and cursed silently. Damn it, why did he have to be so compelling? It was disconcerting to distrust him so much and feel this attraction to him at the same time.

I would be smart to ignore his appeal and concentrate on the fact that he considered me a murder suspect, someone who would flee the scene to avoid his cop questions.

The two officers who had just arrived were preparing to dust the front stair rail and doorway for fingerprints. Jensen asked them to also survey the neighbors and take note of anything unusual while they waited for the county coroner to arrive. Tommy and the chief followed me back to the station in their SUVs.

Fifteen minutes later, we all pulled into the parking lot of the Lighthouse Cove Police Station. I saw my uncle Pete's truck and figured he was here, too. I was happy to have all the support I could get. I just hoped they hadn't stopped at the pub first to start a new betting pool.

"I'd like to go over it from the beginning again," Chief Jensen said as he flipped a page in his notepad. "What were you doing out at the Boyers' house on a Sunday afternoon?"

It was the fourth or maybe fifth time the chief had posed the same question over the past two hours. Was he trying to get me to flub my answers? He'd also been called out of the conference room twice, something that unnerved me because I was stuck waiting and wondering what would happen next. Maybe he was getting reports from the crime scene or stories from other witnesses, whoever they might be. Maybe he'd found the real killer. So what was I still doing here?

The last time he'd left the interrogation room, I had asked him to please send my father and uncle home. It was no use having them hang around and wait for me. I would fill them in on things once I got home. *If* I was ever allowed to go home.

I gazed at the chief and tried to appear patient and helpful—if you ignored my clenched teeth. "As I already told you, I got a call from Mr. Boyer, who asked me to swing by and check to see if there was water running somewhere in the house. He said he was still in San Francisco and couldn't get here for a while."

"And he heard about the running water from a neighbor."

"That's what he told me."

Jensen skimmed a few pages of his notepad. "We've talked to all the neighbors and nobody claims to have called the owners."

I frowned at him, confused. This was the first time I'd heard that. "But that's what Stan told me. Why would he lie? He said that one of his neighbors called him. You should track him down and ask him the same question.

Or maybe your guys missed one of the neighbors. You might want to follow up with them."

He ignored my useful suggestions as he scanned his notes. "Did Mr. Boyer reach you on your home phone or your cell?"

"My cell phone." *My cell phone!* I quickly rummaged through my purse and pulled it out, feeling victorious. I slid my finger across the screen and handed it to him. "See? Here's my list of recent phone calls."

He stared at the screen for a long moment and I wanted to snatch it back from him. Was I showing him too much? Was he memorizing the names of the other people I'd talked to recently? But then he tapped the Boyers' icon and it took him to another screen that listed whether the call had been incoming or outgoing, the time and date of the call, and how long it lasted.

He took his time studying the info screen, then wrote the details down on his notepad. He handed the phone back to me and I let go of a breath I didn't realize I was holding. "So that proves it, right?"

"There's still the matter of that death threat on the beach."

Could he see the steam coming out of my ears? How many times did I have to explain myself? "I've already gone over that with you," I said carefully. "What else do you want to know?"

"You must've been pretty angry to resort to threatening him with murder."

"Haven't you ever been that furious with someone?"

"No."

I scoffed. "I don't believe you."

His eyes narrowed. "I'm a sworn officer of the law. We never lie."

I couldn't help it. I started to laugh.

"You don't believe me?"

"No," I said, still laughing.

He pursed his lips and watched me without saying anything. It was so unnerving, I wanted to shake him. But then I spotted what might've been a twinkle in his eye. So maybe he was kidding around with me? I hoped so, but, darn, the man had a devastating poker face.

"Where were we?" I asked.

"Were you angry?"

"Oh yes." I paused, wondering how much I should say and decided to go with the honest truth. "I was very angry. I was furious. And scared. He was a big, vicious jerk. He expected me to fall into his arms because he bought me dinner? I can buy my own damn dinner, thanks."

"I'm sure you can."

"You bet I can. He tore my best blouse and I still have black-and-blue marks where he grabbed me. If you don't believe me, just ask any of the dozens of witnesses who were on the pier when he attacked me. I feared for my life in that moment and I don't have a single regret about kicking him in the . . . you know. Not that I actually kicked him there, but nobody believes me when I deny it and, besides, a bunch of people won the pool at the pub, so I don't want to bum them out, but . . . Oh, never mind."

I could see him biting his cheeks. To keep from laughing? I hoped so, even if he was laughing at me. I didn't care. I couldn't have the new police chief annoyed with me, especially since I'd been dumb enough to threaten someone who later was murdered.

He kept on taking notes, and when he finally looked up, his expression was placid. "Tell me about that pink pipe wrench left at the scene."

I sighed. "It's mine, obviously. Nobody else uses pink tools but me, and everyone in town knows it."

"Why pink?"

Because I'm a girl, I wanted to say, but refrained from stating the obvious. "When I was little, my dad used to take my sister and me to work with him. I guess the construction guys thought it was cute, because they started bringing us little pink tool sets and things. Hard hats, goggles, tool belts—all pink. When I got older, Dad continued the tradition, so I've got pink everything. Power drills, sockets, hard hat, even a big rolling tool chest. You name it. I've got plenty of regular tools, too, but the pink ones are just as sturdy and the guys don't tend to walk away with them."

"No, I don't suppose they would."

"I told you I keep a set of my tools on-site."

"You mentioned it."

"So, I figure whoever was after Jerry just grabbed the heaviest thing he could find."

"That's one theory." He smiled.

"Well, it's a damn good one. Do you think I'd be stupid enough to use my own pink wrench as a weapon and then leave it at the scene?"

He sat back in his chair and folded his muscular arms across his impressive chest. "I think you're far from stupid, Ms. Hammer. But I've got a job to do. A cold-blooded murder to solve. I'm trying to get a complete picture of what occurred in that basement so that a murderer doesn't go free. I don't like murder happening in my town."

"It's my town, too," I grumbled. "I've never heard of a murder happening here before."

"Until now."

We stared at each other for several long seconds, until I blinked and looked away. I hated losing a staring contest, but I was getting a little freaked-out. Was he going to throw me in a cell? He wouldn't, would he? Didn't he know I was a completely trustworthy, lifelong resident of this town? I belonged to the Rotary Club. My company was accredited by the Better Business Bureau. I paid my bills on time and I didn't go around killing people as a general rule. But he wouldn't know that about me.

I reached for the small paper cup of water and took a quick sip to soothe my parched throat. "How long have you been living in Lighthouse Cove?"

He gazed at me without answering. Was I not supposed to ask him questions? I wasn't under arrest, right? So we could have a pleasant conversation, couldn't we? I gave him an encouraging smile.

Finally he gave in. "I moved here two months ago, right after Chief Raymond retired."

"I've seen you around town. But obviously we've never met."

"Guess you've managed to stay out of trouble until now."

I didn't like the sound of that. I leaned forward and clutched the edge of the table with both hands. "I'm not *in* trouble, Chief Jensen. Just because I was a good citizen and reported finding Jerry's dead body doesn't mean I killed him. I'm worried that while we're sitting around twiddling our thumbs, the real killer's running loose around town."

"Twiddling our thumbs?" he said quietly.

"Metaphorically speaking." Discomfited, I waved off the comment and sat back in the chair. "You know what I mean."

"Yeah, I do." He closed his notebook. "Believe me, I'm not twiddling my thumbs, Ms. Hammer. I've got my entire workforce making calls or out in the field, checking into every aspect of this case. We will find the person who killed Mr. Saxton."

"Good. Because it's not me."

The door opened and I recognized Sally, a longtime member of the police force, standing there. "Hey, Shannon."

I waved.

She turned to Chief Jensen. "Chief, can I see you out here for a minute?"

For the third time, Jensen left the room. Ten minutes passed and I was getting more nervous by the second. I stood and paced, feeling like a jailbird.

But after another minute of circling the room, I realized I was wasting my time. Rather than worry and complain, I needed to sit down and figure out for myself who in the world had killed Jerry Saxton.

The problem was, all the circumstantial evidence pointed directly at me. My biggest fear was that Chief Jensen would take the lazy way out and arrest me without delving any deeper.

Frankly, he looked like the furthest thing from lazy, but that didn't matter. He obviously considered me a person of interest, so how was I supposed to convince him that I wasn't? There was only one way. I knew I hadn't killed Jerry, so it was up to me to figure out who had.

When I met with the girls last Friday, Marigold had suggested that there might be another woman out there who had suffered from Jerry's cruelty. And Penny Wells, the loan agent at the bank, didn't like him, either. Were there others? Maybe one of those women had wanted revenge. Or maybe one of them had a husband or a father who was angry enough to do the job for her.

It wouldn't be too hard to find some answers. Between my girlfriends and me, we knew most of the people in town. We would just have to ask the right ones the right questions. Not that I was anxious to accuse anyone else of being a murderer, but at least I could deflect the chief's focus from me. Now if only I could escape this interrogation room and get started.

Another five minutes passed and I was considering my chances of making a run for it, when the chief strolled back in, as casual as could be.

"Look, Chief Jensen, I—"

"You're free to go, Ms. Hammer."

I blinked in surprise. "What? Why?"

He showed the barest hint of a grin. "Did you want to stick around?"

"No, it's just that—"

"We could tidy up one of the cells for you."

"No, but thanks. I'm happy to leave, but I'm a little confused. What happened? Did you find the killer? Did someone confess?"

"Not yet," he said. "Now, you ought to get going before I change my mind."

"Jeez." I scowled as I grabbed my purse off the back of the chair. "I'm going."

Before I could make it out the door, he said, "And don't leave town."

I turned and glared at him. "Seriously? I was born here, I live here, and I work here. I have friends and family here, so I'm not going anywhere. And, by the way, I'm not guilty of whatever you think I did."

He actually smiled at me. "That was sort of a joke. I don't actually think you'll take off."

I tried to cool my jets. "So that was what—cop humor?"

"Something like that." His smile broadened and it was a sight worth waiting for.

"Oo-kay then." I gave a little wave. "I'll see you around."

"No doubt."

I walked out and took a deep breath of freedom. When I saw Tommy kibitzing with another cop by the front counter, I grabbed his arm. "Walk me to my car."

"Huh? What?"

I dragged him outside, and when we got to my car, I turned on him. "What's going on? Why did he let me go? Did you find the killer?"

"Slow down, Shan," Tommy said. "You know I can't tell you anything."

"I just spent more than two hours being grilled by that guy. Besides, you owe me, Tommy."

He looked uncomfortable. "Yeah, sorry about that. When I heard what you did to that guy on the beach, I was damn proud of you. But I probably should've kept my mouth shut."

I couldn't disagree. But to be fair to Tommy, Thor had admitted he'd already heard the story from someone else. "Just tell me what's going on. I have a right to know and I won't get anything out of your irascible boss."

"He's cool, right? Did you know he surfs?"

My eyes widened in mock amazement. "That's so awesome, Tommy."

He laughed. "I know you don't care. But I gotta tell you, it's great to have a regular guy in charge after all those years with old stick-up-his-butt Raymond."

"I'm glad you're happy," I said, and meant it. "But can you just tell me why he let me go?" I wanted to know whether to keep looking over my shoulder or not.

Tommy glanced around the parking lot, as if someone might be eavesdropping. Finally, he whispered, "The coroner just called with his preliminary report. He thinks the body's been lying there in that basement since around nine o'clock last night. You've got an alibi for that time frame. Lizzie told us you were at her house from six until about midnight."

"We had dinner and then watched a movie," I said, remembering how the girls had teased me about my big Saturday-night plans with Lizzie and Hal and the kids.

But Lizzie was one of my best friends. Why would Jensen believe her? I asked Tommy that very thing.

He looked embarrassed. "He wasn't inclined to believe Lizzie, but then Hal corroborated the story."

Oh, fine. It figured Jensen would put more faith in Hal's story than Lizzie's. But, then, I probably would, too. "So that's it? That's why he let me go?"

"Well." Tommy wore that same pained expression as he scanned the parking lot again. It was fully dark now and clouds were rolling in. It looked like it might rain. Tommy leaned closer. "We also found out that Mr. Boyer wasn't calling you from San Francisco like he told you. He made that phone call from Sweet River. He was shacked up at the Cliff Hotel with someone who wasn't Mrs. Boyer."

"Whoa." Sweet River was south of here, about fifteen miles down the highway. Stan Boyer could've made the drive there and back with plenty of time to spare. But why? "So, what are you saying? Is Stan a suspect?"

Why would Stan Boyer kill Jerry Saxton? And in his own house?

Tommy scowled at me. "Damn it, Shannon, I shouldn't have said anything."

"My lips are sealed, Tommy. I swear." I stretched up and kissed his cheek. "Thanks. You're a peach."

"Just stay out of trouble, kiddo."

Chapter Four

The next morning I woke up early and after a long shower and a healthy breakfast of coffee and Pop-Tarts—blueberry flavored, to get my daily requirement of fruit—I headed for another one of my work sites. While it remained a crime scene, the Boyers' house was in limbo, so I'd shifted my men around to other jobs in town.

As I drove away from my house, I remembered Tommy's warning from the night before to stay out of trouble. But come on. When had I ever been in trouble? It still galled me that Chief Jensen had actually told me not to leave town. *My* town! Sure, he'd claimed he was just kidding, but I'd bet there was some truth in there. So what was with the cops around here? Honestly, if I had a nickel for every time I'd caused *trouble* in this town, I'd have maybe one or two nickels at the most. Of course, Jensen had no way of knowing that.

Chief Jensen knew nothing about me and that was starting to become a problem. Maybe it was time to ask my friends to talk me up to him. It might help him see me in a more positive light. Because, frankly, I figured the only reason he'd allowed me to go home last night was because Boyer had lied, not because my alibi had been so strong.

I needed to win him over to my side. How hard could it be? After all, the pitiful truth was, my life was the proverbial open book. I was friendly to everyone. I didn't drive too fast or drink too much or tell lies or party too heartily, ever. Oh, sure, there might've been a few wild teenage moments in high school, but seriously, they weren't all that wild. In fact, I hadn't done anything truly wild in years, if ever. I certainly hadn't killed anyone, even if I'd threatened to do so the other night. In front of witnesses.

Did that make me sound boring? Well, not the threatening-to-kill part, but the rest of it? Because I didn't feel boring. I loved my life. I had a great job and wonderful friends. I was close to my family; I loved my house and my dog and my cat and my town. I was healthy. I had money in the bank. Okay, maybe I wasn't *blissfully* happy, like rainbows and unicorns happy, but who was?

"Stop it," I murmured, scowling at myself. I was happy enough. Hell, I was downright perky most of the time.

I turned up the radio to distract myself and cruised through downtown past the town square on my way to one of my houses a few streets north of Main Street.

The town square was practically deserted at this time of the morning. Charming shops and cafés faced the pretty central park, where a large gazebo was set beneath sheltering trees. During the summer, free band concerts were held there on the weekends. Everyone in town turned out, carrying their lawn chairs and picnic hampers. The ice-cream shop on the corner did a bumper business on those nights. Some of my earliest best memories had taken place right here. Fireworks. Marching bands. My mom and dad holding hands. Ice cream.

Now, though, the square was silent. I scanned the area, anyway, on the off chance that I'd catch a glimpse of one of my girlfriends opening her shop, but the only place open was the Cozy Cove Diner on the corner. The other shops on the square wouldn't open for business for another two hours or more.

It was just as well, I realized as I drove on. I should probably avoid the area for the next few days. I knew my gossip quotient had skyrocketed since I'd stumbled over Jerry's body on Sunday. Everyone in town would be vying to get the inside scoop from me, but I dreaded the whispers and questions that would follow. I had to endure scrutiny and doubt from the new police chief, but not from people I'd known my entire life.

It was a good thing I had a strong alibi for the time Jerry had died, at least according to the county coroner's estimate. Otherwise, I would probably be bunking in the town jail by now. Despite my alibi, I had a feeling the chief would keep me on his suspect list until someone else confessed to the crime.

After a few more turns, I found Cranberry Circle and parked in front of the work site. The house was a beautiful pale blue Queen Anne Victorian with white trim, a charming porch on the ground floor, and a rounded balcony on the second floor of the tower. It was part of a small group of homes my father had built almost twenty years ago and it was a concept he'd repeated in other areas of town. Here there were sixteen homes, all grouped around a small park and playground. With only one entrance into the neighborhood and the street circling around the park, it was safe for the kids to play and ride bikes. A small coffeehouse thrived on the corner.

The owners wanted a new paint job, and we also needed to replace half a wall's worth of rotted wood siding and cedar shingles. Even though the house was relatively young, it was located at the west end of the block closest to the ocean. Despite being more valuable because of its desirable location, this house had suffered more exposure to the elements than the others. The stiff winter breezes and constant salt spray had damaged some of the western-facing exterior, causing the wood and paint to fade faster than the rest of the houses on the street.

The baby blue–and-white facade had been a popular combination twenty years ago. These days, though, many Victorian homeowners wanted more vivid colors with numerous contrasting hues on the windows, doors, and framing.

I climbed out of the truck and saw Billy and Sean already hard at work. The three of us had gone to school together and they were two of the best on my crew. Perched on the scaffolding, they were using claw hammers to pull off the most damaged cedar shingles.

"Hi, guys," I shouted.

Billy shoved his hammer into his tool belt and rappelled down the scaffolding like an expert rock climber. "Hey, Shannon, honey. You okay?"

Sean followed right behind him. "Yeah, we heard what happened." Always the straight shooter, he added, "Whoever offed Jerry Saxton did the world a favor. Maybe I shouldn't speak ill of the dead, but that guy was a tool."

"You knew him?" I asked.

"Yeah, I knew him." He scowled. "Remember Luisa Capello?"

"Sure. She went to school with us."

"Right. She was a year younger and best friends with my sister." Sean unwrapped a piece of gum, popped it into his mouth, and chewed as he talked. "Anyway, Saxton dated her for a while, and I got the feeling she was crazy in love with him. He led her on, promised her the moon, gave her all sorts of gifts and stuff. She was planning to marry him until she found out he was fooling around with not one, but two other women."

"Jerk," I muttered, shaking my head.

"And guess who spilled the beans to Luisa about Jerry's cheating." Sean scowled. "It was yet another woman he was cheating on."

"How many was he stringing along? Three? Four?" Billy pulled his baseball cap off and scratched his head. "I can barely handle the one I've got."

Sean chuckled but quickly sobered. "Just about broke Luisa's heart. She was seeing a doctor for depression for a while, but I think she's finally over him."

"I'm sorry for Luisa," I said, remembering the pretty, tenderhearted girl from high school. Her parents had moved here from Italy to open a branch of the family restaurant. They were extremely protective of their three thoroughly Americanized children. "She didn't deserve that."

"No, she didn't," Billy said. "I didn't know her as well as you two did, but that's a real drag."

"Oh, and one more thing," Sean said with an evil grin. "Did you know that Saxton was also screwing around with Joyce Boyer?"

My ears perked up. "What?"

"Oh yeah," Billy said, nodding sagely. "Joyce is another one of his conquests."

"Joyce Boyer." It wasn't possible, was it? Joyce was Stan Boyer's wife. The wife that Stan was cheating on last weekend while Jerry Saxton was being murdered. In their new house! "How did you hear about her and Jerry?"

"From Johnny," Sean said, naming another longtime member of my crew. "Ask him. He and Todd and the other guys working on the Boyer house got an earful of Joyce and Jerry carrying on last week."

An *earful*? I wondered what that meant.

"Yeah," Billy said. "The guys were laughing about it last Friday night at the pub. Hey, we missed you there, by the way. But I guess we know why you didn't show up."

"Believe me, I'm sorry I couldn't make it," I said, lamenting that I hadn't been there to hear about Joyce and Jerry. I'd avoided the pub—and every other public place—last Friday because of my infamous fight with Jerry the night before. "So, Jerry was screwing around with Stan's wife. Wow."

"That's what Johnny said. Apparently the two of them were having sex in one of the upstairs bedrooms while the guys were working there."

I grimaced. "That is the tackiest thing I've ever heard. I mean, besides the fact that a bunch of guys are working there, those upstairs bedrooms aren't even finished yet. It's a mess."

"I know," Sean said, laughing. "The guys were afraid they'd come away with splinters in their private parts."

I covered my ears. "Oh, ick."

"It's cheesy, for sure," Bill agreed, and all of a sudden he looked embarrassed. "The thing is, Shannon, we were talking about Jerry because of your run-in with him."

"That's okay." I patted his arm. "Everybody else in town is talking about it, too."

"The good news is that you gave him exactly what he deserved out on the beach the other night."

Sean chuckled. "Yeah, you nailed him, boss. Every woman he ever cheated on is praising your name these days."

I didn't deserve the praise for *nailing* him, but at this point, it was too much trouble to correct that generally held belief. I hadn't even intended to bring up the subject of Jerry, but now I couldn't let it go. "So, Jerry fooled around with a lot of women?"

"He was notorious," Sean said. "Ask anyone."

"Married women, too?"

"Well, there's Mrs. Boyer," Sean said, as if that settled it.

"Sounds like everyone in town knew he was a player." Everyone but me, obviously. And Lizzie.

"A lot of guys knew," Billy said.

Sean nodded. "Mainly because he liked to brag about it at the pub."

"Yeah, he kind of had a big mouth," Billy said.

Sean snorted. "'Cuz he was kind of a big ass."

"Did you ever hear of anyone claiming that he hurt them physically?"

Sean looked uncomfortable. "Well, it's not like I'm definitely pointing the finger at Saxton, but Luisa showed up with a black eye once. She said she fell down."

It didn't take much of a leap to conclude that Jerry had given Luisa that black eye, but it was too late now for the police to do anything about it. I would love to talk to Luisa about it, though. And while I doubted she would ever hurt a fly, I was putting her on my personal suspect list.

Luisa was a real softie, so it was a long shot. In fact, I almost smiled at the picture of her bashing Jerry over the head with a pipe wrench. She'd barely be able to lift the thing. But Jerry might've pushed her to the limit.

And if Luisa hadn't been pushed that far, perhaps her two brothers or her protective father had been.

As I was leaving, three more of my crew drove up. I rolled down my window to let them know that I'd see them all later in the week. As I drove off, I made a mental note to run by Luisa's place sometime this week and catch up with her.

Billy's words circled through my mind. He'd sworn that Jerry had a big mouth and was always bragging about his conquests. But if that were true, why would Lizzie have ever set me up with him? I couldn't believe she'd never heard the rumors. She knew this town as well as I did. On the other hand, Lizzie and Hal rarely hung out in the pub, where they might hear the stories. Their lives revolved around their kids. I didn't have that excuse and I'd never heard the rumors either, so who was I to talk?

So, how did Lizzie meet Jerry? And why had she set me up with him? Someone must have suggested him as a good date possibility, probably because, sadly, Lizzie was always in the market for new and interesting men to match up with her girlfriends. But who in the world would recommend Jerry?

It was time to ask Lizzie that question. I also knew I would have to tell Chief Jensen what I'd heard about Mrs. Boyer. *Is he already aware of Jerry Saxton's affair with her?* I wondered. I hated the idea of being a snitch, but why should I be the only person on his suspect list? It wasn't fair.

A few minutes later, I pulled up in front of Paper Moon, Lizzie and Hal's bookshop on the square. I almost hated to walk inside because I never walked out without buying something fabulous. The shop was filled with books and beautiful cards and paper items and unusual gifts. But I was on a mission.

The store wasn't open yet, but I knew Lizzie would be working in the back office. It was quieter here than at home, where Hal would be getting their two kids ready for school. She always did her paperwork and bills here in the mornings.

I walked down the passageway between two shops and found the back entrance.

"Knock, knock," I shouted as I rapped loudly on the door.

Moments later, Lizzie called out, "Who's there?"

"It's Shannon."

She opened the door to let me in and quickly locked it behind us. Not that our tiny town was dangerous or anything—Jerry Saxton's murder notwithstanding—but Lizzie loved locks. She was our safety girl and liked to lecture us on personal safety. She knew every type of locking mechanism known to man and probably could have gotten a job at Fort Knox.

"What are you doing here?" she asked over her

shoulder as she led the way back to her small office. "Not that it's not wonderful to see you."

Today Lizzie wore a simple outfit of mossy green jeans and a matching sweater. I knew she thought the one-color scheme made her appear taller, but she still looked like a perky elf with attitude. Not that she didn't look clean and classy and ready for business. She did, as always. I was the perfect contrast to her in old work boots with thick socks, jeans, and a flannel shirt over a faded blue thermal henley. In my defense, I was dressed for business, too. Just a different kind of business.

Lizzie poured a cup of coffee with cream for me and we both sat.

"I'm so sorry," she began, and I saw that her eyes were bright with unshed tears. "He was a horrible man and it's my fault that he hurt you, and now he's dead. And I'm glad, damn it. Now that I've said it out loud, I don't care if anyone knows how I feel. Nobody hurts my friend and gets away with it."

I frowned at her. "You didn't kill him, did you?"

Her look of shock was priceless. "Good God, no. Did you?"

"No." I laughed, grabbed her hand and gave it a squeeze. "So no more apologies from either of us. It's not your fault that he attacked me. I know your heart was in the right place when you set us up and I know you'd never do anything to hurt me. That's not why I'm here."

"All right, okay. I just felt so bad about your horrible date." She brushed at her eyes and sniffled once. "And then when I heard that he was dead, wow." Her face contorted in dismay.

"Tell the truth. Did you think I did it?"

"No!"

"It's okay if you did. The new police chief thinks I did it."

She gasped. "No, he doesn't."

"He did for an hour or two last night. I was the one who found the body, after all. And plenty of people overheard me threatening him."

"You've never been a violent person. I can only imagine that awful man must have hurt you pretty bad."

"He did," I said quietly. "And what hurts even more is that I bought into his whole act."

She buried her face in her hands. "Oh, God, it's all my fault."

"And we've come full circle."

"Okay, I'll stop," she said, holding up both hands like a traffic cop. "We will never talk about Jerry Saxton ever, ever again." She swept her shaggy bangs off her forehead and straightened her shoulders, refreshed and ready to change the subject. "So, what's up? Why are you here? Not that it isn't a thrill to see you."

I laughed softly. "I want to talk about Jerry."

"Shannon!"

"I just need to know how you met him. Why did you set me up with him? Who introduced you? Did one of your friends tell you he was a good person?"

She looked puzzled. "I didn't tell you? He came into the store a few weeks ago and introduced himself. He was so charming and gorgeous that I immediately thought of you. I wanted you to meet him."

"So nobody recommended him to you as good blind-date material."

"No."

I nodded and drained the last of my coffee. "And you didn't ask anyone about him after you met him."

"You mean, did I do something smart like gather some character references? No. I got a positive feeling about him from the very beginning. He was such a good listener." She rolled her eyes in disgust. "So much for my ability to judge character."

"You're a perfectly good judge of character, Lizzie. So am I." I stood and gave her a tight hug. "I guess we had to find out the hard way how charming a sociopath can be."

Being a good citizen and informing the police of a new clue didn't turn out as well as I'd hoped. I had driven directly to the police department and politely requested a few minutes to talk to Chief Jensen. Naturally, the infuriating man completely misinterpreted my news.

"Are you conducting your own murder investigation, Ms. Hammer?"

"Of course not," I stammered.

"Sounds like it to me," Chief Jensen said.

"I'm just trying to help. I came across some information that might be useful and I thought you should know about it."

"Information? Is that what it's called?" He sat back in his chair. "Sounds more like gossip to me."

The man made me so angry! Yes, he was gorgeous, and yes, my heart did beat a little faster whenever I looked into those searing blue eyes of his, but enough was enough.

"So what if it is?" I jumped up and paced in front of his desk while I talked, waving my arms for emphasis. "Gossip can be informative, right? And I thought you'd want to know that my men witnessed Mrs. Boyer and Jerry Saxton carrying on with each other. I thought that was information you could use." I stopped abruptly and shook my finger at him. "And you're a fine one to talk about gossip. Apparently you listened to plenty of gossip concerning my fight with Jerry Saxton on the beach the other night. I'll bet you found it highly entertaining."

"I found it highly motivating."

"Motivating?" I was puzzled for a second, but then I realized what he was saying. "Ah. As in *a motive for murder*. Really, Chief? Haven't we moved beyond all that?" My shoulders drooped and I slid back into my chair. I was mostly playacting for his benefit, but part of me was bummed. When would he stop giving me grief?

His lips twitched but he refused to smile. "Why didn't you file a police report after the fight?"

I scowled, mostly at my own forgetfulness. "I meant to. I told Lizzie I would. You can ask her. Liz Logan. You know her, right?"

"Yeah, I know her."

Of course he did, I realized. She and Hal had provided my alibi for the night Jerry was killed. "Well, you should ask her. She was going to come with me to the police station to file the report, but I got caught up in work stuff and forgot. Next thing I knew, the guy was dead."

"We'll follow up on your information." He sounded so condescending, I was surprised he didn't put air quotes around the word *information*.

"That's great," I said, trying to keep the sarcasm out of my voice as I stood to leave his office.

He stood also. "Thank you for coming by, Ms. Hammer."

I tried to hide my shock. He was being courteous?

"I mean it," he said, reading my expression. "I realize it wasn't easy for you to share what you heard, so I appreciate your effort."

My head was practically spinning from the warm cordiality. "You're welcome."

I was driving out of the police station parking lot when I remembered that my new tenant, Wendell Jarvick, would be arriving around noon. I had only an hour to prepare myself for another onslaught of negativity. Having just dealt with Chief Jensen, I figured today was my day to confront people in grouchy moods.

An hour later I watched from my front window as Wendell Jarvick drove into my driveway and parked his oversized luxury car halfway between the street and my garage. He was prompt, anyway. He sat in the driver's seat and waited for several minutes before finally getting out of the car. He was almost six feet tall, and skinnier than a stick of licorice. His dark hair was coiffed—there was no other word for it—into a kind of pompadour, à la Elvis. He wore skintight plaid pants and a long-sleeved white shirt buttoned up to the collar. I imagined he fancied himself a hipster.

He glanced around again, probably wondering where the servants were hiding, then popped the trunk and pulled out six pieces of matching luggage. Then he stood and waited. I had to wonder what he would do if nobody ever showed up. Would he call me? Knock on my front door? Or just keep waiting out there?

If Wendell expected valet service, he should've booked the Ritz-Carlton a couple hundred miles down the road.

I inhaled deeply, then exhaled slowly, counting to ten. Pasting a bright smile on my face, I strolled out to the driveway with my arm extended to shake his hand. "Hello, Mr. Jarvick. Welcome back to Lighthouse Cove."

He ignored my hand.

"I'm Shannon Hammer," I continued, mentally gritting my teeth. "I'm your host for the next two weeks. Let me show you the way to your room."

I turned and headed for the garage stairs.

"Wait just one minute, young lady," he said imperiously. "Did you not notice that I have luggage?"

"Oh, I can help you with that." I picked up two of the smaller suitcases and walked to the garage stairs.

He was already grumbling under his breath when he caught up with me on the stairs. I had a feeling his visit was not going to end well. I wasn't the most experienced hotelier in town, but I'd always enjoyed having guests stay here. In almost all cases, I knew they went away happy. I was almost certain that Wendell would not end up on the happy list.

He would be here for only two weeks. I could put up with anything for two weeks.

"I was promised an ocean view," he said, panting for breath as we reached the top of the stairs.

"There's a beautiful view from inside. Let me show you." I unlocked the door, swung it open, and preceded him into the room. I set the two suitcases down near the closet and walked over to the bay window. I pulled up the blinds to reveal a charming view of the Victorian rooftops of the neighborhood, beyond which was the wide blue ocean, a mere two blocks away. To the left were steep green hills topped by a forest of glorious redwood trees.

"Isn't it lovely?" I said brightly.

"Why aren't you closer to the beach?"

"It's a short walk and very refreshing. Less than one block away is Main Street and our town square, where you'll find loads of wonderful shops and restaurants. But I don't have to tell you that. You come here every year, so you must love it as much as we do."

He stared down his nose at me. "Will I be allowed any privacy at all?"

"Of course. I'll leave you to it. If you have any questions, just give me a call. The notebook by the phone has pages and pages of things to do and places to go and any phone numbers you might need. My number is at the top of the page. There's also a TV listing and emergency numbers, in case you need those. Enjoy your stay."

I escaped down the stairs and back into my house. The phone was already ringing. "Hello?"

"I need the rest of my bags."

"I'll be happy to help you carry one of them upstairs. I'll meet you at your car." I quickly hung up the telephone. I didn't want to be rude, but I also wasn't going to carry all of his luggage upstairs for him. It wasn't my fault he'd brought six freaking suitcases.

I met him at his car and carried one of the last two suitcases upstairs. When we reached the apartment I dropped the suitcase by the closet and smiled. "Just one last thing and I'll let you enjoy your privacy. You'll need to remove your car from the driveway because it's blocking my access in and out."

"You expect me to park on the street?" He looked horrified.

I swallowed a laugh. "The streets of Lighthouse Cove are the safest in the country. Your car will be fine."

I knew I was on thin ice with him, but that was too bad. Not only did I need ready access to my truck, but my father often parked his RV in the driveway.

I was pretty sure I wouldn't be receiving any stellar recommendations from Wendell Jarvick, but I didn't think he had any right to complain. I knew my two guest suites were well-appointed, clean, and comfortable. The neighborhood was quiet and the view was unsurpassed. All we were missing was a bellman and an elevator.

I met Jane right on time for dinner at Bella Rossa, our favorite hole-in-the-wall Italian place on the square. It helped that it was owned by Uncle Pete, who also owned the wine bar next door and Bella Rossa Winery outside of town. He'd started out growing grapes for the local wineries, but when our very own Anderson Valley became the newest hot spot for wine tasting, Uncle Pete had bitten the bullet and built a small winery, where he started making his own wines.

The winery became so popular that he opened the wine bar on the square, next door to Bella Rossa. He had never had kids of his own, so he'd named the winery after me. In a manner of speaking, that is. *Rossa* was Italian for "redhead." These days, I was the only redhead in the family, since Dad's and Uncle Pete's hair had turned gray and Chloe had dyed her hair blond the minute she got to Hollywood. It suited her, though, just as my red hair suited me. I was born with it and had the freckles to prove it.

Even though he didn't have an Italian bone in his body, Uncle Pete was always shouting out Italian phrases and mild swearwords, much to the delight of his customers. My family was 100 percent Irish, but nobody seemed to notice at Bella Rossa.

Uncle Pete greeted us with hugs and big kisses before taking us to our table. Jane and I ordered a half bottle of a good Sonoma Pinot Noir, an antipasto appetizer, and pasta pomodoro for the main course. A busboy brought a basket of crunchy sourdough bread and a crock of butter, along with water glasses and a bowl of briny olives.

As soon as he left the table, Jane demanded answers. "When I saw you Friday morning at the tea shop, you were traumatized by Jerry's attack. The next thing I hear a day later is that he's dead. What happened?"

"How should I know?" I popped an olive into my mouth. "Why are you asking me?"

"Because you always know everything."

I leaned in and whispered, "If you're asking whether I killed him or not, I didn't."

Her eyes widened. "Of course you didn't. Why would you even say that?"

"Because there are people who think I did."

"Well, they're insane."

I glanced around the restaurant, hoping nobody could hear us. "The police chief is one of them."

"That's ridiculous," she said, laughing. "Eric would never think that about you. He's a sweetie pie."

A *sweetie pie*? "So you've met him."

"Of course I have," Jane said, smiling. "We're neighbors. He couldn't be nicer."

"Sounds like you know him pretty well."

"He's been living here for two months. And he's kind of hard to miss, if you know what I mean."

"Unfortunately, I do."

The waitress brought our wine and we both took hearty sips before continuing the conversation.

"What did you mean by that?" Jane whispered once the waitress was gone.

"By what?"

"You said, *unfortunately*."

"He hates me." It hurt to admit that. I set my glass down and took a slow breath. "I was interrogated for hours the other night, plus some more today. In case you haven't heard, I'm the perfect suspect."

"That's crazy."

"It's not. Will you do me a favor and tell Chief Jensen how wonderful I am?"

"I will," she promised. "Oh. He just walked in." She jumped up, and before I could grab her she dashed over to greet the chief. When he saw her, he smiled broadly and gave her a friendly hug. Apparently, Thor did have a warmer, friendlier side—I just hadn't been privy to it.

I turned away so I wasn't watching and slugged down a long drink of cold water. I was taken aback, to say the least. I'd never seen him smile so easily. But who wouldn't smile at Jane, my tall, blond, beautiful, easygoing friend?

Seeing him smile like that was a revelation. Tonight

he wore a thick fisherman's sweater, casual jeans with faded boots, and a scarred leather jacket. The look was so appealing that it caused a little tempest of nerves and excitement to swirl around inside me.

I shifted in my chair to watch them. Jensen continued to smile as Jane gestured with her hands and talked animatedly. But then his forehead furrowed. He leaned to his left and stared beyond her, right at me, meeting my gaze with a frown.

Great. So she'd mentioned my name to him and he'd instantly morphed from smiling guy to grouchy bear. So much for him being a sweetie pie.

We managed to nod at each other. Jane glanced over her shoulder at me and I signaled for her to come back. She said good-bye to the chief. And when she got to our table, I said, "See? I told you he hates me."

She wore a thoughtful look as she sat down and reached for her wineglass. "I don't think he hates you, Shannon."

"No, he just suspects me of murder," I said, and dolefully lifted my wineglass. "Cheers."

Chapter Five

Over thick, buttered bread and tangy antipasti, I told Jane everything that had happened since I saw her Friday morning until now. I replayed my adventures in the grim darkness of the Boyers' basement and then later in the interrogation room at police headquarters.

When I was finished, I was a little winded and my throat was so dry, I had to drink down half a glass of water.

"I still say he likes you," Jane said as she casually chewed on a breadstick.

I almost choked on the water. "Did you hear a word I just said?" I hissed. "He interrogated me for more than two hours. For good reason, too. I threatened the dead guy with murder and then tripped over his body. That makes me look really suspicious. One of these days I expect Chief Jensen to show up at my house with a search warrant."

She smiled softly. "I expect him to show up with flowers and candy."

"Oh, Jane." I shook my head. "Poor, sweet Jane." Jane was a big romance-novel reader and I'll admit she shared them with me occasionally. I found them enjoyable, especially the endings when the guy had to grovel to get the girl. But Jane took it to a whole new level. She was totally in love with the idea of finding one's own great romantic love, and yet I was pretty certain she'd never actually been there. High school crushes didn't count.

I broke a thick chunk of bread into two pieces and gave her one. "You've been inhaling too many paint fumes. It's affected your brain."

She laughed, but after a minute of silent munching, we both agreed not to talk about the murder again. The restaurant was filling up and I couldn't forget that Chief Jensen was sitting a mere thirty feet away. Yes, he was in the other room, but that was still close enough to make me nervous.

As we drank wine and ate more bread, my mood gradually lightened. Our pasta was served, and we chatted about family and friends and the upcoming Harvest Festival parade. I entertained her with my impression of Wendell Jarvick's attempts to make me carry all his luggage upstairs.

I knew Jane wanted to ask me more about the murder, so when dinner was over, we walked the two blocks back to my house for ice cream. Once our bowls were filled with scoops of sea-salted caramel and chocolate mint ice cream, we sat at my big, old kitchen table, and Jane asked the questions that had been on her mind all evening.

"So, who do you think killed him?"

"I have a list of names if you'd like to hear them."

"Very funny."

"I'm not kidding."

"Well, maybe we can go over them later." She skimmed her spoon over the scoop of caramel and nibbled it slowly. "What did it feel like when you found the body?"

"It was horrible," I said, remembering the terror I felt as I stood in that dank, dark basement. "It scared the crap out of me. My first thought was that whoever knocked him off was still hiding down there and I was next." I shivered at the memory. I told her about tripping over the arm, then seeing the body, and then realizing that it was Jerry Saxton. Dead. I couldn't get out of there fast enough. Once I was back outside, I had to call the police.

"So, tell me for real now," she said. "Who do you think killed him?"

"I really do have a list of possibilities. The names are all in my head right now, but maybe it would help to write them down."

I pulled out a notepad and handed it to Jane, who wrote as I spoke. I named every woman I'd heard of who had been linked with Jerry. "The women's fathers and husbands and brothers would be out for revenge, too, so let's add Luisa's dad and her brothers, Buddy and Marco, to the list, along with Stan Boyer."

"Okay." When we were finished, she looked up at me. "We know most of these people."

"I know," I said, feeling the guilt seep in. "I'm sure they're all innocent, but so am I. So while I'd love to talk to them all, I can't exactly run around interrogating them. Especially after what Chief Jensen said about me running my own investigation."

"Maybe you can't go around snooping, but I can," Jane said with a determined smile. "And so can Lizzie and Marigold. And Emily, too."

"I can't ask you guys to do it." But I'd had the exact same thought when I was stuck alone in the interrogation room the other night. It made sense. Among us, my girlfriends and I knew every single person in town. Why couldn't we get some answers?

But then I grimaced as reality set in. "No, it's too dangerous. In case you've forgotten, there's a killer running loose. What if he finds out you're all asking questions? He could get angry or suspicious or worse."

"Come on, Shannon," she said reasonably. "You know everyone in town is talking about the murder. This is Lighthouse Cove. We thrive on gossip. We live for it. Let's take advantage of the situation and join in the conversation. We'll look perfectly innocent doing it, and one of us might find out something important that'll get you off the hook for good."

I didn't want to pin too much hope on it, but I had to admit that talking to Jane was helping me let go of some of the anxiety I'd been carrying around. The thought of doing something proactive was exciting, and it was nice to know that my friends might be willing to help.

"And you could be our liaison to Chief Jensen," I said brightly. Better Jane than me, after all. I didn't want to see what he'd do if I brought him more "information"—in air quotes—about other possible suspects.

"My pleasure." Jane took our bowls to the sink. "I mean, it's not exactly a hardship to look at him."

"I have to agree. So, why didn't Lizzie try to set one of us up with him? Or is he married?"

"He's divorced," she said, "and I have a feeling it was an ugly one."

"That's too bad."

"I know. That wouldn't have stopped Lizzie, though. The fact is, she did ask him if he'd like to meet some nice women in town and he said, and I quote, '*No*.'"

I started to laugh. "Just like that, he told her no?"

"Pretty clear-cut, right?" She smiled. "He had no idea that an answer like that would just embolden Lizzie."

"I'm afraid to see what her next move will be."

"Me, too." Jane shook her head. "But he's obviously not interested in dating right now."

I agreed and allowed the subject to drop. Reaching for the notepad, I read off the long list of possible suspects. Jane helped me choose which of us five girls knew each person best and could get answers from them more easily than anyone else. When we were finished, Jane made phone calls to Lizzie and the others to set up a meeting the next morning at Emily's to go over our big plan. I wanted them to be comfortable with what we were thinking of doing. Jane assured me that they would.

Putting down my pencil, I took a deep breath and let it out. We were taking action and I felt . . . relieved. It was the first time I'd felt that way in days.

At Emily's tea shop the next morning, my friends enthusiastically accepted their assignments from Jane.

"This is going to be fun," Lizzie said, practically bouncing in her chair. "It'll be good to do something positive after all the negativity that's been going around town."

Marigold stirred her tea. "I just received a new shipment from Lancaster County, so I have an excuse to call Susan, the woman I told you about. After we talk business, I'll ask her if she heard the news about Jerry's murder and see what she says."

Emily was eager to help, too. She was friendly with Luisa's father and brothers, who operated a pizza kitchen on the other side of the town square. "We have our restaurant-association lunch this Thursday, so I'll chat them up and see what pops."

"I'll talk to Penny at the bank," I said. "She told me she worked with Jerry on some home loans, so she might know something about his business connections."

"Good," Jane said, checking another name off the list.

"I'll talk to Joyce Boyer, too," I added. "And Stan. I want to find out why he lied to me on the phone."

"Just be careful," Lizzie said.

I felt a cold chill and realized I'd forgotten to say something important. "Promise me you'll all be careful. One of us might be confronting a killer."

"We'll be fine," Emily said, trying to sound light-hearted as she glanced around the table. "We'll approach it as though we're having a wee chat. Sharing a bit of gossip. Nobody will be the wiser."

"That's right," Lizzie said. "Just having a friendly conversation. I'll run over to the Cozy Cove later and see if Cindy knows anything."

"Good idea," Jane said, making a note.

"Thanks, everyone," I said. "I'm beyond grateful."

"Don't be silly, love," Emily said, squeezing my arm. "You'd do the same for any of us."

What she said was true, so I left it at that.

Jane brought up the subject of Police Chief Eric Jensen and everyone made happy noises. So it was true. He was super nice to everyone in town but me. Didn't that just figure?

"He's got a bug up his very attractive butt about Shannon," Jane said. "He doesn't know her, so I suppose he can be forgiven for thinking she actually could've killed that horrible man. But as soon and as often as possible, we all need to let him know how wonderful Shannon is and how she wouldn't ever dream of killing a single soul."

"Even if I did threaten to do so," I muttered.

"Oh, don't worry about that," Jane insisted. "We all know you never would have carried out the threat."

"People talk like that all the time," Marigold put in. "Just yesterday I heard Hazel Williams threaten to murder little Stevie Johnson if his ball landed in her garden again. *Nobody* takes those kinds of threats seriously."

"Except Chief Jensen," I muttered. "He doesn't trust me."

"He doesn't know you," Lizzie said. "Once he does, he'll realize that you could never hurt anyone like that."

"Well, now, she did kick the man in the bollocks," Emily said.

"I didn't," I insisted, then laughed shortly. "Thanks for that, Emily."

"Just keeping it real, love," she said with a wink.

Later, as everyone was leaving, Emily pulled me aside. "Come to dinner tonight."

"Here?" I asked, glancing around the tea shop.

"No, no. My place. I'm trying out a new luncheon recipe. Scottish-style beef stew."

"Sounds wonderful. What makes it Scottish?"

"An extra bottle of ale."

I laughed again. "I can't wait. Thanks, Emily."

She pushed my hair back from my forehead like somebody's mom would and gave me a tight hug. "Stiff upper lip, m'dear."

I nodded firmly. "You bet. See you tonight."

From the tea shop I drove out to Sloane's Stones, the huge brickyard where I liked to buy the floor tiles and granite or marble slabs for my clients' kitchen and bathroom counters. Sloane's yard was massive, at least five acres, and filled with every type and color of brick and tile ever made. If I couldn't find it here, they would happily order it from anywhere.

Growing up with a contractor father, I had great childhood memories of my sister and me dashing wildly across the brickyard, playing hide-and-seek among the huge stacks of bricks and slabs of marble, and exploring the different showrooms with their gorgeous wall murals created from thousands of bits of colorful mosaic tiles. We would invariably come home covered head to toe in dusty redbrick powder.

We always had good times when Dad took us somewhere on business. One of our favorite destinations was the landfill, where he would dispose of truckloads of demolished house parts. I shuddered now to think of the dump as another of our childhood playgrounds, but we'd always had fun. These days, though, I let my guys take care of running stuff out to the landfill. Some memories were meant to stay in the past.

After two hours at Sloane's, I had amassed enough tile and counter samples to weigh down the back of my truck. On the way home, I stopped at the lumberyard and picked up several fine wood-grain samples I thought Penny might like to use for her new cupboards and drawers.

Back in town, I parked my truck on the street in front of my house because Wendell's damn Lincoln Continental was hogging the driveway. I knew I would have to lecture him about that eventually, but I didn't want to spoil my afternoon. Climbing out of my truck, I brushed off the worst of the brick dust on my shirt and jeans and walked up to Main Street to Nail It, my favorite day spa owned by my friend Paloma and her mom.

I hadn't always understood the benefits of a good manicure. Back in high school, I'd resisted any kind of pampering as a protest against Whitney and her snotty friends, who enjoyed teasing me mercilessly about my laid-back wardrobe, my messy mass of curly hair, and my less than meticulous manicures. At that point, if I had dared to show up at school wearing designer jeans and painted nails, I would've received even more grief.

During my brief sojourn in San Francisco, I had worked for a large construction firm. There I'd made friends with the office manager, Debby, who insisted that I join the office girls every Thursday night for mani-pedis and margaritas. Who could pass up an invitation like that? The sneaky little side benefit was that my nails and hands were no longer cracked and red and dry from working all day long with power tools.

Paloma brought the mani-pedi experience to a new level of bliss by wrapping me up in a warm robe and then smearing some wonderfully scented waxy substance all over my feet and hands. I thought there might also be seaweed involved, but I couldn't say for sure. After a twenty-minute shoulder and neck massage, Paloma would peel off the wax and rub more lotions and potions onto my skin. Eventually she would begin painting my nails, but I was usually fast asleep by then. When I awoke, I was fluffed and folded and buffed and ready to face the world again—and happy that I no longer gave a damn what Whitney and her mean-girl posse thought of me.

That night, over bowls of hearty beef stew, crusty bread, and a lovely Rhône, Emily entertained me with tales of all the customers she'd chatted up about the murder that day. I knew how wonderful my friends were, but my affection for them was renewed when I saw how determined they were to keep me out of jail.

"Everyone has her opinions, of course," Emily said. "Natty Terrell believes it was either Mr. or Mrs. Boyer, or maybe they were in on it together. According to her son, Colin, who works part-time at the flower shop, Joyce Boyer was in there yesterday to order flowers for her mother. She was boasting about the fact that Jerry was killed in their basement. Poetic justice, she called it, and said 'good riddance.'"

"'Good riddance'? Joyce said that? Wow." I shivered.

"It's a bit gruesome, isn't it?" Emily said, nodding. "Colin also reported that Joyce was quite tearful as she spoke. So was she happy he was dead, or sad?"

"She was crying?" I thought about it. "It's an awfully cold statement to make in public, especially by a woman rumored to be sleeping with the man. Maybe she realized what she'd said out loud and it upset her."

"But what does she mean by *poetic justice*?" Emily shook her head. "She sounds angry and guilty to me."

"I would love it if that were true, if only to stop the police from suspecting me. But I don't believe she would talk like that if she really did kill him."

"No, probably not. Despite her big mouth, she doesn't seem like a stupid woman."

"On the other hand," I mused, "she *was* having an affair with Jerry."

"True. So how smart can she be?" Emily took a small bite of tender stew meat and chewed it before continuing. "Phillippa Baxter told me that Jerry had the hots for her, as well."

"Oh, dear."

"Yes. But she assured me she wasn't about to fall for any of his fancy words. She's apparently well versed in the wicked ways of evil men."

I shook my head. "Flipper has always imagined that every guy in the universe is after her body. She's kind of insane."

"But highly entertaining."

"I suppose," I said cautiously. I'd gone to high school with Phillippa Baxter, or Flipper as we called her. The poor girl had been delusional about men forever.

Emily set down her fork. She took a sip of wine and leaned closer. "Honestly, Shannon. These people confide their deepest secrets to me. It's a bit shocking, really. I feel like the vicar in the confessional."

My laughter was strained. "I just hope the police don't get wind of our little investigation."

"The police?" She brushed off my concerns. "They won't take notice of some small-town gossip. And my teetotalers love chitchatting with me. Who knows? One of them might just drop a vital clue that leads to some fabulous revelation."

"As long as you're careful. Don't forget, there's a murderer out there somewhere."

"Yes, I tend to forget from day to day that we're harboring a killer." She pondered that dark thought for a moment, then smiled brightly, reached over, and patted my hand. "Ah, well, as long as we can keep you out of the pokey, that's what matters most."

I woke up the next morning to a cold gray sky with more fog rolling in. I added a thermal T-shirt under my usual henley and flannel shirt, then drank an extra cup of coffee to keep myself revved up. Foggy days often made me want to stay inside with a cozy blanket and a good book.

I spent the first half of the day driving from one end of town to the other and back again, checking on my six main job sites. I also met with the architect on the Main Street Brownstones project. My company had been hired to do the rehab, and I was eager to find out what obstacles, if any, he might've discovered in his research.

Thank goodness I had plenty of work to do besides sit around and try to avoid a certain hunky police chief.

That afternoon, I stopped at the Boyers' house in South Cove. I spotted Wade Chambers, my head foreman in charge of this job site, standing on the front porch, talking to one of the cops who was still there collecting forensic evidence.

The place was still a crime scene, so I had cut the crew down to two guys, plus Wade, who traveled between sites. The basic assignment here was to make sure that none of the police fell through the feeble floorboards or tripped down the basement ramp.

Wade checked in with the police every day to see if they were finished with their evidence collecting. We were all eager to get back to work inside the house.

Wade saw me and waved, said one last thing to the cop, and carefully jumped off the porch. "Hey, boss, I was just going to call you. The police still have the interior cordoned off, but they gave us permission to work out here. I thought we should go ahead and tackle the front stairs. What do you think?"

Frowning, I gazed up at the house. It wouldn't do much good to start reinforcing the sagging porch roof if we couldn't even get up to the porch without risking life and limb on those stairs. "I agree. Let's get started on the stairs."

Two police squad cars were parked out front, so there had to be at least four cops somewhere on the property, probably downstairs collecting more evidence. Lucky for them, we'd already done the preliminary work of jacking up the basement ceiling and adding four new support posts down the center of the room. We'd rebuilt the main header beams and repaired several damaged joists, all before Jerry Saxton was killed down there.

With an old house, we always followed the golden rule of triage: first, stop the bleeding, so to speak. Whenever I took on a new job, I prioritized the work according to structural urgency. In other words, a coat of paint might make the place look nice on the surface, but if a wall or a load-bearing beam was weakened by age or termites or water damage, the house wouldn't survive much longer without fortification. And that had to start at the bottom, with the basement. With so many police officers traipsing through the kitchen, going up and down that precarious ramp, and then moving themselves and their equipment around the big, dank basement space, all three floors of the house would've collapsed on top of them if we hadn't done the reinforcement work first.

"Have the owners been around much?" I asked, as Wade escorted me back to my truck.

He shook his head. "Todd said Mrs. Boyer was here for a little while on Monday. She wasn't in the best mood, apparently."

I tried not to show any reaction. "It must be weird to know that someone was killed in your own house."

"According to Todd," Wade said quietly, "she wasn't any too sad about it. Apparently she made quite a point of telling the men how much she hated the guy. The statement was sort of ruined when she burst into tears, though."

"She was crying?"

"That's what Todd said."

"So she hated Jerry Saxton, but she was crying about it." I shook my head. "I understood the two of them were having an affair."

Wade was too much of a gentleman to say anything overly inflammatory about anyone, but the news about Joyce and Jerry's relationship was all over town. As far as I was concerned, Joyce had every right to hate Jerry after finding out about his many affairs—if only she hadn't been carrying on her own extramarital affair at the same time. But it sure seemed odd that she'd been canoodling with him a few days before his death and now, all of a sudden, she insisted she hated him. It didn't make her a murderer. It just made me wonder. Especially when I kept hearing that she was bursting into tears all over the place.

I left the Boyer house in Wade's good hands and drove out to the Paradise Lane work site a mile east of the center of town. On the drive, I pondered the information Wade had shared. Emily had heard the same basic story from Natty Terrell, whose son had heard Joyce call Jerry's death a "good riddance." Was Joyce simply jealous that he had been fooling around with other women? Again, since she was married, she couldn't complain too much, could she?

Apparently, she could.

And I still didn't know why Stan Boyer had lied to me about his whereabouts when he called me last Sunday. Not that I would expect him to tell me he was having an affair, but he didn't have to say he was in San Francisco, did he? I supposed some people felt the need to embellish their lies in order to make themselves sound more plausible. I wouldn't know. I couldn't lie worth beans. Oh, I tried to every so often, but I usually ended up sounding ridiculous.

I pulled to a stop on Paradise Lane, climbed out of my truck, and stared at the property in front of me. This house was among the oldest Victorians in town and one of the "grande dames" of Lighthouse Cove. If you took one of the historical tours that were offered around town, this house was always featured. It was built in 1867 by a prosperous Danish dairy farmer, Herman Clausen, otherwise known as the Butterfat King and one of the earliest settlers in the region.

The house was a gorgeous example of the Stick-

Eastlake style, whose most notable features were elaborate fretted woodwork, fanciful carved moldings, and stunning spindle-wood gables. The style epitomized the gingerbread look for which so many Victorian homes were noted.

The new owners had insisted that they wanted only the simplest updating done to the house. I had hesitated to take the job until they assured me that they loved every aspect of the design. Some new owners of vintage homes wanted to strip away those froufrou details that made some Victorian homes so unique and valuable. I usually didn't take those jobs.

This home still had the original stained-glass panels on the front door and side insets. The intricate stick work that framed the porch eaves was in remarkably good condition. The pitched tin roofs over the dormer windows needed only modest repair and repainting. The new owners thought those features were delightful and just wanted them lovingly restored to their original charm.

That worked for me.

I tracked down Carla Harrison, my second foreman, at the back of the house and almost forty feet up in the air, where she was inspecting one of the third-floor gables with the owner. They stood inside the basketlike platform of our articulated boom lift, one of my favorite pieces of equipment and a real thrill ride. The steel-encased platform held two people comfortably as the powerful motor and pump allowed the mast and riser arms to stretch as far as fifty-one feet into the air.

I greeted Douglas, the crew member assigned to watch the lift and operate the lower controls in case of a glitch. Even though the upper platform had its own controls, it was important to have another person on the ground checking that everything ran smoothly.

The articulated lift was a necessity for any company that worked on Victorian houses as much as mine did, since many of the homes stretched three stories high and had roofs so steep that it was impossible to scale them. They were often irregularly formed as well, with balconies and turrets in the oddest places, so scaffolding wasn't always possible. The boom lift solved all those problems.

Carla was pointing out some aspect of the intricate woodwork to the owner and explaining something I couldn't hear. But I knew that all that whimsical woodwork—I think we counted 312 unique pieces—would have to be pried off individually and stripped of paint, the cracks would have to be filled and sanded, and then all would be sealed and repainted and put back where they belonged.

When the boom brought them back down to the ground, Dan, the owner, looked slightly shell-shocked. I assured him that it was all part of the service and included in the price they were paying for the rehab.

Dan gave me a weak smile. "It's a little overwhelming."

"It'll be beautiful when we're finished," I assured him, but I knew how he felt. It was a daunting job to fully restore a historic home to its original luster. I was so glad that Dan was determined to have it done the right way.

After he walked off, Carla and I strolled over to her

truck to talk privately. She was the daughter of my dad's old foreman so we'd grown up together, part of each other's families.

We talked about a small hitch she'd run into on the job site and the fact that she was still on schedule, a minor miracle. I got Wade on the phone and the three of us arranged a meeting for Sunday morning. We usually tried to meet every two weeks to go over the schedule and work out any crew or subcontractor issues the two of them had. We would determine which job got what heavy equipment for the week and which homes needed extra crew. And I wanted to talk about the slowdown at the Boyers' house.

As I was leaving, I looked up and saw my guy Johnny kneeling on the flat porch roof. He'd been assigned to the Boyers' rehab but we'd moved him over to this job site while the crime scene was in effect. I waved to him and he acknowledged me by holding up a brush and can of rubberized sealant. He was applying it to the seams of the roof to prevent water from leaking into the eaves, in advance of the change of seasons.

"Good job, Johnny," I shouted.

"I do it all for you, boss."

I smiled as two of the other guys laughed. They were repairing the porch balusters and doing a really good job, I noticed before jogging back to my truck.

From Paradise Drive I drove seven miles south to the Point Arlen City Hall. There was a snafu on a construction permit for a family who wanted to build a Craftsman home there, and while I didn't expect it to be an insurmountable hassle, I wanted to show up at City Hall early enough to work out the problem and have the permit issued right then and there.

I wouldn't have time to stop by the owners' property today, but as soon as I got my hands on the permit, I would give them a call and figure out a start date.

It always gave me a thrill to work on a Craftsman home, although I didn't get the chance very often because they weren't my professional specialty. I'd been born and raised in Lighthouse Cove, so the Victorian design was my main area of expertise. And since the entire town had been designated a National Historic Landmark District for its plethora of well-preserved Victorian homes and businesses, I was right where I needed to be. Still, I was excited at the opportunity to design and construct a Craftsman home. It was a chance to show off my carpentry muscles. Luckily, the city clerk was able to clear up the snafu in record time.

On the way back home, I got a call from Marigold, who invited me to dinner with her and her aunt Daisy. She indicated that she had some news to share, but refused to spill it over the phone. I couldn't blame her, even though I was frustrated the whole way home. I couldn't wait to find out what my friend had discovered.

Thanks to my brilliant, nosy pals, motives for killing Jerry began to spring up all over town. Jane even went to the trouble of making up a detailed spreadsheet of all of them to give to Chief Jensen. I hoped he fully appreciated her diligence.

Marigold's customer Susan had called Jerry selfish, narcissistic, and manipulative. And those were nice terms compared to what some of the other people had used to describe him. Susan had confessed to Marigold that she had bought into his song and dance and succumbed to his questionable charms. He'd been rather cruel afterward, but she refused to go into detail, despite Marigold's less than subtle questioning.

It was alarming to discover just how many women were being serviced by the phenomenal Jerry Saxton, many of them concurrently. The women were married, single, old, young, rich, poor—you name it. Jerry was an equal-opportunity womanizer.

If the number of Jerry's sexual encounters was shocking, something equally alarming cropped up in our investigations. Through one of Lizzie's business connections, we found out that several unwarranted home foreclosures had occurred as a direct result of Jerry's allegedly shady dealings.

I remembered on the night of our date, Jerry had talked about some of the property deals he'd handled in Lighthouse Cove, but I hadn't realized there were so many. And I'd certainly never thought he might be doing anything illegal with them. Then again, I didn't really know the man at all.

I was beginning to think it might be easier to find someone in town who *didn't* have a motive to kill Jerry.

By the end of the week, there were still too many questions in my mind. But now I knew exactly who to talk to in order to get some answers.

Chapter Six

Friday night I finally showed my face at the pub. Jane and Emily flanked me as I walked inside and was greeted by many of the friends and neighbors I'd been avoiding all week. There was plenty of good-natured ribbing, but nothing too outrageous. Jerry's death had clearly put a damper on any teasing I might've received for kneeing him that night on the beach.

We left our name with the hostess and found a spot at the bar to have drinks while we waited for a table. I glanced around to see if my dad was here, but didn't spot him. I saw plenty of other people, though. Penny was sitting in a booth with two people I recognized from the bank. Joyce and Stan Boyer sat across from each other at one of the bar tables, talking animatedly while they drank cocktails and shared an order of French fries. I would've loved to get close enough to listen in on their conversation, but they would probably notice and shoo me away.

Police Chief Jensen stood at the far end of the bar, talking to Tommy and another cop. I figured the three of them were off duty, given that they all had beer bottles clutched in their hands.

Jane waved to Chief Jensen, who grinned at her and then acknowledged me with a somber nod. I smiled at Tommy just as Whitney approached him and whispered something in his ear. He chuckled at whatever she said and gave her a sweet kiss on the cheek. She turned and looked directly at me, smiling smugly. I rolled my eyes and gazed in another direction. The woman was relentless in her need to prove to me how much Tommy adored her. I simply didn't care, but I would never be able to convince her of that.

A minute later Whitney was joined by Jennifer Bailey and their friend Trina, another member of their rich-girl posse from high school. All three women were overdressed for a night at the pub, but that was typical. Whitney wore a sleeveless baby blue beaded top to show off her tanned, perfectly toned arms, along with white skinny jeans and terrifyingly high stiletto heels. Her sleek dark hair was tucked coquettishly behind her ears. The other two women were both dressed in shimmering black from head to toe, including the requisite stiletto heels. Tommy ordered drinks for the women, and when the cocktails arrived the three of them moved away from the cops to talk more privately.

"She's still a piece of work, isn't she?" Jane murmured, shaking her head.

"Yeah." I glanced down at my clean blue jeans, navy sweater, and black ankle boots and wondered briefly if I should start wearing clothes with sparkles on them. I'd probably get laughed out of the pub.

"She's scared to death that Tommy is still in love with you," Emily said.

I blinked at her. "That's crazy."

"No, it's not," Jane said. "It makes perfect sense."

"Except for the fact that Tommy is deliriously happy with both his marriage and his family."

"That may be true," Emily said, "but she's too insecure to see it."

I glanced over my shoulder at Whitney, then turned back to my friends. "Possibly," I hedged.

"Let's change the subject," Jane said. "How's your chef hunt going, Emily?"

Emily regaled us with the disastrous results of her search for a second cook for the tea shop. "Needless to say, the past few days have been a complete fiasco. But I have prospective cooks coming in every day next week, so please pray that none of us gets food poisoning or a knife shoved into her gut."

"That's a lovely picture," Jane said, laughing.

I shivered at the thought. I guess it was too soon for me to find jokes about murder funny.

I took a sip of my wine and gazed across the room in time to see Wendell Jarvick saunter imperiously into the bar and collide right into Whitney. Her drink, some cranberry-and-vodka concoction, splashed all over the front of Wendell's crisp white dress shirt and dripped down his perfectly creased khaki pants.

"You stupid bitch!" he shouted, his facing turning as red as the stain.

"It's not my fault," she yelled back, outraged. "You weren't looking where you were going."

"You saw me and deliberately got in my way."

"That's ridiculous." She set her empty glass down on the nearest surface. "You owe me a drink."

"Oh yeah?" In an instant, Wendell grabbed a ketchup

bottle off a nearby table and shook it. Whipping the top off, he flung the contents at Whitney, leaving thick red blotches spattered across her sparkly top. She gaped at her top for a second or two, then screamed and grabbed for his throat.

Wendell shoved her away from him.

I flinched. "Oh, my God. He's horrible."

"You'll pay for that," Wendell said in an ominous tone as he brushed the excess liquid off his shirt.

"You're going to die!" Whitney screamed, and leaped at him again.

"Hey, hey," Tommy said, grabbing Whitney around the waist and pushing Wendell back a foot. "That's enough."

Chief Jensen stepped into the fray. "You okay?" he asked Whitney, who nodded silently. He turned to Wendell and pointed to the door. "You. Out."

"Why should I go?" Wendell demanded. "She's the one who threw her drink at me."

"I did not!" Whitney cried. Tommy wrapped his arm supportively around her shoulders. Whitney breathed heavily, her face pale from the shock of Wendell's attack.

Wendell glanced down at his stained shirt. "This is a two-hundred-dollar handmade shirt and it's ruined. I demand that she pay for it."

"Good luck with that," Jensen said dryly. "Everybody saw you run into her, so it's your own fault. Now do yourself a favor and get out of here before I decide to let her throttle you after all."

Wendell's teeth were clenched and he was trembling with anger. He had to know it would be folly to continue arguing with someone as big as Eric Jensen, even if he didn't realize the man was the chief of police. So after a long, charged moment, he pivoted and stomped out of the bar.

The room erupted in applause.

Trina handed Whitney a clump of paper napkins and she began to wipe the ketchup off her top. She looked so numb, I actually felt sorry for her.

"Wow," Emily whispered. "That man is pure trouble."

"Yeah," I said, feeling a little shell-shocked. "He's also my tenant for the next two weeks."

"If he lives that long," Jane muttered.

Saturday morning I called the person I most wanted to talk to about Jerry Saxton. She couldn't meet me until noon, so in the meantime I took a walk over to the Cozy Cove Diner to have breakfast with my dad and Uncle Pete. The two men met there every morning unless they were away on a fishing trip, which was more often than not lately.

"Morning, Shannon," Cindy the waitress said. "I'll bring you some coffee."

"Thanks, Cindy."

"There's my girl." My dad waved me over to the booth he was sharing with Uncle Pete.

"Got time for breakfast with the old man?" Dad asked.

"Of course." I gave them each a smooch on the cheek and slid into the booth next to Dad. "What are you two rovers up to?"

"Going fishing," Uncle Pete said, and checked his watch. "Leaving in an hour."

"I'm shocked."

They both chuckled as Cindy poured coffee into my waiting mug.

Once I'd moved back to town from San Francisco and Dad's health had improved, I'd taken over the house and the business and he'd bought the massive Winnebago he'd always wanted. It had long been the plan for him and my mom to raise us kids and then take off to see the country in their RV.

With Mom gone, Dad had still been determined to hit the road. Halfway to the Oregon border, though, he'd realized he wasn't so keen to leave his hometown and see the world after all. Not by himself, anyway. Besides, the Winnebago was huge and he didn't feel comfortable driving it much over twenty miles an hour. So he turned it around and headed back to Lighthouse Cove.

Most often he parked it in my driveway and that was fine with me. Dad liked living in what he called his Rolling Man Cave with its big-screen TV and comfortable furnishings. His construction-crew buddies and Uncle Pete met there once a week to play poker, watch football, and share their opinions about what I should be doing with my life. Every month or so, Dad would indulge his wanderlust by driving the Winnebago up to the river or down to the beach to go fishing with Uncle Pete or one of the other guys.

I ordered the hash and eggs and listened to Dad and Uncle Pete talk about the two lovely ladies they'd met at my uncle's wine bar the night before.

That was something else in which my dad and uncle shared an abiding interest: the ladies. And why not, since they were both good-looking, eligible bachelors? They were sweet men and always treated women nicely, but it was funny to hear them talk about their strategy as though they were planning a reconnaissance mission into enemy territory.

I told Dad about Wendell parking in the driveway and Dad brushed it off. "We're leaving this afternoon to go fishing so I'm not worried about a parking space."

"Probably be gone a week or so," Uncle Pete said, after taking a big bite of bacon.

"Will you be okay while I'm gone?" Dad asked.

"I'll be fine. I'm hoping for a lot less excitement than we had last week."

"Damn straight," Dad said, then lowered his voice to add, "But if that police chief comes sniffing around, accusing you of anything again, you call me. I'll race back here and give him a piece of my mind."

I smiled. "Thanks, Dad."

At noon, I drove over to meet Penny at her house. My main objective was to find out more about Jerry Saxton and the rumors about the foreclosures he might've manipulated. But I hadn't mentioned that subject when I spoke to her on the phone, hoping I might bring it up more casually at some point. Instead, I'd told her I had the samples I'd gathered for her counters, floor, and backsplash. I had wood-grain samples, too, from which she could choose her cupboards and drawers.

"I'm sorry I have only an hour to spend," she said, slinging her suit jacket and purse over the back of a dining room chair. "It's crazy busy at work today. And I just realized I've been saying that a lot lately."

"I guess being busy is better than the alternative."

"Absolutely," she said with a grin. "I should be used

to it by now, but I'm always surprised at how many people like to bank on Saturdays."

I checked the clock. "I think we can get through all of this with time to spare."

"Sounds good." She sat down at the table and pulled an apple out of her purse. "I hope you don't mind if I munch while you talk."

"Please do." I placed the heavy box of samples on the table and pulled the tiles out one by one. I discussed the pros and cons of each floor tile and counter sample, weighed the benefits of travertine versus ceramic tile, and discussed prices. I laid the tiles down on the kitchen floor for her to imagine how they might look. "I'll leave all of these with you for you to play with during the week."

"Thanks." She pointed to one of the squares on the floor. "I love that rust-colored travertine, but I'm not sure the color will go with everything else I like."

"I brought another book with additional colors for you to look through."

Her eyes lit up. "You think of everything."

"That's my job," I said with a smile.

We went through the same process with the marble and granite samples for the kitchen counters. She picked out a beautiful black-and-red-speckled granite that I knew would go perfectly with the vertical-grain Douglas fir she'd chosen for the cupboards and drawers.

"If you're not happy with something, I'll keep looking," I assured her.

"I'm happy, I promise." She stood and pulled her jacket on.

"Okay, but you can always change your mind." I stood, too, and grabbed my purse. "I'll give you another week to go through the books, and if you're still happy with these choices, I'll start ordering."

"Sounds great."

As she led the way outside, we talked some more about a tentative schedule for the work. Then I broached the real topic I'd wanted to discuss with her. "Hey, do you mind if I ask you a question about Jerry Saxton?"

"Ugh," she said, making a face. "No, I guess not. Have the police talked to you yet?"

"Oh yeah. Two hours the other night at the police station, plus a few minutes the next day. I doubt it'll be the last time they question me."

"Unfortunately, you're probably right," she said. "They talked to me for a while, too. I'm glad they're being thorough, though. It's creepy to know there's a killer on the loose."

Very creepy, I thought, barely suppressing a shiver.

"Anyway," I said, getting back to the subject, "I heard a rumor that Jerry pulled some shady maneuvers with some of the bank loans. I'm worried that a few of my clients might've been affected."

"Oh, God." Her shoulders sagged slightly. "It's all true, but you didn't hear it from me. I'm not at liberty to discuss it, but, believe me, if Jerry wasn't already dead, my bank president would gladly kill him."

"That sounds bad." I grimaced, wondering if the bank president should be considered another suspect.

"It's beyond bad," she assured me with a serious frown. "Besides being a jerk and a womanizer, the guy was a crook."

"That sucks for the bank," I said, then added, "But on the bright side, at least you didn't date him."

She began to laugh. "No, thank God."

I sighed. "I guess I'd be laughing, too, if I didn't have the cops breathing down my neck about it."

She gave me an encouraging smile. "Don't worry. They'll figure out you're not guilty and move on to someone else pretty soon."

"Hope so."

She opened her car door, and with a wave good-bye I headed for my truck.

"Oh, wait," she said. "I wanted to ask you something."

I turned. "What is it?"

"I think we go to the same gym. Flex-Time over on Old Cove Road?"

"Yeah, that's the one I go to."

"I just joined last week and I thought I saw you driving out of the parking lot a few nights ago."

"Probably so," I said. "It's a nice facility."

"Do you want to meet there sometime and work out together? We can spot each other."

I thought about it. I could never get my friends to go with me. Penny was new in town and probably didn't know a lot of people, so I was happy to say yes. "That sounds great."

"I usually go after work on Tuesdays and Thursdays and Sunday mornings."

"Okay, I'll try to be there Tuesday afternoon. About five?"

"Wonderful," she said. "I'll see you there."

When I arrived home, Wendell Jarvick's car was parked in my driveway. For the fourth day in a row! My shoulders stiffened instantly. I was so sick of him and there was nothing I could do to get rid of him. At least I wasn't alone in my feelings. There wasn't a hotel in town that would give him a room.

He had complained about Robbie barking at him, but who could blame the little dog? I'd seen Wendell glaring at poor Robbie and I wouldn't put it past Mr. Dog Hater to try to kick my little guy when I wasn't around.

I'd had to laugh, though, when I saw Tiger approach Wendell and start winding her way around his ankles, tripping him up as he was walking to the stairs. Wendell began to swear at the cat, who dashed away. By the time Wendell reached the top of the stairs, he was sneezing loudly. My Tiger knew exactly whom she was dealing with.

Maybe on a world-hunger scale, it was no big deal that Wendell's car was blocking my access to the garage. But in my little world, he was a major pain, deliberately obtuse and disrespectful. Not only to me, but to my father. And my animals. And half the people in town. I thought back to that scene with Whitney and wondered what would've happened if Tommy hadn't stopped her from strangling the man.

Before I lost my nerve, I decided to confront the passive-aggressive jerk.

I just wished Dad hadn't left to go fishing with Uncle Pete, so he could park his gigantic RV right behind Wendell's car, blocking him in. That would get Wendell's shorts in a twist.

I ran upstairs and knocked on his door, but there was no answer. It was early afternoon, so he was probably out having lunch somewhere. Or perhaps he was off annoying some shopkeeper in town. I decided to watch and wait until I saw him arrive. I'd forgotten to check the mail the day before, so I walked out to the mailbox and that's when I saw him strolling up the sidewalk without a care in the world.

"Hello, Wendell," I said with forced cheerfulness. "Now that you're home, you can move your car."

His face scrunched up and I could tell he was insulted by the demand. "I refuse to allow you to treat me this way. It's not right to ask a guest in your home to park on the street."

Aggravated, I clamped my teeth together so tightly, I had to wonder if I was wearing out the enamel. "Technically, you're *not* a guest—you're a tenant. You're renting a room from me for two weeks and you're bound by the contract you signed when you first made the arrangements."

He sniffed at me. "There was nothing about assigned parking space in the contract."

"Exactly my point. You're *not* assigned a parking place so you can't park here."

"That's a stupid argument."

"This is private property."

Out of the corner of my eye, I saw my next-door neighbor Jesse walk out to check his mailbox. From twenty feet away, he asked, "Everything okay here, Shannon?"

"Everything's just great, Jesse."

Then Mrs. Higgins from across the street toddled down her walkway and stood at her picket fence to watch. Mrs. Higgins was in her late seventies and hardly ever left her property, yet she always seemed to know everything that was going on in town. By osmosis, maybe?

The two senior citizens had the biggest ears in Lighthouse Cove. I should've lowered my voice, but I was so angry, I no longer cared who heard me.

I turned back to Wendell. "I'm asking you nicely to move your car, so please do it now or leave my premises."

"I don't know why you're complaining," he said, shifting his shoulders for emphasis. "At least my car looks good. Better than that hideous truck you drive."

Okay, now he was just being nasty. My truck was in perfect condition, and I washed it regularly.

I could feel my nostrils flaring like those of a bull about to attack. "I don't care what you think of my truck. It's *my* truck and I'll park it in *my* driveway whenever I want to."

"Whatever." He brushed me off with a sweep of his hand. "I'm going to go take a nap."

"Don't you walk away from me." I could feel my blood pressure spike and I shouted, "You are not authorized to park on my property. If you don't move your car this instant, I'll have it towed."

He whipped around. "You tow it and I'll sue you."

He would *sue* me? He couldn't sue me, could he? Did I care?

He reached the garage and walked haughtily up the stairs. His chin was stuck up in the air like that of some pissy six-year-old pretending to ignore me.

"Just move your damn car!" I yelled.

He got to the top of the stairs, unlocked the door to the suite, and disappeared inside.

I let out a frustrated scream.

"He's not a very nice man," Mrs. Higgins cried out from across the street. "You should tow his car."

"Thank you, Mrs. Higgins," I said, waving at her. Just

what I needed was advice from a veritable shut-in. Even though she was right.

"That reminds me," she said loudly, her elderly voice shaky in the chilly air. "Did you two hear about the strange man who bought the old lighthouse mansion?"

"What?" I asked, thinking she must be deluded. "Jesse, do you have any idea what she's talking about?"

He shrugged. "Some movie star just moved here. That's what I heard up at the diner."

"Really? Where have I been?" But I knew the answer to that. I'd been running around town, trying to find out who killed Jerry Saxton. And I'd been squabbling with Wendell Jarvick in an attempt to get his stupid damn car off my property. I stared up at his room over the garage and wondered what to do next.

Jesse followed my gaze. "He's something else, that guy."

"I can't stand him."

"So tow his car like you threatened to do," he said, leaning his elbow against his mailbox. "Gus'll take care of it for you."

Gus was the auto mechanic who'd been servicing my vehicles since high school.

"I know, but I have a feeling it would cause more problems than it's worth." I yanked the mail out of the box and slammed the door shut. "I just want Wendell to go away. Forever."

"You can't always get what you want, kiddo," Jesse said.

"Don't I know it?" I muttered, and walked back into the house.

* * *

That night I went to dinner at Lizzie and Hal's for the second time in a week. Don't get me wrong—I wasn't complaining. Lizzie was a great cook and Hal liked to grill steaks, so why would I say no to their invitation?

Still, I was more than a little suspicious. For some reason, each of my friends had invited me over for dinner every night that week. Did they think I couldn't be trusted to dine alone? Did they think I was lonely or nervous about being by myself in that big house of mine?

Maybe I should've been nervous. After all, the police hadn't arrested anyone for killing Jerry yet.

And then there was Wendell. I hated having him stay in my pretty garage apartment so maybe it was just as well that I was away from home tonight. I was ticking off the calendar days until he departed Lighthouse Cove and, if I had my way, he would never come back again. I had only to avoid him for nine more days, but it wouldn't be easy. He seemed to thrive on stirring up negative feelings wherever he went. That seemed like an inherently dangerous way to live one's life.

After giving hugs to Lizzie and Hal and their two kids, Marisa and Taz—short for Tasmanian Devil, Hal always said—I handed Lizzie the bottle of wine I'd brought along with a small pink box of cookies.

"Are those cookies?" Taz whispered reverently. "Thanks, Aunt Shannon."

"You're welcome, sweetie," I said, ruffling the eleven-year-old's hair and getting a little choked up that he was still young enough to call me his aunt. "Good grief, he's almost as tall as you are, Lizzie."

"I'm taller," Taz said, grinning.

"Don't remind me," Lizzie said, as she hung up my coat in the front closet.

Her very grown-up thirteen-year-old daughter, Marisa, took hold of the pink box. "I'll put them in the fridge, Mom."

"Thanks, honey. And no sampling, please." Lizzie walked with me over to the kitchen bar. Hal had just poured glasses of wine so the three of us had a toast to the first lovely hints of fall in the air.

"I heard you had another run-in with Wendell," Lizzie said after she'd taken a sip.

"How could you have heard that? It happened only a few hours ago."

Lizzie gazed at me quizzically. "I'm sorry—where do we live again?"

"Small-town America," I said, groaning. "But, come on, the only people watching us fight were Jesse and Mrs. Higgins."

She gave me that same look and I held up my hand. "I know. They're the town criers. They were probably on the telephone within seconds."

"I found out about it at the market less than an hour ago," Lizzie said.

"Ridiculous." I sighed. "I don't want to talk about it. But he's a horrible man. We fought over something really stupid, but he made me so angry, I wanted to slap him. Really hard. I mean, really, really hard. And you should've seen what he did to Whitney at the pub the other night. What a jackass."

I was pounding my fist into the palm of my other

hand with enough force that Lizzie began to frown. "But you don't want to talk about it?"

"Oh, hell." I placed both hands flat on the bar counter to calm myself. "Let's change the subject."

"Yes," Lizzie said, smiling, "because I have something interesting and fun to talk about."

"Hooray." I took a seat on one of the barstools. "Let's hear it."

"Okay, you've heard of MacKintyre Sullivan, right?"

"The writer? Of course. I love his books."

"I do, too." Her eyes lit up and she waved her hands excitedly. "Well . . . he's moving to Lighthouse Cove!"

"Moving? Here?" I shook my head in confusion. "Why?"

"Why not? We have a wonderful little town."

"Of course we do," I said, "but he belongs in Hollywood or New York, doesn't he?"

"No," she said quickly. "I mean, yes. Okay, I was a little shocked to hear it, too, because what are the chances, right? But isn't it awesome? I just reordered a bunch of his books for the store last week. Everybody loves him. Hal loves him, too. Don't you, honey?"

Hal turned from the stove, where he was stirring something that smelled fantastic. I could detect the aroma of onions and garlic, so I was happy. He turned down the heat and joined us at the bar, where he'd left his wineglass. "His books are great."

MacKintyre Sullivan was a famous crime novelist whose books were always winning awards and hitting bestseller lists. His main character, Jake Slater, was an ex–Navy SEAL turned private detective who specialized in lost causes. When things got really rough, he would call on a motley group of misfits from his black-ops days to help him right the wrongs of the world. Sullivan's first book had been made into a blockbuster movie and Jake Slater was getting to be as popular as James Bond and Jack Reacher.

Lizzie rested her elbow on the counter. "I love Jake Slater. Rich, gorgeous, brave, dashing."

"And fictional," I said, smiling.

Marisa turned from the stove, where she had taken over stirring the onion mixture. "That movie was so awesome."

"It was," I said. I was a sucker for action films.

"You should see him in person, Shannon," Lizzie whispered ecstatically. "He walked by the store this afternoon and looked inside the window. We made eye contact and he smiled and waved at me." She patted her chest. "Oh, God, he's soooooo cute! And he's single! I heard he was engaged but it didn't work out. Which means there's no woman in his life. Currently."

"Don't even think about it." I happened to glance at Marisa, who was rolling her eyes at her mom. Laughing, I said, "But he is awfully cute, at least according to his book jackets. I'm sure I'll get a chance to see him eventually."

"Of course you will," she assured me. "Oh, and Cindy at the diner told me he likes to be called Mac. She said that while he was eating lunch, people came up and asked for his autograph and he was perfectly happy to give it. He's not stuck-up or anything."

"That's nice to hear."

"And she agreed that he's incredibly handsome."

I glanced over at Hal. "Did you get a chance to see him, Hal?"

"Yeah."

"What did you think?"

He pressed both hands to his cheeks. "OMG, Shannon! He's such a dreamboat."

I laughed again. "You sound just like Marisa."

Marisa turned and glared at me. "I resent that."

"It was a compliment," I said. "Your father's funny."

"I know. He makes me laugh all the time." She ran over and wrapped her arms around her dad's waist.

I shared a sentimental glance with Lizzie, who knew how lucky she was. Even though Marisa had recently become a teenager, she was still a sweet girl and hadn't yet turned into a raging hormonal monster.

I took a sip of wine. "Do you know where he's . . . Oh, wait a minute. MacKintyre Sullivan didn't just buy the old lighthouse keeper's house, did he?"

"Yes!"

Mystery solved, I thought. Although the fact that Mrs. Higgins had heard the news before I had was just so wrong.

Our famous lighthouse had been standing out on the bluff since 1870 and the home attached to it was nearly as old. An earthquake had almost destroyed it, but instead of tearing it down, the town decided to refurbish it with steel reinforcement rods encased in concrete. It had lasted more than one hundred years and was still in fine shape.

The year I was born, the town of Lighthouse Cove acquired the lighthouse and attached mansion from the U.S. Coast Guard. In recent years, the light itself and the foghorn had been replaced with new technology that was maintained by the lighthouse trust. Recently, the trust had begun to search for a new owner for the mansion, a person who would agree to live next door to an operational lighthouse with its thriving gift shop and small museum.

Apparently they'd found a buyer.

"Do you think he means to live there?" I wondered aloud. "Or will he just fix it up and try to flip it?"

"I haven't heard," Lizzie said. "I hope he stays. And I hope he comes into the store soon. We have all his books in stock and I'd love to get him to sign them."

"If he's as wonderful as you've heard he is," I said, "I don't know why he wouldn't want to."

Lizzie tucked her arm through Hal's. "He's still not as nice and cute as you are, honey."

"Nobody is," Hal admitted with a sigh. He lifted her off her feet, gave her a semihot kiss on the lips, and walked away. Lizzie stared at his back until he disappeared down the hall.

"You're so lucky," I said, smiling at the glazed look in her eyes.

"I know." She blinked a few times, then pulled utensils from the drawer. "Come help me set the table."

Lizzie pushed the swinging door open and we walked into the dining room. I grabbed place mats and napkins from the sideboard. "So, tell me more about our new celebrity resident."

She patted her chest. "Seriously gorgeous, Shannon. Let me know if you want to meet him."

"Of course I want to meet . . ." I blinked at her. "No. I'm warning you, Lizzie. You're not going to set me up on another date again."

She laughed. "I didn't mean I would set you up. I just meant, you know, introduce the two of you."

"But you haven't even met him."

"True, but chances are, I'll meet him before you do."

She was probably right, but still. "I'll run into him eventually on my own."

"Of course you will. But I don't see why you wouldn't want to go out with him, just as a friendly gesture. He probably doesn't know anyone in town."

"You are incorrigible," I said, folding another napkin before calling for help. "Hal, I need more wine."

To my delight, Hal came running through the swinging door with the bottle and filled my glass and Lizzie's. "Honey, Shannon just had a bad experience and she isn't ready to date anyone else just yet, so let it go."

"Are you listening in on our conversation?" she asked.

Hal chuckled. "Of course."

She sighed and looked at me with some regret. "Okay, I'm sorry."

"No problem."

"But whenever you're ready . . ."

"Stop!" Hal and I said it in unison.

She laughed. "All right, all right. But, dang, I don't see why you wouldn't want to go out with Mac."

"Maybe because he dates supermodels and heiresses?"

"Does he?" She frowned. "He doesn't seem that superficial."

"He's a man," I whispered.

"True." She gazed lovingly at her husband. "But so is Hal and he's wonderful."

I smiled. "Yes, Hal is wonderful. And rare."

"Thanks, pal." He winked at me and headed back into the kitchen.

When the door swung closed, Lizzie added, "You know, Police Chief Jensen isn't bad, either."

"Oh no." I smacked my forehead. "You did not just say that."

"I did." She smiled brightly. "Just say the word and I'll work my magic."

"Your magic?" I laughed. "Besides, I have it on good authority that you already asked him if he'd like to be introduced to anyone and he said no."

"True, but I haven't given up hope." She placed the last utensil on the napkin in front of her. "You have to admit he's awfully good-looking."

"Oh, sure. That's all I could think about when he was looking at me the other night like I might be a stone-cold killer. Nothing better than having a hottie investigating you in a murder case."

"You did get to know him in kind of a different way," she mused. "That can often be the beginning of a wonderful relationship."

I studied her for a moment, not quite believing we'd been close friends most of our lives. "When did you go crazy? I missed it. And by the way, for a married woman you're awfully fascinated by all these other men."

"I'm not dead yet." She set a pair of salt and pepper shakers on the table. "Jane thinks the chief is interested in you."

I folded another napkin. "Liz, he's interested in me as a murderer. It's not a compliment."

"At least he's paying attention to you. For some women, that would be enough."

"Are you listening to yourself?"

She laughed. "Yes, and I'm kidding. I just want you to be happy, that's all."

"With a man who considers me a flight risk? Oh, be still my heart."

Within a day, the gossip around town about Jerry's murder was eclipsed by the latest buzz concerning the mysterious stranger who'd bought the old lighthouse mansion out on the bluff. I already knew who the stranger was and tried not to get too wrapped up in the gossip. I also tried to forget Lizzie's threat to introduce me to the stranger, the great MacKintyre Sullivan, but the thought wouldn't leave my head.

Maybe because I'd always had a tiny bit of a crush on the man. Did I say *tiny*? The author photograph on the back of Sullivan's books was positively mesmerizing. There, I said it. Mac Sullivan had to be one of the best-looking men I'd ever seen. And that was only the two-dimensional picture of the man. What would I do if I ran into his real, live, three-dimensional self somewhere in town? Faint? Hyperventilate?

"Get a grip," I muttered. The photograph was probably a fake, anyway. Didn't they do that all the time on book covers? If readers knew the author was gorgeous, wouldn't that make for better book sales? Except that Lizzie had already confirmed that the guy was stunningly handsome, so there went that theory.

As I toasted bagels and set up the coffeepot, I realized that it wouldn't be a problem for me because the great MacKintyre Sullivan would never even bother to notice me. He was a wealthy new resident. I was a working-class local, a townie. The two sides rarely met. And that was fine with me. So there, I'd worked it all out.

Carla and Wade showed up at ten o'clock for our meeting and we spent an hour going over crew schedules and equipment inventory. Because my pink wrench had been used to kill someone, I was in favor of a new rule of not only locking up our toolboxes but also of putting them all in a safe, secured place after finishing work each day.

"Jeez, boss," Wade said as he poured more coffee into his mug. "That wrench thing was just a fluke, don't you think? I'd say as long as we lock up our own toolboxes and lock the main doors to the houses, which we always do, we'll be all right."

Carla nodded. "I agree. The chance of anyone using one of our tools like that again is a million to one, so let's not overreact."

I thought about it. Was I overreacting? Maybe, but it was *my* wrench, after all, and it was *my* sorry butt being scrutinized by the police. So to speak. But Carla and Wade were right. I didn't have to force everyone else to go to extremes just to solve my problems.

"Okay," I said. "If you'll make sure things are locked up when you leave at night, we should be fine."

Carla licked a bit of cream cheese from her thumb. "So, did you guys hear that they sold the lighthouse mansion?"

"Are you kidding?" Wade said. "That thing's been empty forever."

"I heard." I set down my coffee as something occurred to me. I would've thought of it sooner if I hadn't been so distracted lately. "And I'm guessing they'll be doing an extensive rehab."

"Oh, you've got to bid on that project, Shannon," Carla said excitedly. "That place could be so beautiful."

"I know." I felt anticipation building. The lighthouse mansion was Victorian in age, of course, but not in the ornate style of the grande dames that were featured on the local Victorian-house tours. No, the mansion had simple, uncluttered lines, but it also had the most wonderful veranda, wide enough to use as another room in the summertime if you filled it with some chairs, a lounge, a dining table, and maybe even a swing. At least that was my vision for it. It faced west, of course, with a dramatic view of crashing waves against the rocky coastline.

As fabulous as the veranda was, there was also a jewel of a solarium, small and classically Victorian, connected to one side of the house. The story went that the navy had constructed it especially to raise citrus trees year-round for the sailors once stationed there.

"I might take a drive out there to get a feel for it."

"Great idea," Carla said, gathering up her notebook and purse. "I'd offer to go with you, but Keely has a ballet recital this afternoon."

"Oh, that's so sweet," I said, smiling at the thought of her tiny five-year-old wearing a tutu. "Take pictures."

"Are you kidding?" She laughed. "Chase bought a brand-new video camera just for this moment."

We talked about their kids as I walked Carla and Wade outside—and came face-to-face with Wendell's car, still parked in my driveway.

"Damn it," I muttered.

"Whose car is that?" Carla asked.

I bared my teeth like a feral cat. "It's Wendell Jarvick's and I've warned him every day this week that he can't park there. He's just too damn special to listen."

"So tow it," Wade said. "What the hell?"

"That guy is the biggest jerk," Carla added in a low voice. "Chase and I were having dinner at Lindy's on the pier last night and he was there. He made the biggest fuss about some stupid sauce on the fish and disrupted everyone's dinner."

"He did something even worse the other night at the pub." I told them what happened to Whitney. "I think we should banish him forever."

"That's a great idea," Carla said. "I'll start a petition."

After another minute, we were laughing about it. The two of them took off and I walked back inside. But now I was frustrated with Wendell all over again, so I decided I would go to the gym and work off my irritation. And afterward, I would drive out to the lighthouse mansion and see what things looked like out there.

I slipped into my sweats and grabbed my gym bag. Before leaving, I stuck a notepad and pen into my purse to jot some notes down once I got out to the mansion. Then I locked up and headed for my truck. But when I turned the ignition, all I heard was a vague clicking sound.

My weekend was complete. The battery was dead.

Chapter Seven

"It's not the battery," Gus Peratti, the mechanic said. "My guess is the alternator or maybe the starter. I'll let you know after I've checked it at the shop."

The shop. You never wanted to hear those words from a mechanic. Even one you knew and trusted.

"You have to tow it?"

"Yeah," he said. "I don't want to take the chance of starting it here and having it conk out on the road."

Oh, man. "I appreciate that."

Gus's auto shop was on the outskirts of town, about a mile east of my place on the way to the highway. Gus, or Augustus, as his mother called him, was another one of the locals I'd grown up with and an all-around great guy. He owned the garage with his father and uncle and always took good care of his customers. We chatted as he attached the giant hook to the front of my truck and slowly lifted it off the ground.

"I'm sorry I dragged you out here on a Sunday," I shouted over the noise of the tow crank.

"No worries, babe. I was working today, anyway."

He'd been calling me *babe* since he was ten years old.

Some men were just born to be chick magnets, and Gus was one of them. He was tall, with wavy black hair, dark eyes, and a sexy smile, and he always wore his T-shirts a touch too tight over his muscular arms and chest. Unlike half of the women in town, I had never been involved romantically with him, so maybe that's how we had managed to remain such good friends.

"I should have it ready for you by Tuesday afternoon. You need a loaner for a few days?"

"No, I'll manage," I said. But I gave my shiny chrome baby one long, sorrowful look as Gus readied her for her trip to the car spa. "Thanks for coming to my rescue."

"Always," he said, and after a quick hug, he drove off with my truck bouncing along behind his tow truck.

"Now what?" I wondered aloud. The day was too pretty to stay in the house all afternoon. Besides, I needed to move around and work off some of the negative energy that Wendell had infected me with.

I could ride my bike. A Sunday bike ride was the perfect solution. I wouldn't have time to drive out to the lighthouse to see the mansion, but I could get some exercise and see what was going on around town.

This would also be a good time to stop at my friends' shops and drop off the herb and flower cuttings I'd worked on a few weeks ago. They had been hanging from the rafters all this time and would be dry enough to display by now.

After changing into jeans and a light sweater, I wheeled my bike out of the garage and secured the three bundles of flowers and herbs in the big white basket attached to the handlebars.

My father had bought this retro bicycle for me last

Christmas. It had three gears, wide white-wall tires, and a comfy seat for easy riding. And it was pink, of course.

Before going into town, I rode down to the bike path that loosely paralleled the boardwalk and breezed along the beach for over a mile. Gaining speed, I felt the wind rush past me before I slowed down to turn around and head back to town. It wasn't the most grueling workout ever, but it made me feel better.

After locking my bicycle to one of the many bike posts scattered around the town square, I walked into Paper Moon. Hal was busy at the cash register and Lizzie was helping a customer pick out the perfect note cards, so I carefully set on one of the display shelves the little old teapot filled with dried red tea roses interspersed with sprigs of lavender and rosemary, and headed for the door.

"Oh, that's adorable," Lizzie's customer said. "How much is it?"

"Shannon," Lizzie called. "How much shall I charge for this beautiful thing?"

I turned and smiled. "It's just for display, not for sale."

"I'll give you forty dollars for it," the woman countered immediately.

Lizzie flashed me a brief but meaningful look, then turned to the woman. "Sold."

I laughed and walked out. I'd fished that old teapot out of a neighbor's trash bin, knowing I could use it for dried flowers. Lizzie and I would work out the details later, but I knew she would insist on giving me the money—which I would use to buy more trinkets and old bottles to fill with flowers for her store.

At Emily's place, I set a shallow wicker basket filled

with long, graceful stalks of dried lavender on top of the deli case near the front door. I caught Emily's eye as she was taking an order and she smiled and waved. I knew she would divide up the stalks later and put them in tall bud vases around the shop.

Next door at Marigold's Crafts and Quilts, I dropped off my last delivery: a small wooden box filled with dried rose petals, lavender seeds, bay laurel leaves, and some dried spiny pods from my sycamore tree.

"Smells wonderful," Marigold said as she sniffed the concoction. "So fresh and light." She set it down on the front counter near the cash register. "I'm putting it right here so I can enjoy it. Thank you, Shannon."

Marigold was the only one of my friends who could actually take the herbs and flowers I gave her and turn them into pretty, flower-strewn soaps. It was something she'd learned to do as a child growing up in an Amish community.

The store was empty, so I was able to spend a few minutes catching up with Marigold on the latest news. She, too, had blown off all talk of the recent murder in favor of gushing over MacKintyre Sullivan's move to town. That was fine with me. I would much rather chat about the popular author than the fact that I was still uncomfortably high up on Chief Jensen's list of suspects.

When three new customers walked into Marigold's store, I took off and headed for the diner. I'd decided to treat myself to Sunday lunch.

Before I'd gone halfway down the block, I saw Luisa Capello climbing out of a navy blue Porsche her older brother was driving. She wore a light pink sweater over dark jeans, and was still as fragile and pretty as she'd been in grammar school.

"Luisa?" I said.

She turned and her eyes lit up. "Shannon. It's great to see you."

"How are you?"

"I'm good." She glanced at her big, handsome brother. "Buddy, I want to talk to Shannon for a minute. Why don't you go meet Mama and Papa at the café? I promise I'll be quick."

"Yeah, okay. Hey, Shannon," he added before strolling to the restaurant.

Luisa watched until Buddy was far enough away for us to talk without being overheard. "We're having Sunday lunch at the Blue Moon Café."

"I like that place," I said.

"Me, too." She pressed her lips together pensively, then blurted, "I wanted to call you this week, Shannon, but I . . . I couldn't get up the nerve."

"Why not?" I asked, playing dumb. "What's up?"

"I heard what happened to you with Jerry. I'm so glad you defended yourself, but it never should've happened. I should've warned you. I should've warned every woman in town about him. He was a manipulative predator." Her breath trembled and she had to swallow a few times before continuing. "For months I was so afraid of saying anything to anyone for fear of him coming back and . . ." She couldn't complete the sentence, and I thought the worst. Would he have beaten her? Killed her?

I'd meant to call her last week, too, after Sean told me

that she'd shown up with a black eye and her family had suspected it was from Jerry. I didn't want to say anything now, though, because my reasons for contacting her hadn't been the most noble. I had wanted to gauge her anger at Jerry in the hopes that the police would add her to the suspect list. It was no fun being on the list all alone.

"Well," she continued, after shaking her head in self-disgust, "it might be terrible of me to say so, but I'm happy you kicked him. I wish I'd been there to see it."

I had to ask. "Luisa, did Jerry hurt you physically?"

Apparently, the question was traumatic, because she seemed to gasp for air, taking a few deep breaths before she could finally make eye contact. "Yes. He punched me in the face. More than once. I still can't see very well out of this eye." She touched the left side of her face. "The doctor says I'll be fine, eventually, but it was so awful, Shannon. And now I'm always flinching at noises and things. I hate that."

"Your parents and brothers must've been furious."

"They wanted to kill him," she said, then pressed her fingers to her lips. "I shouldn't have said that. And I didn't mean it. Not really. I mean, yes, they were furious with Jerry, but that's just natural. The police even talked to them because they had told people how much they hated him. But, luckily, they all have alibis."

"I'm glad."

"Me, too." She glanced around to make sure we were alone. "I know they didn't kill Jerry, but I also know they wanted to. And I hate to say it, but a small part of me wanted them to do it, too. That's a horrible thing to confess, but it's true. I was so angry at him, and even more angry at myself for allowing it to happen."

"I know how you feel," I said, grabbing her hand and squeezing it. "But you were smart and brave to stop seeing him."

"Not really," she whispered. "I went back to him after he hit me the first time. He promised never to do it again. And I really thought I loved him. He was so handsome and such a good listener. But then he hit me again. I'd heard of women getting caught in that cycle, but I never thought I would be one of them. I'm lucky I escaped before anything worse occurred."

"I don't care what you say. I still think you were brave to walk away from him." But now I had to wonder why she'd never pressed charges against him. Why hadn't her family? What were they afraid of?

"Do the police know who killed him?" she asked in a low voice.

"No," I said. "They're still investigating."

She nodded. "If you find out, will you call me?"

"Sure."

"Good," she said firmly, as her hands bunched into fists. "I want to know who to thank."

My breath caught, but before I could respond, she grabbed me in a tight hug, whispered, "Thanks, Shannon," and let me go. She walked quickly down the sidewalk and across the street.

I stared after her, still unsure what to make of the conversation. Especially her last statement. So much for that shy, fragile facade of hers. Shaking off my perplexity, I walked the rest of the way to the diner.

"Howdy, Shannon," Cindy called. She stood in front of the order spindle, looking into the kitchen. "Sit anywhere you'd like. I'll be right over."

The entire front counter of the homey restaurant was filled with diners, as were most of the booths and tables. I glanced around and saw Penny sitting at the far end, talking with two women I recognized as tellers from her bank. She saw me and waved, so I approached her booth.

After greeting them all, I turned to Penny. "I'm glad I ran into you. I won't be able to make it to the gym on Tuesday. My truck has a dead battery."

"Oh, so that's why I saw you riding your bike earlier," she said.

"Yeah, that'll be my transportation for the next few days."

"At least it's a really cute bike." She briefly described my pink retro bike to her friends.

"Can we do the gym on Thursday instead?" I asked.

"Sounds good." She gave me a sympathetic smile and went back to her conversation.

I walked over and sat at a small booth by the bay window and perused the menu, just to find out if anything on there had changed lately. I was impressed to see that they had added some local wines to the list. We were only a short drive away from the Anderson Valley, the latest wine-growing region to hit the big time, so some of the newer wineries were now represented on the list.

"What's it gonna be, hon?" Cindy said, her notepad and pen ready. She wore the world's largest frilly handkerchief corsage with her name tag pinned to her white uniform. Her blond hair was pulled back in a neat ponytail. She was somewhere in her forties and had been working at the diner since I was in high school.

"I'll have the cheeseburger, medium-rare; crispy fries; and a root beer float."

"Onion on the burger?"

"Why not? A big slice of raw onion, please."

"Sounds like heaven," she said, grinning. "I'll bring you some water."

"Thanks, Cindy."

As I waited for my order, I thought about Luisa. She claimed that her father and two brothers each had an alibi. But what about Luisa herself? As soon as I asked the question, I felt guilty. There was no way Luisa could have killed Jerry Saxton. Despite her heated statement about wanting to thank his killer, she was simply too sweet and passive. And short. Heck, she probably couldn't even lift my pink wrench, let alone swing it hard enough to smash his head in. Not like I could, anyway.

And wasn't that a miserable thought? To distract myself, I pulled out my smartphone and scanned through my appointments for the week. Since I wouldn't get my car back until late Tuesday, I would have to plan the early part of my week more carefully. I studied my calendar entries, trying to figure out where I could shift things around.

Generally, I didn't approve of people mindlessly fiddling with their smartphones in restaurants, but I was willing to break my own rules to keep my mind from wandering back to the murder scene.

"Hey! Are you deaf or something?" a man at the counter snapped angrily. "How many times do I have to tell you I want another cup of coffee?"

I looked up and almost lost my appetite. The loudmouth was Wendell Jarvick. I was surprised I hadn't seen him when I first walked in. He sat alone at the end of the counter, looking utterly outraged that Cindy wasn't paying enough attention to him. I'd been on the receiving end of that pinched look of his more than once over the past week, so I felt for Cindy. But as usual, she handled it professionally.

"Right away, sir," she said cheerily. "I was just brewing another pot and you'll get the first cup." Her soothing tone should have calmed him down, but this was Wendell. He continued to fume.

Cindy grabbed the full pot of coffee and poured it neatly into his coffee mug. Wendell didn't acknowledge her speed and efficiency, just muttered, "About damn time."

He reached for the cup and took a big gulp. Suddenly, he spewed liquid across the counter and jumped up from his seat. "It's too damn hot! Are you trying to kill me?"

Cindy's eyes widened as the color in her face drained. "I'm sorry, sir, but you were demanding coffee so I gave you the first cup off the burner."

"You bitch!" Wendell grabbed his water glass and gulped down the entire thing—to cool his mouth, I assumed.

It wasn't the first time I'd heard him shout that offensive word. Besides the world in general, he seemed to have a particular problem with women.

I could see Cindy's hand shaking. She backed away and set the pot back on the burner.

"Don't you walk away from me," he shouted. "Bring me more water."

"Right away, sir."

He pounded his fist on the counter. "The service in this place sucks."

The kitchen door swung open and Rocky the cook and owner walked out to the front counter. "Is there a problem, sir?"

"You're damn straight there's a problem," Wendell bellowed. "This bitch was trying to burn my mouth with that crappy coffee you serve."

"You're welcome to leave," Rocky said. "Coffee's on the house."

Wendell's shoulders tightened in aggravation. "I'm not leaving until I finish my lunch."

"That wasn't a suggestion," Rocky said, standing directly in front of Wendell. "Lunchtime's over."

I could almost see Wendell's devious mind spinning as he scrutinized the situation. This time the obnoxious jerk wasn't facing down a woman like me or even a well-mannered police chief at the pub. No, Rocky was a 250-pound ex-Marine with a tattoo of a snake on his neck.

Wendell turned around and slowly panned the room, glowering at every single person in his line of sight. His face turned redder and redder, and when he saw me, I thought his head might explode.

"God, I hate you people," Wendell said, his voice dripping with malevolence. Without warning, he grabbed his coffee cup and dumped the hot liquid on the floor where Cindy and Rocky were standing. Then he flung the cup against the wall, causing it to shatter, and stormed out of the diner.

"I hate him more," Cindy said, scowling at his back.

Rocky watched him leave. "Don't go away mad," he taunted loudly.

"That guy is a menace to society," one of Penny's friends said.

"You should warn the police about him," another customer suggested.

I'd never seen Cindy so angry. Her lips trembled and I thought she might start to cry.

"What an ass," Rocky said, glancing out the door to make sure he was gone for good. "I don't want to see that guy back here again."

"You and the whole town, Rocky," one of the guys said.

Rocky's voice softened. "You okay, Cin?"

She sniffled but nodded briskly. "I'm fine. Thanks, Rocky. I'll be around to serve y'all in a minute."

There was a moment of silence and then everyone in the restaurant burst into applause.

"Good riddance," someone shouted.

Cindy looked ready to cry again, so she grabbed a mop and began to sop up the dark liquid off the floor. The busboy ran over and nudged her aside. "Let me do that."

Through clenched teeth, she said, "Thanks, Kenny." She took a few seconds to breathe before going right back into service mode. She picked up the coffeepot and, pasting a bright smile on her face, walked around the restaurant, refilling coffee cups.

When she got to my table, her gaze narrowed in on me. "Do me a favor, will you, Shannon, honey?"

"Anything you want."

She glared at the doorway where Wendell had exited, then looked back at me. "Next time you're looking to emasculate someone, you give *that* one a swift kick in the you-know-what for me."

Later, as I rode my bike home, I couldn't help but dwell on the irrefutable fact that I wanted to get rid of my hateful tenant. I couldn't help it. He'd been a complete ass with me, but what he'd done to Cindy and Whitney was a crime. And I didn't even like Whitney! But nobody had the right to treat another person like that. I thought of him spewing ketchup at Whitney. And then to dump the coffee on the floor of the Cozy Cove and smash the cup? Maybe Wendell hadn't been potty-trained as a kid, because something was horribly twisted inside his head.

Monday morning, I was halfway through my usual getting-ready routine before I remembered that I didn't have my truck. It didn't really matter, since there were no high-powered business meetings scheduled today. But I'd been planning to swing by some of my job sites to check on things and I supposed I could use the bike for those trips. My guys wouldn't dare make fun of me.

Who was I kidding? They *lived* to make fun of me. Out of love and respect, of course.

As I poured my second cup of coffee, the phone rang.

"Morning, Shannon." I recognized Tommy's friendly voice.

"Hey, Tommy, what's up?"

"I'm calling to give you the go-ahead on the Boyers' house. It's no longer a crime scene, so you and the guys can go back to work."

"That's great, Tommy. I appreciate it."

I hung up and immediately phoned Wade to tell him the good news. We had planned for this eventuality at our Sunday meeting, so he was prepared to call his crew members to alert them to the change of assignment.

I pulled out my computer tablet and made some minor adjustments to the crew list and the Boyers' estimated completion date. Then I contacted Carla and gave her the same information.

I let both of my foremen know that I was without a car today, but I would be willing to stop by a few of the nearby places on my bike. The one exception was the Boyers' house. I could make the trip, but I didn't want to take the chance of running into the Boyers on my bike. For reasons I couldn't quite explain, I wanted to present the most professional image I could to them, at least until the murder of Jerry Saxton was solved.

Both Wade and Carla insisted that they had everything under control on all the jobs. I knew it was true, but that didn't mean I could shirk all the other duties I had to take care of today. Like payroll, for instance. I could always stay home and write checks and clean up some paperwork.

And I would. Maybe this afternoon. But what I really wanted to do this morning was check out the lighthouse mansion. It was less than three miles up the coast, so I could make the trip there and back, along with an hour of wandering around the house itself, in a few hours. The road twisted and turned in a few sections, but the surface was smooth most of the way and the ride was partly downhill on the trip back.

I worried for a minute that I might run into the new owner, but decided it wouldn't happen. The house wasn't livable yet, especially for a pampered celebrity author like MacKintyre Sullivan. No, he was most likely staying at Glencannon Green or the Royal Coast Hotel up near Mendocino, both of which were world-class establishments.

Since I would be gone most of the morning, I packed

some munchies and a bottle of water in a small backpack and tucked it securely in the bicycle basket.

I wore jeans and a sweater topped by a down vest
that I could take off once the cool marine layer dissi-
pated.

I paced myself for the ride north, coasting leisurely
along the bike path until it ended and I crossed onto the
Old Cove Highway. Traffic was light this early in the
morning and I felt safe as long as I kept within the narrow
lines of the bike lane painted along the edge of the smooth
blacktop surface. Going around some of the curves
freaked me out a little, so my brakes got a good workout,
especially when the occasional truck rumbled by.

For the next mile and a half, the highway twisted and
inclined gradually so that by the time I reached the turnoff, I'd gotten a good workout. I waited for a milk truck
to pass and then crossed the highway and turned onto
Old Lighthouse Road and headed toward the ocean.

The condition of the old road had not been improved
since the first time I remembered coming out here with
my family when I was five years old. Dad would park the
station wagon along the dunes and we would trudge
over the hills of sand to watch the waves crash against
the craggy breakwater. It never got old.

The road was still crusty, pockmarked and pitted with
bumps and cracks and gaps along the edges. Sand had
blown across the surface recently, so I took it nice and
slow in case my tires lost their grip. The flaws in the road
made me wonder about our famous new resident. How
much time would pass before Mac Sullivan demanded
that the county repave this road? Maybe he had already
done so.

I followed the narrow lane as it curved along the dunes for another quarter of a mile. Finally there was a break in the line of tall cypress and redwood trees and I stopped in the middle of the road to breathe in the cool, sea-scented air and take in the overwhelming, up-close sight of the lighthouse tower.

Even though the tip of the lighthouse could be seen from the highway, this first up-close, full-length view was always spectacular.

The tower rose one hundred feet into the sky and stood as straight as an arrow, thanks to a series of steel reinforcement rods encased in concrete. Inside the walls of the tower was a solid stone-and-iron spiral staircase, which I had climbed twice in my life. Gazing up at the top of the structure, I could see that the narrow balcony surrounding the glass-walled lantern room appeared to be in good condition. I itched to inspect it more closely, but that moment would have to wait. Not long, hopefully—assuming Sullivan allowed for open bidding on his rehab job.

The tower was separated from the house by only a few feet, a convenient commute for the lighthouse keepers of times gone by. As I leaned my bike against the aging latticework frames that camouflaged the subfloor area under the front porch, my only thought was that those frames would have to be replaced.

After carefully testing the stairs, I walked up to the front door. The veranda was just as spacious and potentially fabulous as I remembered it. Its wood-plank floor was basically solid. To augment my notes, I took out my phone and snapped photos of everything I saw, from the worst problem areas to the unexpected delights.

Crossing to the opposite side of the house from the tower, I peeked through the glass walls of the small solarium. It was empty except for its old brick floor, but I could already imagine it filled with lush greenery and a wonderful chaise longue or two for reading and napping.

Wandering around to the back, I noticed several shutters leaning drunkenly from their window frames and suspected they were rotting from years of rough winds, salt air, and neglect. One of the three chimneys had bricks missing and I worried that they'd fallen through the roof. Everywhere, the serviceable white paint was faded and peeling off the wood siding. Adjacent to what I thought might be the kitchen, a thick wooden door leading to a root cellar had been broken off and left to deteriorate, leaving the old concrete stairs within accessible to the elements.

I rubbed my arms briskly to banish the cold shivers I got from staring down those steps, which led to darkness. God only knew what was down there. Dead animal carcasses? Spiders? Rats? Humans?

I backed away fast. Who needed a real body in a basement when I could use my own imagination to scare myself to death?

"I'm done here," I muttered, and scurried around to the front of the house. I checked my notes to make sure I'd written down everything that I wanted to remember. Reaching again for my phone, I scanned the photos I'd taken, then took a bunch more of the house from every angle.

Turning away from the house, I took shots of the spectacular views: the ocean waves spewing white foam against the rough rock barrier to the west; the weathered cypress, pine, and redwood trees bordering the property to the east; the soft curve of the coastline to the south.

Without access to the house's interior, I'd done as much as I could do here today. Standing my bike up, I packed my notebook and phone securely in the basket and walked the bike to the end of the driveway. At Old Lighthouse Road, I put my foot on the pedal, eased onto the seat, and began to ride back home.

I was going downhill now, but I rode the hand brakes, trying to hold back from gathering too much speed because of the difficult twists and turns of the highway.

About a mile into the trip, I approached one of the more treacherous curves and gripped the brakes tightly to slow down.

Nothing happened.

I continued to gain speed and pumped the brakes as hard as I could, but I felt no connection reaching the tire walls. I downshifted to second gear and then to first. That helped slightly, but then the road declined more steeply around another curve and my pace accelerated again. I tried to press my foot down against the road's surface, but my foot kept bouncing up. I couldn't get any traction. I was going too damn fast. This was going to end badly if I didn't come up with a plan quickly.

A car passed me and honked.

"Not helpful," I shouted. Careening downhill, trying to stay within the narrow bike lane, I had to think fast. Coming up in less than half a mile was Travers Meadow, a pastoral field that belonged to one of the local dairy farmers. The meadow was relatively flat and if I could find a break in the short steel posts that lined the curving road, I would be able to coast to a stop.

My front tire wobbled over a patch of pebbles in the road and I had to strengthen my grip on the handlebars to keep control of the bike. I rounded another curve and now I could see the meadow a few hundred yards away. I steadied my nerves, knowing I would have to swerve quickly to angle the bike through one of the breaks in the row of barriers.

I counted the posts, held my breath, and veered sharply right. My thigh slammed against one of the steel barriers and I felt my jeans rip, but I didn't care. I'd made it through the break and hit the open field with a jarring bump. The bike and I continued to bounce across the wet, uneven ground until my front wheel hit a gopher hole and abruptly ejected me.

As I flew through the air, my only thought was *Don't land on your head. Don't land on your head.* I was wearing a helmet, but that wouldn't be enough to protect me at this velocity.

For a few seconds it felt like I was moving in slow motion. But then I hit the ground fast, breaking the fall with my hands and left shoulder. I tumbled another few yards in an awkward somersault before skidding for a few feet on my hands, arms and stomach and finally collapsing in the muddy grass, facedown.

I lay unmoving, my cheek pressed against the wet, grimy ground, for a few long, humiliating minutes.

I wanted to cry. The palms of my hands were already stinging and I knew they had to be scraped bloody. I could feel the cold grass against my knees, which meant that my jeans had ripped there, too. My chin had taken a hit, as well, because my jaw was stiff and my neck felt jarred.

But I could breathe, so chances were that I hadn't broken any ribs or collapsed a lung. A small victory.

I heard car brakes squealing along the highway, but ignored them.

After a minute, I lifted my left shoulder an inch to test whether it was broken or not. I did the same with both arms and legs, and then arched my back slightly to make sure I hadn't damaged anything else too badly.

Sudden footsteps pounded on the ground and a man yelled, "Are you all right?"

I was alive, so yeah, I was all right. I held up my hand as well as I could, given my awkward position, and waved to let him know I was conscious.

I hoped it was a friend or even a stranger, because then it wouldn't matter that I wasn't exactly looking my best. As long as it wasn't someone horrible from town who would ridicule me and make sure everyone knew about this.

You're an idiot, I thought, and shoved those concerns aside. Because who cared what I looked like? I was alive. Hallelujah.

Still, I had to look awful, what with my face caked in mud and stained with grass and dirt. But again, who cared? It wasn't like I was trying to impress anybody with my grace.

It must've been quite a sight, though, to see me flying off my bike and landing in a heap. Pure elegance. Ugh.

I flinched when a warm hand touched my back. "Hey, are you okay? Can you move?"

"I'm fine." I struggled to push myself off the ground and managed only to make an *oof* sound.

"Fine, huh? Hold on," he said, pressing his hand down more firmly. "Don't move yet. Can you tell if anything's broken?"

"I don't think so."

"Let me check." His hands moved gently up my back, along my spine, across one shoulder, then the other, and down my arms. He had a firm, expert touch, but still managed to be gentle, like he did this sort of thing every day. I'd never felt anything so wonderful in my life. Which was a little pathetic, but I wasn't going to complain.

"Really, I'm okay," I said.

"Yeah, I think you are," he said. "You took quite a leap there. I passed you on the road, but then I caught a glimpse in my rearview mirror from the top of the hill. You really went flying."

"And all in front of an audience."

His chuckle was deep, sexy. He continued to rub my back lightly. "Can you turn over for me?"

For that amazing voice, anything, I thought dreamily, then wondered if maybe I'd hit my head after all.

He helped me roll over, his arm cradling my back to cushion me until I was settled on the ground. That's when I got a close-up look at him for the first time. And almost groaned out loud.

It was MacKintyre Sullivan, world-famous author and newest resident of our little village. Oh, lucky me.

He was so much more handsome than his book covers portrayed him. Everything about him was more intense, more striking than those posed Photoshopped pictures could've ever revealed. His hair was darker, richer, short cropped, and utterly masculine. He always looked so dangerous and serious on his book covers, so when he flashed me an easy smile, it was startling. His teeth were white and straight and his soulful dark blue eyes actually twinkled. He had a shadow of a beard, which gave him a rugged, heroic look that made me want to crawl into his strong arms and stay for a long, cozy nap.

Good grief. Where were all these fanciful thoughts coming from? I had definitely hit my head on something.

He shifted his weight until he was sitting companionably on the ground next to me. Shoving up the sleeves of his faded forest green cable-knit sweater to reveal tanned, muscular arms, he gently brushed my cheek with his fingers to get rid of some attractive dirt clods or weeds that were still stuck to my skin.

"So, what happened here?" he asked.

"My brakes gave out."

"You were going awfully fast."

I sighed. "I didn't want to, but I couldn't stop."

"Scary."

"I was terrified."

"Good thing you were wearing a helmet. And you're sure nothing's broken?" He reached over and lifted my leg at the knee, moving the joint up and down. "Does that hurt?"

"No." I didn't mention the thousands of tingles I felt from his touch. I figured they weren't related to the fall.

He did the same with my other leg. Nothing was broken or sprained.

"You were lucky," he said.

"Except for having my brakes go out, I guess I was."

"My name is Mac, by the way," he said.

"I'm Shannon."

He grinned. "Irish. It suits you. So, let me know when you're ready to stand up, Shannon."

"I think I'm ready."

"I'll help you." He rose easily to a standing position and held out his hands for me to grab hold of.

Once I was on my feet, he gripped my upper arms until I was no longer swaying. When he took a step back, I tried to roll my shoulders, but the slight movement had me biting back a moan. "That hurts," I admitted.

"You'll probably be aching for a few days." He walked over to where my bike lay fallen in the grass. Lifting it effortlessly, he checked the tires, then played with the hand brakes. Standing the bike up with its kickstand in place, he gripped the left brake line between his thumb and index finger and followed it all the way to the back wheel.

"The brake wire is frayed right here. A strand of this thin plastic coating is all that's holding it together."

"How can that be possible?" I wondered. "The bike is less than a year old."

"I'm familiar with this model," he said, running his hand over the bike's wide back bumper. "It's expensive."

"I wanted a good one," I said, slowly bending at the waist to test my stomach muscles. "I like to ride."

"Yeah, me, too." He got down on one knee to take a closer look at the fraying and I stepped next to him to see what he was looking at. After a moment he glanced up at me, a frown marring that gorgeous face. "See this row of indentations on the wire? Looks like the brake line was cut intentionally."

Chapter Eight

Wendell.

That was my first thought, that Wendell had sabotaged my bike. Maybe it was because I'd been consumed by his negativity all week. But it took only a few more seconds to realize that Wendell Jarvick would never waste his time and energy trying to hurt me *physically*. That would shine too much attention on *me*. His world revolved only around *him*.

"This is fascinating," Mac said, as he casually turned the brake wire this way and that to study the striations on the thin plastic covering.

"Fascinating?" Was he crazy? "The only thing that's fascinating is that you actually think someone did it on purpose. I don't believe it."

His expression was mildly curious. "Do you have enemies, Shannon?"

"No. I mean, not really." I wasn't about to mention Whitney or her annoying friends to him and, to tell the truth, I didn't believe they would want to get their hands dirty fiddling with my bike. "I mean, well, there's nobody who would deliberately try to injure me. Unless . . ."

His eyes brightened. "Unless *what*? Tell me everything. Don't hold back."

I laughed. He wasn't even trying to hide his eager interest. I don't know why I found it so honest and charming. "Somebody was murdered recently and I've been asking questions around town."

"Ah. And somebody out there doesn't want to provide the answers. I'm intrigued."

"You would be," I said acerbically, then blanched. "I mean, because you write mysteries."

"You know who I am?"

"Of course I do. You're MacKintyre Sullivan. Everybody in town knows who you are."

"They do?"

I smiled. "You don't come from a small town, do you?"

"No."

"We're all talking about you. It might take some getting used to." Then, because I wanted to hear him say it, I asked, "So, it's true? You really are moving here?"

"Yeah. I've always loved this part of the coast. I grew up in Oregon and I've stayed overnight in Lighthouse Cove a few times on my way home. I really like it."

"That's wonderful. I hope you'll be happy here."

"How long have you lived here?"

"My entire life."

"Ah." He chuckled. "And you don't think you have enemies?"

I frowned at the implication. "I didn't think so, but after today . . ."

He picked up the bike. "How about if I drive you and your bike back to town and you tell me all about it?"

"I'm not sure there's much to tell, but I would appreciate the ride. Oh, wait." I saw my notebook splayed nearby and grabbed it, then carefully checked the surrounding area. "I think I've lost my phone."

He set down the bike and pulled his phone out of his front pocket. "What's your phone number?"

I blinked at the impulsive question, but then realized what he meant to do. I rattled off my number, he called it, and seconds later, I heard my phone's distinctive ring. It had sailed another twenty feet beyond where I'd fallen.

"That was smart."

He grinned. "I used that little trick in a book a while back."

"Oh." I thought about it for a moment. "Wasn't that in *Dead Shot*? I loved that book."

His eyebrows shot up. "You read it? Hey, thanks."

"You can't be surprised. You must know that everyone loves your books."

"Not everyone," he said, his lips twisting ruefully. "But I am surprised. I've been writing for fifteen years and I still react with shock when someone tells me they liked one of my books."

"You must live in a constant state of astonishment."

His laugh rumbled out, full and deep. "It never gets old—that's for sure."

He hefted the bicycle up with one hand and we slowly crossed the field. Now that I was walking—or, rather, limping—I realized how badly I'd banged up my left knee. Both knees had been bloodied in the fall, but now I was concerned that I might've wrenched something.

Mac slowed down to match my pace and finally

wrapped his arm around my back to support me. "Looks like you're in worse shape than you thought. Where does it hurt?"

"My left knee, mainly." I was unable to keep from hissing when I took my next step.

Without warning, he set my bike down and lifted me up in his arms. "If you wrap your arms around my neck, you'll be more comfortable."

"Oh no," I protested, mortified by his intimate move. I wasn't overweight, just tall and healthy and pretty much the opposite of petite. But he seemed to hold me with little effort. Either that, or he was really good at masking his own pain. "Please, this isn't necessary."

"You shouldn't walk on that leg," he said sensibly as he headed for his car. "Besides, it's faster this way."

"I'm perfectly fine to walk on my own."

"No, you're not. You're injured. The sooner I get you back to town, the sooner you'll be able to see a doctor."

"It's probably just twisted or bruised." I wasn't sure why I was complaining. He smelled wonderful. Not from cologne, but more like he'd gone walking through a redwood forest and had captured its essence. I caught a hint of bergamot and leather, too. I gave up protesting, wrapped my arms as he instructed, and just breathed him in until we reached his car. When he let me go, I almost whimpered.

"Thank you," I managed as I regained my balance.

He smiled. "You're welcome. My pleasure." Pulling out his keys, he clicked the doors open. "Go ahead and climb inside. I'll get your bike."

His car was a big black SUV, so it was a little tricky sliding into the passenger's side with my left knee beginning to throb badly. I finally turned around and faced the back of the car, and tried to lift my right leg instead. I managed to get my foot onto the running board and then I reached inside and gripped the overhead security belt with both hands to hoist myself up. When I had both feet on the running board, I rotated slightly and dropped into the seat. It was exhausting, but I gave myself a mental high five for my own ingenuity.

Mac returned and lifted the tailgate, slid my bike into the space, and slammed the tailgate shut. A few seconds later, he was in the driver's seat, starting the engine. As he eased onto the highway, he flashed me a quick grin. "We've got time now. Feel free to tell me all about your enemies. Don't hold anything back."

"I don't have any enemies," I said, and tried to change the subject. "Isn't this a beautiful day?"

"Yeah, beautiful." He reached over and squeezed my hand. His touch was light, but I felt a definite connection. "Shannon, I don't want to scare you, but I think someone tried to hurt you deliberately. I'd call that person an enemy."

I wasn't willing to accept it. "Maybe it was an accident."

He glanced at me sideways.

"All right," I grumbled, knowing he wouldn't let up until I told him my story. Maybe it was because he was a writer and used to wangling all sorts of deep, dark secrets out of people. Not that I minded sharing the gruesome facts with him. After all, he had just moved to town. He was one person I *knew* didn't have a grudge against me. It was more than that, though. I could tell instinctively that he was one of the good guys. Still, I had a feeling he would be relentless if he needed to be.

"I went on this date last Thursday," I began, and went through the whole sordid history of threatening Jerry Saxton and later finding his body. And of calling the police, only to wind up a main suspect in the murder.

"You were lured to that house, Shannon," he said after listening to my entire account. "And you were lured down to that basement. You were meant to find his body. Somebody planned that."

I rubbed my stomach, feeling like I'd taken a blow. "I hadn't thought about it like that, but . . . yes, I guess you could make the case that I was. What do you think it means?"

He came to a stop on the northern edge of the town square and turned to meet my gaze. "It means you have an enemy."

When we got to my house, Mac parked, but instead of getting out of the car, he spent a full minute staring up at my refurbished Queen Anne house. "Wow, this place is fantastic. That bay window is something else."

"Thanks. I love it." I was truly proud of the work I'd done on my house and absurdly thrilled that he liked it. When I had taken over the place from my dad, I did a little refurbishing, just to put my own stamp on the place where I'd grown up. I had removed three small single-pane sash windows and their frames in order to add the large bay window Mac was talking about. It was built into the tower and the glass itself bowed gracefully around the curve. It had been a major pain in the butt to install, but the result was fantastic.

Mac climbed out of the car and jogged around to my side to assist me.

"I can walk," I protested weakly.

"I don't know." He glanced at the house and back at me. "Those stairs look like killers to me."

I frowned. Mac was right, of course. It would take me a week to climb those ten stairs in my present condition. But the reason I was frowning was that I was starting to wonder why he was being so nice to me—although why I would *frown* at the thought of someone being nice to me was a question for the headshrinkers. But, really, did he like hanging around murder suspects? Maybe he thought he could get some good ideas for his next crime novel.

You should just stop thinking, I thought, shaking my head.

I let him lift me out of the passenger's seat and carry me up the stairs to my front door. He set me down and I unlocked it and turned to say good-bye.

"Can I get a tour sometime?" he asked. "I just bought a house and I'm looking for ideas."

"You bought the old lighthouse mansion."

"How'd you know?" He snapped his fingers. "Oh yeah. Small town."

"Yes. But also I'm a general contractor. When a house sells, I usually hear about it, especially when it's one that might be up for rehab. I specialize in old Victorians."

"You're a contractor."

"Yes."

He looked around the porch again and ran his hand along the painted window frame. "You did this."

"Yes." I pushed open the door and stepped inside. "I won't be able to give you much of a tour in my present condition, but if you want to see the front room, come on in."

He followed me through the foyer, past the staircase with its impressive iron balusters, and into the living room—or what the Victorians would've called the front parlor. He wandered around, checking out all the classic Victorian features. Crown moldings, medallions on the ceilings, the massive fireplace, the wainscoting throughout.

Despite those touches, I hadn't kept entirely with tradition in this room. There were no dark wood walls or heavy patterned wallpaper. No clutter on the tables or Oriental carpets, although I appreciated all those charming facets of the era. But the bay window was so big and allowed so much indirect sunlight into the room that I had decided to go with a different feeling altogether. Light taupe with white trim for the walls and coffered ceiling, and comfortably contemporary furnishings: a pale khaki overstuffed couch; two fat, comfy chairs; light wood tables. The window seat was wide enough to nap on and cushioned in a pale buttercream. I'd added splashes of color with throw pillows and artwork.

Other rooms in the house were more classically Victorian, and I loved them, as well, but this was the room I lived in most of the time. I sat down at one end of the long couch and stretched my leg out while Mac studied the elaborately beveled wood around the fireplace and the heavy marble mantel. I'd stumbled upon that unique chunk of thick marble at the landfill a few years ago and had to bring it home.

He sat down at the opposite end of the couch. There was plenty of space for him, so why did the couch and the room and everything around me seem smaller with him here?

Tiger came from out of nowhere and pounced up onto the couch. Instead of coming my way, she went immediately to Mac, and who could blame her? She stood and stared at him until he pulled her into his arms. I had to bite my tongue to keep from saying *Awwwww*.

"What a beauty you are," he murmured as he stroked her fur. Then he looked at me. "Her coloring is remarkably similar to yours."

"My father picked her out for that very reason."

"Two beautiful redheads," he said to the cat. "How did I get so lucky?"

The lucky cat settled in his lap, her petite frame appearing even smaller than usual. Maybe it was because Mac's imposing presence filled the room, overwhelming everything. Including me, apparently.

"So, you're a contractor," he said, and laughed. "I'm stating the obvious again. Sorry. I've just never met a female contractor before."

"There are a few of us," I said, struggling to sit up straighter. It was time to pull myself together and act like a professional, despite my torn jeans and grass-streaked face. He was, after all, a potential client. "I grew up working with my dad, mostly building or restoring Victorian houses."

He scanned the room again. "Damn, I'm slow. It's still sinking in that you did all this. You're hired."

I laughed. "You might want to check out a few other builders before you make your choice."

"But I like you best," he said, grinning boyishly.

"You don't know that yet."

"I do. But fine, we'll do it your way." He shifted in his seat and faced me directly. "Do you have a résumé I can review, with a list of your latest projects?"

"Yes, I do."

"Okay, good. Do you want to tell me where it is, or would you like me to carry you around the house until we find it?"

Yes, please, I thought, but said, "That won't be necessary." I struggled to stand and stopped him when he moved to help me. "I need to do this. It's going to be fine; I'm just a little achy."

"I admire your spirit, but I don't believe you."

"I'm trying to be optimistic here," I said, making a face as I took a step toward the doorway.

"It would help if you didn't limp."

I laughed as I limped down the hall. "My office is right through here."

I led the way to the alcove off the kitchen where I'd built a desk and shelves to fit the compact space. Pulling open the top drawer of my file cabinet, I took out a business-sized portfolio that held my résumé, a list of clients and projects, and several sheets of before and after photographs. "Here you go."

He scanned the front of the professionally designed folder and opened it to the first page. He gazed at me and smiled. "So you're Hammer Construction Company. Very nice to meet you, Shannon Hammer."

I held out my hand. "Nice to meet you, too, Mac-Kintyre Sullivan."

"My friends call me Mac," he reminded me as he shook my hand.

"It was kind of you to rescue me, Mac," I said, and wondered when or if he would let go of my hand.

"I'm glad I found you," he said warmly. His gaze was drawn to the kitchen window. "You have a garden."

"I do."

"It's impressive." He looked thoughtful as he glanced down at our hands. Finally he let mine go before walking over to the window to get a better view. "Do you take care of it yourself or is there someone else?"

"It's all mine."

He turned to me. "You have many talents."

I happened to catch a glimpse of Wendell walking down the garage stairs and grimaced.

"What's wrong?" Mac checked the window again. "Oh. Who's that guy?"

"I rent my garage apartments to tourists. Occasionally I get one who's a real pain in the neck."

He glanced up. "Those are apartments?"

"They're more like guest suites. They're nice and spacious and the ocean view is wonderful."

"That's worth some change." He tucked my business portfolio under his arm. "Well, I ought to let you get on with your day."

"Okay." I followed him to the front door. "Wait. I've got to get my bike out of your car."

"Since you can't ride it, anyway, I'd like to hold on to it for a day or two. Do you mind?"

"What are you planning to do with it?"

"I've got a buddy who's ex-FBI. I thought I'd show him that brake line. See what he thinks."

"That seems like a whole lot of trouble for nothing."

"You think so? Then I won't bother mentioning that I'm going to show it to the police, too."

Somehow I made it up the stairs and started running the water for a bath. I was so shaky that I had to sit on the edge of the tub for fear of fainting dead away. I'd never fainted in my life, but, then, I'd never gone flying off a bike before, either. When I finally got a look at myself in the mirror, I wanted to cry.

"Way to make an impression, Shannon," I muttered to myself. If only there were just grass stains, but no. My face and neck were streaked with brown mud and guck. A small clod of weeds and dirt was stuck in my hair. And speaking of hair, mine was no longer merely wavy, but had moved unswervingly into Bride of Frankenstein frizz. It wasn't a good look for me.

Shaking my head in disgust, I moved away from the mirror and stripped out of my ruined clothing. Clipping my hair up off my neck, I poured half a box of Epsom salts into the stream of hot water and added a handful of girly bath salts for good measure. I stepped gingerly into the warmth and moaned out loud, it felt so good. I really needed to take baths more often, but who had the time?

Sinking down until the water covered me up to my chin, I closed my eyes and rested my head against the curved rim of the tub.

And thought of Mac.

MacKintyre Sullivan, my hero. Just wait until Lizzie heard about this one.

But now at last I could worry in peace. Would Mac really take my bike to the police? What would Chief Jensen say when Mac demanded that they check out the cut brake line and dust the whole thing for fingerprints? It wasn't like someone had cut my *truck's* brake line. It was just a bike.

Would Chief Jensen laugh him out of his office? I didn't think so. In fact, maybe it was a good thing that

Mac was the one taking my bike in. Chief Jensen would listen to him when he might not listen to me.

Of course he would listen to Mac. The man was awesome. An ex–Navy SEAL, a crime writer, a cool guy. A nice guy. He probably knew as much about police procedure as any officer on the force.

On the other hand, I wasn't sure Mac's theory was correct. First of all, why would someone deliberately try to hurt me? And second, if they really were out to injure me, why would they cut the brake line on my *bicycle*? It seemed like such a silly thing to do. At the most, I would call it malicious mischief. And who in my world was capable of doing something petty like that?

I would've loved to blame Whitney and Jennifer, but I knew they wouldn't go to the trouble. And I barely had anything to do with the other mean girls in their circle. Two of them, Lindsey and Cherise, hadn't been around lately. I think they were busy being stay-at-home moms.

And then there was Wendell.

"Ugh." I took a few slow, deep breaths and tried to concentrate on something else besides that jerky tenant of mine. Flowers. Balmy ocean breezes. Ice cream. Mac Sullivan.

Much better.

Tuesday morning my knee was marginally better, but I was still so achy in every last corner of my body, I could barely move. After popping some ibuprofen and brushing my teeth, I managed to dress myself and hobble downstairs. Once I reached the kitchen and had my first cup of coffee, I accepted the fact that I wouldn't be going anywhere today.

Which was just as well, since I had no means of transportation until my truck was ready sometime tonight.

I called Carla to let her know I was housebound for the day.

"Everything's cool over here, boss," she said. "Don't worry about a thing. You just take care of yourself."

"Thanks. I will."

She chuckled. "You know, I figured something must be up with you."

"What do you mean?"

"Well, Jesse told Jane, who told Emily, who told my mom, who told me that a man was seen carrying you up your front stairs yesterday. It was a real Rhett and Scarlett moment, according to Jesse."

So my darling old next-door neighbor had spread the word about me and Mac. Great. I could feel my cheeks heating up. As a true redhead with the requisite smattering of freckles across my forehead and nose, my skin tended to turn pink at the slightest hint of embarrassment.

"Um, yeah, about that," I stammered, then tried to brazen it out. "Here's the thing: I fell off my bike and thought I sprained my ankle. The guy who found me was nice enough to, you know, carry me up the stairs. Otherwise, I would've had to crawl. It wasn't pretty. He did me a favor."

"A favor." I could tell by her tone that there was no way she was buying my lame explanation. Even though it was essentially true. "So who was the guy?"

"Nobody."

"Oh, Shannon," Carla said, and started to laugh.

"Really," I said, assuming an air of nonchalance. "It was nothing. Doesn't matter. Move along now."

She laughed. "Your protests will just force us to dig farther."

"I'm not protesting," I protested. "Go ahead and dig. You won't find anything."

She chuckled softly, but said nothing else, which scared me, frankly. She deftly changed the subject to the new cedar shingles on the Paradise Drive house. After we hung up, I just had to hope she'd decided to buy the sprained-ankle story.

Not that it mattered. Jane and Emily would be pumping me for information within the hour. If they were smart, they'd bring Lizzie along. Eventually, I would break.

I poured another cup of coffee and called Wade at the Boyer house to tell him I wouldn't be out there today.

"No worries, boss," he said. "But you might be interested in something that happened here yesterday."

I sat up straighter. "What happened?"

"Joyce and Stan were here and they couldn't stop sniping at each other. They were like a tag team. First Joyce would start chitchatting with one of our guys and end up ranting about something or other. Then Stan would come over, tell her to shut up, and start in on his own rant. This went on for a couple of hours."

Probably slowed down the work on their house, too, I thought. That would be the only reason Wade would pass along idle gossip. I would have to tell the Boyers to leave my workers alone if they ever wanted their house to be finished.

"That must've been pleasant," I said.

He snorted. "It was entertaining, anyway."

Wade said that both Stan and Joyce seemed anxious

to divulge all the details they'd heard about the murder investigation. They had both been brought in for questioning, of course. Joyce was extra vocal about her negative feelings for Jerry, blathering to anyone within hearing distance about what a slimeball he was.

"I think you were the one who set her off, Shannon," Wade said somberly. "You might want to be a little careful around her."

"Me? What did I do?"

"According to Stan, it was after your scene on the beach with Jerry that Joyce went ballistic. I guess she had a date with him the next day and confronted him about his cheating. Jerry blew off her tantrum, told her she was in no position to complain about him seeing another woman when she was married to another man."

I did the math and realized that their date was on the day that Jerry died. "But just to be clear, you don't think she's angry at me specifically, right? I just happened to be the one woman she found out about."

"No, I think her anger is specifically aimed at you," he clarified. "You represent all the other women he's been seeing. Probably because you're the one who nailed him in public."

"I didn't," I said, groaning inwardly at the ongoing myth. "Never mind."

"Whatever happened in reality, in Joyce's mind you personify Jerry's betrayal to her." Wade paused and then lowered his voice to add, "So I really think she's got it in for you now."

"But why?" If she had half a brain, she'd be thanking me for kicking him. "I refuse to believe she didn't know Jerry was cheating on all those other women."

"I guess the others didn't make quite the splash you did."

"Thanks a lot."

He chuckled. "Sorry, boss."

I didn't blame him for laughing, but I wondered if I would ever live down that awful scene on the beach. Was it possible that my evening with Jerry had led directly to his murder? What if Joyce killed him and was trying to make me look guilty? Had she somehow arranged for Stan to lure me to their house? Did she set me up to find Jerry's body in the basement? Was she angry enough to come after me next? I thought about my bicycle's damaged brake line and shivered a little.

But that was just an accident, I tried to convince myself for the umpteenth time.

"Meanwhile," Wade continued blithely, "Stan was making his own snide comments on the side."

I tried to concentrate on his words. "You guys must've been shaking your heads at all this."

"We were," he said.

"I'll have to find a way to ask them not to come around. We'll never get their house finished at this rate."

"Good luck with that," Wade said. "Oh, but there's more. Stan was listening to everything Joyce was ranting about and finally he gets right up in her face and says to her, 'You're such a bitch, I'm surprised the guy didn't kill *you*.'"

"Whoa."

"Yeah. It got a little dicey there for a few minutes. She threatened to punch Stan, and he dared her to try it. I had the guys circle around them in case we had to pull one of them off the other."

"Aren't they a fun couple?" I was starting to get a headache.

Wade chuckled and I thanked him for that lovely golden snippet of gossip, even though it was more disturbing than I was willing to admit to him.

A minute later we ended the call, and as I drank the rest of my coffee, I thought about Jerry Saxton and what a jerk he'd been. And besides being a jerk, he really knew how to pick his women.

Was it just me, or was it getting more obvious every day that Jerry had driven some woman over the edge? And whoever that woman was, she'd seen no other way out than to kill him.

Chapter Nine

The sound of ringing dragged me out of an intense, weird dream in which Joyce and Stan Boyer were chasing me around their dank, shadowy basement, waving my own pink wrench at me.

As I fumbled for the phone, I tried to adjust my vision to the total darkness of the living room. Where had the sun gone? "Hello?"

"Ms. Hammer, it's Chief Jensen."

Was this part of my weird dream? No, pretty sure I was awake. I shook my head back and forth to restart my brain. "Hello, Chief Jensen."

"Sounds like I woke you up," he said. Was it my imagination, or did he sound judgmental? "I'm sorry about that. I heard about your trouble yesterday."

"You did?" So maybe it was my imagination, after all. "I guess I'm still a little sleepy. I took some aspirin a while ago and fell sound asleep."

"That's probably a good thing to do after what you've been through."

I felt my way over to the end table and turned on the

lamp. Was he being sympathetic? Should I be worried? "How can I help you, Chief Jensen?"

"I was speaking with Mac Sullivan a little while ago."

"Yes?" *Here it comes,* I thought, sinking back onto the couch. I was going to get a lecture on wasting the police department's time and energy. Robbie and Tiger must've sensed my unease, because they both jumped up and cuddled next to me.

"Yes. I'd like to come by your place with two of my officers and dust for fingerprints in your garage. I understand that's where you keep your bicycle."

"Oh." I was shocked, although I probably shouldn't have been. Mac was pretty darn persuasive, after all. Still, this was Police Chief Jensen, not exactly my number-one fan. "Right now?"

"If it's convenient."

I brushed my unruly hair back from my face and checked the clock on the mantel. It was only a few minutes past five. The days were getting shorter, the sun setting earlier. In a few weeks daylight saving time would end and it would be even darker by now. "Sure. That would be fine."

"Good. We can be there in—"

"Oh, wait." I pressed my hand to my forehead. "I'm so sorry. I forgot I have to pick up my truck at the shop in a little while. Can we do it tomorrow?"

He paused for a moment, maybe to check his calendar. "Early morning okay for you?"

I tried to think fast, but it wasn't easy. "Yes, early is better than late. I usually like to leave the house about eight-thirty, but I'll be happy to stick around for as long as it takes."

"We'll be there at eight." He hesitated, then asked, "Do you need a ride to the auto shop, Ms. Hammer?"

"What?" Was he honestly willing to give me a ride? He was being so nice. Who was this guy? "Um, no. My friend Jane is taking me. But thank you for offering. I appreciate it."

"You're welcome. I'll see you tomorrow morning, Ms. Hammer."

I sighed. "You should call me Shannon, Chief."

"I'll do that," he said cheerfully. "Take care, Shannon."

"Thanks, Chief. You do the same." When he hung up, I stared at my phone for a minute or two, trying to decide if I were still dreaming or not.

Miracle of miracles. When I got home from the auto shop, Wendell Jarvick's car was gone. I gleefully pulled my truck into the driveway, being careful to leave absolutely no room behind me for another car to park. Wendell would just have to leave his hotshot luxury car out on the street. Bummer for him.

Jane had generously offered to cook dinner for me, but I begged off, knowing I wouldn't be good company. I just wanted to order a pizza and watch TV in my pajamas.

Since I had to get up early the next morning, I had a few pieces of pizza, most of a small salad, and one measly glass of wine. Soon after that, I turned off the television and crawled upstairs to bed. I doubted the police would find anything incriminating in my garage tomorrow, but I was thrilled that they were at least willing to look. And maybe I was being overly optimistic to think it meant I was no longer a suspect, but I had to believe it was a step in the right direction. And I was pretty sure I had Mac Sullivan to thank for that.

The doorbell rang at eight o'clock sharp the next morning, just as I knew it would. I set down my coffee cup and moved as quickly as I could to open the door. "Good morning."

"Good morning," Chief Jensen said, glancing around. "This is quite a house."

"Thank you."

He was smiling, which did wonders for his looks. His blue eyes were streaked with shards of soft gray, and the rays of morning sun had turned the tips of his dark blond hair to gold. Tiny laugh lines gave him more allure than any man deserved and he carried an aura of power that his relaxed smile couldn't disguise.

What had happened to the dour, suspicious police chief I'd just started getting used to? Never mind. I liked this one better. I just hoped he would stick around.

Robbie came scurrying down the hall to sniff around the newcomer.

"Who's this?" Chief Jensen asked.

"That's Rob Roy, but we call him Robbie. He's very friendly."

"And good-looking, too," he said, squatting down to ruffle Robbie's scruffy white coat and play for a minute. That, naturally, caused me to like him even more than I did a minute ago.

"Do you and your officers want some coffee?" I asked.

"That would be great. Thanks." He stood and pointed

over his shoulder with his thumb. "They've already started working on the surface areas around the garage door."

I glanced past him, down the driveway. "I'd better unlock the door so they can get inside."

"That would help. Thanks."

I grabbed the key and my down vest and followed the porch around to the backyard. Here there were only three steps to descend as opposed to the ten steps out front. I took them carefully, still feeling tender from my short flight off the bike the other day.

"Maybe you can show us where you keep your bicycle."

"Sure."

He started to introduce me to the officers, but I stopped him. "That's okay, Chief. I've known these two for years."

"That's right," Mindy said, grinning as she snapped on a pair of thin rubber gloves. "Jeb went to high school with Shannon and I was two years behind them. And Jeb's brother, Todd, works on Shannon's crew."

Jeb chuckled. "Gotta love a small town."

"I do," Chief Jensen said, surprising me again. Maybe there was hope for the chief yet.

"How are you, Shannon?" Mindy asked.

"Pretty good." It wasn't true, of course, but I wasn't about to go down the list of my aches and pains and worries. "How have you been?"

"Can't complain," Mindy said.

Jeb snickered. "Right, 'cuz nobody listens."

Mindy smiled. "Isn't that the truth?" She flicked what looked like a very small duster over the surface of the windowsill next to the garage door. Black dust particles remained in her wake. She studied the surface, pulled out a clear piece of tape and applied it to a section of the sill. Then she pulled the tape up. "Got some clean prints here."

"They're probably mine," I muttered.

Chief Jensen turned to me. "Are your fingerprints on file somewhere?"

"They should be. I'm bonded and licensed by the state."

He nodded. "Good."

They continued to work while I showed Chief Jensen where I always parked my bike. "I'm not sure if you'll find anything, Chief, but I appreciate you taking the time to look."

"Mac made a good case for looking," he said. "And maybe you should call me Eric."

That came out of left field and I was certain that my confusion showed. Suffice to say I was really getting to like this new improved police chief. "Really?"

He chuckled. "I'd say we started off on the wrong foot."

"It probably didn't help that my *wrong foot* tripped over a dead body." Did I say that out loud?

"Yeah, there's that." His expression was serious, although there was a hint of humor in his eyes.

Flustered, I looked around and pointed to my favorite pink tool chest. "I'm just going to pack my tool chest in my truck, if you'll excuse me."

"I'll help you."

"That's okay."

"I can see you're still in pain, Shannon," he said softly. "Let me carry it for you."

I didn't mention that I usually carried it out there on a dolly, mainly because he lifted it up as though it barely weighed an ounce instead of sixty-plus pounds. But, then, he probably bench-pressed three times his weight on a regular basis. The man had muscles on his muscles.

As we approached my truck, I noticed for the first time that Wendell had parked his car directly behind my truck in the driveway. I stopped and glared at the hated car. I hadn't seen it earlier because he'd parked at such an odd angle.

"Damn it," I muttered through gritted teeth. "I'm going to kill that guy."

Eric turned and looked at me. "What's wrong?"

Oops. "I didn't mean that," I said in a rush. "But this car isn't supposed to be parked here."

"Do you want us to tow it?"

"I would love it."

He started to move and I held up my hand reluctantly to stop him. "But you'd better not. It would cause more problems than it's worth."

But I could feel anger coursing through my system. My shoulders were tight and my jaw was clenched. I felt so powerless. How could something this petty fill me with such fury? Because it was Wendell Jarvick. He was a horrible man. If only I could have him banned from the town forever.

"I can't wait till he's gone," I said.

"Is he the guy that caused the ruckus at the pub the other night?" Eric said.

"That's him. A real piece of work."

"He won't be around much longer, hopefully."

"That moment can't come soon enough."

We got to my truck and I pulled the tailgate down. As Eric loaded my tool chest into the truck bed, I wandered over to Wendell's car. I was truly tempted to do some damage, so I kept my hands firmly inside my pockets.

Maybe I could dig up a bunch of worms in my garden and put them on the driver's seat. Happy at the thought, I tried to glance inside the car, but along with having tinted windows, there was a layer of condensation on the glass, so it was hard to see. Without thinking, I tested the driver's door and found it unlocked. I pulled it open and stared in shock at what I saw on the front seat.

I jumped back and screamed as loud as I'd ever screamed before. If they weren't awake already, I probably woke up half the folks in town.

"What's wrong?" Eric shouted. "What happened?"

Dizzy and sick, I slammed the door shut and shook uncontrollably. This couldn't be happening. I took a couple of big gulps of air and waved at the car door. "In there."

Eric came around and pulled open the door and took a step back. I summoned enough courage to venture another peek inside — and was sorry I did.

Wendell Jarvick lay sprawled on the seat, his eyes open as though he were staring right at me. Blood was smeared across the smooth taupe leather seats. Something was protruding from his neck and I could feel my heart sinking in my chest because I recognized the tool. It was my extralong pink Frearson screwdriver.

My contractor's brain kicked in to remind me that the Frearson differed from a Phillips-head screwdriver because of its more pointed, V-shaped head. *The better to stab someone in the neck,* I thought.

I squeezed my eyes shut but the image wouldn't go away.

"Shannon." Eric's tone was a warning and his arm blocked me from moving any closer, as if I wanted to. "Don't touch anything. Step back now."

"Is he . . . ?" It was a stupid question.

Eric leaned in and pressed his fingers against the pulse point on Wendell's neck, a few inches away from where the screwdriver protruded. "Yeah."

No doubt about it, Wendell Jarvick was dead.

Stumbling over to the garden wall at the side of the drive, I lost the cup of coffee I'd gleefully chugged a half hour ago.

An hour later, I was cooling my heels inside the house as my yard was turned into an official crime scene. The county coroner's van was parked in front of my driveway and four police cars surrounded it, blocking off as much of the view from the curious public as possible. That didn't stop any of my neighbors from lining up along the sidewalk on the other side of the street. I glanced out the window and saw a few folks still wearing their bathrobes at almost ten o'clock in the morning. Good grief. Some of my neighbors were real slackers.

Someone pounded on my front door and I checked to see who it was before opening the door. "Thank God it's you guys. Come in."

Jane and Lizzie scurried inside and I shut the door quickly because, despite what Mr. Bennet claimed in *Pride and Prejudice*, I did not live to make sport for my neighbors.

"We came as soon as we heard," Jane said, tossing her purse on the chair.

Lizzie glanced out the bay window. "Shannon, what in the world happened?"

"You won't even believe it," I muttered.

"I just saw you twelve hours ago," Jane said. "How could so much pandemonium occur between then and now?"

"Heck if I know," I said, throwing both hands high. "Do you guys want some coffee?"

Lizzie shook her head. "No."

"Talk," Jane said, sitting down.

I told them everything that had happened from the time I parked my truck in the driveway last night until the moment this morning when I pulled open the car door and discovered Wendell.

"I know how much you hated Wendell," Jane said. "Did you ever have his car towed?"

"No," I said, staring at her in dismay. "And remind me not to use you as a character witness."

"Jane," Lizzie cried. "Shannon didn't kill Wendell Jarvick."

Jane waved her hands in front of her face as if to sweep her words away. "Of course not! I didn't mean . . . Oh, never mind. You know I didn't mean that. Everyone in town hated his guts, Shannon. Not just you. You know I'm totally on your side."

"Yeah, I know," I said, patting her shoulder. "I'm just a little sensitive right now."

"I guess I am, too," she said, dazed. "Sorry."

"Everybody hated him," Lizzie repeated thoughtfully, talking while pacing the length of the coffee table and back. "It'll take the police weeks to investigate everyone who had a grudge against him."

Jane looked at me with concern. "I hope Chief Jensen doesn't consider you a suspect."

"You mean just because the guy was found in my driveway with my screwdriver sticking out of his neck?"

"Oh, gross," Lizzie said. "Ugh."

"Sorry," I said, remembering my own reaction to Wendell's grisly end. "You probably shouldn't repeat that. But hell, yeah, he considers me a suspect. Wouldn't you?"

"Absolutely not!" Lizzie cried. She sank down into the chair. "Was it really a screwdriver? In his neck? Ick."

"Yeah."

We each sat silently with our own thoughts for a moment.

Jane finally spoke. "Your screwdriver? Really?"

"Yes." I caught the look of concern my friends exchanged.

The doorbell rang.

"Saved by the bell," I muttered, and limped over to see who was outside. I swung the door open. "Hi."

"Hi." Mac walked in and headed straight for the living room. "Damn, Irish. I can't leave you alone for a minute, can I?"

I couldn't hide my smile as I shut the door and followed him in, just in time to see Lizzie's mouth drop open. It was a rare sight and so worth waiting for.

"Lizzie and Jane," I said politely, "this is Mac Sullivan. Mac, these are my two oldest friends. Lizzie owns Paper Moon, the book-and-paper shop on the town square, and Jane is about to open Hennessey House, a small hotel over on Apple Street."

"How are you?" Mac said as he shook both of their hands. "Good to meet you."

"How did you—" Jane asked.

"When did you—" Lizzie sputtered.

Mac grinned at me, and I had to admit, it felt good to have him there. He was just so . . . steady. Not to mention gorgeous in a rugged, outdoorsy kind of way. Knowing two of my closest friends were sitting there bug-eyed was pure gravy.

"Lizzie and her husband, Hal, are two of your biggest fans," I explained. "She's hoping you might consent to do a book signing at her store one of these days."

"Shannon!" Lizzie hissed.

"Hey, that sounds great, Lizzie," Mac said jovially. "I could sign some books and also get a chance to meet some of my new neighbors."

"That would be wonderful," Lizzie said, instantly perking up enough to dig one of her business cards out of her purse and hand it to him. "Thank you."

I smiled at Mac. "Thank you."

"For you, Irish, anything," he said with a devilish grin.

Lizzie and Jane exchanged looks of stunned disbelief, which I blithely ignored. Hey, you have to take your fun where you find it.

The good times couldn't last, though. A few minutes later, Chief Jensen knocked on the door to ask me a few questions. He said he wouldn't mind interrogating me right here at the house, and since I considered it a small victory that he didn't instantly drag me down to police headquarters, I agreed. Lizzie, Jane, and Mac took off after I promised to get in touch with them later that afternoon.

I poured the chief a cup of coffee and got myself a glass of water before sitting at the dining room table.

"I know it looks bad," I said, trying to appeal to the new and improved, more agreeable Chief Jensen. "But I didn't kill Wendell Jarvick."

"I believe you."

"I'm sorry?" I rubbed my ear, unsure if I'd heard him right. "What did you say?"

"I believe you," he said again, then added, "I know you didn't kill Jarvick and I know you didn't kill Jerry Saxton, either."

"You do?"

"Yeah. Your alibi for the time of Saxton's death is unshakable, according to the coroner's final report." He lifted his shoulders in a casual shrug. "Alibi aside, my instinct tells me you're trustworthy enough."

I pressed my lips together, feeling immensely relieved. I hadn't realized until then how worried I'd been that he would never really believe I was innocent. "Thank you."

"No problem," he said gruffly. "But that doesn't mean I'm not going to do this by the book. I mean to question you about every single thing you said or did, every interaction that transpired between you and Jarvick."

"Okay."

He pulled out a small notepad and pen. "Right now it doesn't look good and I'm sure you know why."

"Yeah," I said gloomily. "My house. My pink screwdriver. My threat to kill him."

"You ought to stop making those threats," he said dryly, "innocent or not. But let's move forward. I want you to be completely honest with me. I can't do anything to mitigate this situation if I don't have your cooperation."

"You've got it," I said, understanding exactly what he *wasn't* saying: that if I didn't give him every last bit of information I had, I might be going to jail after all. "What do you want to know?"

"Tell me where you were last night between the hours of eight o'clock and two this morning."

"I got home from the mechanic's shop around seven thirty last night. I was able to park the truck in the driveway for the first time in a week. Usually Wendell had his stupid car parked there and he refused to move it."

He glanced up from his notes. "You sound angry about that."

"It was driving me crazy." I blew out a breath, took in another, and let it go slowly. It wouldn't do to start ranting about the man whose dead body had just been found on my property. "Yes, I admit I was angry. Wendell was a horrible person, always pushing people's buttons and leaving chaos in his wake. You saw what he did at the pub the other night, right? He pulled stuff like that all over town. For a little while yesterday, I even thought he might've been the one who cut the brake line on my bike. But then I figured he wouldn't want to get his hands dirty."

I took a drink of water before continuing. "I was literally counting off the days until he finally left town. Most of the people here feel the same way about him. We've put up with his abominable behavior every single year for the past twelve years. He's always unpleasant. You can ask Cindy at the Cozy Cove Diner. He was so awful to her last Sunday, I thought Rocky was going to throw him through the plate-glass window."

Eric stood and removed his brown leather bomber jacket and hooked it over the back of the chair before sitting again. "I'll talk to Cindy, but why don't you go ahead and tell me what happened in your own words?"

"All right." I related the hot-coffee incident in detail. "The place was full so there were plenty of witnesses who saw the same thing I did. I heard that he pulled a number at Lindy's on the Pier, too."

Eric continued to jot down notes in his pad. After a minute, he looked up, frowning. "If you knew what he was like, why did you agree to let him stay here?"

"Good question." I grimaced. "Maybe I shouldn't have, but I couldn't imagine it would be that big of a deal. I mean, I knew he was unpleasant, but wow. The thing is, I joined our local innkeepers' association last year and I wanted to be part of the team. Ordinarily, our policy is that we don't turn away a paying guest, but the group has a whole different set of rules for Wendell. Each member is required to let him stay at their establishment once. After that, they can refuse him a room."

As Eric wrote it down, he shook his head. "Sounds like he might've been more trouble than he was worth."

I sighed. "I was so looking forward to refusing him a room next year."

His lips twisted in a smile.

"But I didn't kill him," I said, repeating myself. Frustrated, I added, "I don't know how I can prove it. He was parked in my driveway and killed by my screwdriver. But I didn't do it. I mean, seriously, would I do something like that outside my own home? And use my own screwdriver? I'm not an idiot, Chief. Er, Eric. Really."

He reached across the table and touched my hand lightly. Trying to calm me down, I figured. Strangely enough, it worked.

"Look," he said, "I intend to follow up on every lead and track down even the smallest clue in order to close this investigation, but let me repeat what I told you before and maybe ease your mind a little. I really don't think you killed Wendell Jarvick."

I looked at him for a long second or two and read reassurance in his steady gaze. For the first time since finding Wendell dead in my driveway, I took an easy breath. "You really don't."

He shrugged. "You said it yourself. You're too smart to kill someone with your own screwdriver and then leave the body in a car parked in your own driveway."

"Thank you." But then something occurred to me. "You don't worry that I might've used my own tools to fool you?"

His smile was placid. " 'I'm not a great fool.' "

"Of course not." My eyes widened. "Wait. I know that line. Are you quoting *The Princess Bride*?"

He grinned and it warmed me down to my ribs. "Yeah. Your remark reminded me of that scene."

"I love that movie."

"Do you remember the next line?"

"I'm pretty sure I know *every* line." I thought for a second. " 'I can clearly not choose the wine in front of you.' "

"Right. It was the battle-of-wits scene between the

Dread Pirate Roberts and Vizzini. So, tell me, Shannon. Are you trying to outwit me?"

"No. God, no." I rubbed my face, feeling nervous all over again, plus exhausted. "Please forget I even brought it up."

"Why did you?"

Because I'm not thinking straight, I thought. But it was time to start. Sitting forward in my chair, I crossed my arms on the table surface. "Because when I look at all the evidence pointing directly at me, it scares me and I get a little loopy. I wouldn't blame anyone for thinking I was guilty. But I'm not."

"Here's what I'm worried about," he said, leaning forward and matching my posture. "With all this evidence pointing at you, I'm wondering who is trying to set you up to take the fall."

"What do you mean?"

"Somebody is going to a lot of trouble to make you look guilty. Who do you know who would go to such lengths?"

"You mean, do I have any enemies?"

"That's another way to put it."

It was exactly what Mac had asked the other day after my bicycle accident. At the time, the only people who had come to mind were the snotty girls who'd ridiculed me in high school. They weren't even worth mentioning. The only other person I could think of was Wendell, but he was no longer a viable suspect, obviously.

Did I dare mention Joyce Boyer? Wade seemed to think that Joyce might have it in for me, and while I was happy to point the finger at someone else besides me, it was sort of ridiculous to think that Joyce would kill Wendell. Jerry Saxton, yes. But Wendell? She and Stan had been sitting in the pub the night Wendell attacked Whitney, but did she know the man? I doubted it. Heck, she barely knew me, except through working together on her house rehab. Would she really go to all this trouble to hurt me?

"I have no idea," I said finally.

"You had to think pretty hard to come up with that answer."

"I've lived here all my life, so naturally I've had runins with people in the past. But nothing that screams Mortal Enemy. And nothing's happened recently that would cause me to point to anyone in particular." I thought about it and frowned. "Well, except for tangling with the two men who are now dead."

"Yeah," he murmured. "Except for them."

Something in his tone made me sit up and take notice. "What are you thinking?"

"I'm thinking that instead of trying to set you up, someone might be trying to help you out by killing off the two men who've been giving you so much trouble lately."

My mouth opened but no words came out. I shook my head in bewilderment.

He leaned forward. "Shannon, think. Is there someone who craves your attention? Someone who might be willing to earn your favor by getting rid of people who bother you?"

"Oh, my God," I said, rubbing my hands together for warmth. "That's so sick."

"There's no accounting for motivations."

I shook my head. "I don't know anyone who would do something like that."

He studied me for a moment. "I hate to upset you, but clearly you *do* know someone who might do that."

I scowled at him. "Why do you think I know this person?"

He tapped his pen against his notepad. "Because of the victims. Because of the use of your tools. Whoever the killer is, he or she came onto your property and killed Wendell Jarvick using your screwdriver as a weapon. Why? It can't just be a coincidence. Something similar happened in the case of Jerry Saxton. I'm not saying that you were meant to find his body, but you were certainly meant to be blamed for his death. He was found in a house you were working on. You had keys to all the doors. And, again, they used one of your own tools to kill him."

I sat and digested that for a moment. "And both of the dead men were bugging the hell out of me."

"Yes."

"So, you think someone is trying, in their own twisted way, to do me a favor."

"It's a possibility."

"But, then, why would they frame me for the murders?"

"I said they were doing you a favor. I didn't say they were brilliant."

"It's horrible! I don't know what to do." I shoved my chair back from the table and rested my elbows on my knees. I stared at the wood grain of the floor. Finally I looked up. "I'm a little freaked-out."

"I don't blame you," he said with a sympathetic smile.

"And it might be related to something altogether different."

"But you don't think so." I thought about the implications of what he'd suggested. "I'd rather have someone trying to set me up to look guilty than to know someone was doing it to impress me. That's just sick and creepy."

"I agree," he said. He closed his notebook.

"Wait a minute," I said. "What about my bicycle? Where does that fit in?"

"We sent the brake wire to the sheriff's office for further examination. It looks like it was deliberately cut, but we want to be sure. They've got a forensics lab that'll be able to look at it microscopically. They'll also be able to pick up any prints or fibers that don't match yours."

"And if it was deliberately cut?"

He rubbed his jaw as he considered. "Then I would say someone is out to hurt you. There's a small chance it might not be the same person who killed those two men, but I'm betting it is. He also managed to get access to your garage, which I imagine you keep locked most of the time."

"I do." I squeezed my eyes shut for a moment. Why was this happening to me? "Okay, so you're telling me that the same person is either setting me up to go to jail or doing me favors or trying to kill me. Or all of the above."

"I've managed to frighten you and I'm sorry, Shannon."

"Yeah, me, too. He sounds schizophrenic."

"It's definitely not a normal scenario." He stood and slipped his jacket back on. "Look, I can't promise you round-the-clock protection, but I can try to schedule a cruiser to drive by every hour or so. In the meantime, I would strongly suggest that you find someone to stay here with you or else pack a bag and go to a friend's house for a few nights."

"My dad lives in his RV and he usually parks it in my driveway, but he's been away for the past few days, fishing."

"Until he gets back, I'd like you to take those extra precautions."

I shifted my gaze from his to the windows overlooking my familiar view of the safe, quiet street I'd grown up on. After a long moment, I looked back at Eric and nodded. "Believe me, I will."

Chapter Ten

Lizzie offered to spend the night at my place, but I told her I didn't want to take her away from Hal and the kids.

"Why do you think I'm offering?" she said, annoyed that I didn't understand her ploy.

"Oops." I laughed. "Sorry."

Jane jumped in. "It's all right, Lizzie. I'll be staying with Shannon for as long as necessary."

"Thank you," I said, having already planned for her to stay. Jane had become almost fanatical in her determination to keep me safe. I got the feeling that she was more worried about me than I was about myself, which was pretty darn worried.

"But I could stay, too," Lizzie said. "We could have a slumber party."

I gave her a big hug, but in the end she went home to her darling family, while Jane and I ordered Chinese food and watched one of Jane's favorite old romantic comedies. We laughed, we cried, and if we'd only had more time, we would've painted our toenails and braided each other's hair. It was girls' night, for sure.

Thursday morning after breakfast, Jane still wasn't

keen on leaving me alone in the house. But since I knew she had an appointment with her landscaper, I insisted that she go home.

"I can cancel the appointment," she said. "You and I can stay here and play cards or . . . something."

"No," I said, shaking my head. "I'll be fine by myself. I've got a bunch of things to do today and besides, nothing's going to happen to me in broad daylight."

"But Eric said—"

"I know what he said and believe me, I appreciate his concern. I've already seen a cop car drive by a few times this morning, so I feel safe right now."

She glanced out the window. "I'm uneasy about leaving you here alone."

"I'm a little anxious myself, but I'll be okay. When I asked you to spend a few nights here, I didn't expect you to stay twenty-four hours a day."

She fiddled with her purse strap, unsure of what to do next. "I feel guilty leaving you."

"No guilt allowed," I said, grabbing her for a quick hug before nudging her toward the door. "You have your own life, and you need to get that garden whipped into shape if it's going to look good by the grand opening."

"What will you do while I'm gone?"

I walked with her out to her car. "I'll be sticking close to home today."

"Can I give you a ride anywhere?"

"No, thanks," I said easily. "I plan to clean up the garage. It's got that black dust everywhere from the fingerprinting. And then I thought I'd better go through my tools. Make sure nothing else is missing."

She grabbed my arm. "Oh, God, Shannon."

"Yeah, I know." If I found more tools missing, I was going to call the police right away.

With a heavy sigh, she climbed into her car. "Okay. I'll be back sometime later this afternoon."

"Thanks, Jane." I watched her drive off, then went back inside the house. I called Penny at the bank to beg off meeting her at the gym.

"Is everything okay?" she asked.

"Oh yeah. I've just got something I've got to take care of at home." I didn't feeling like sharing the details with everyone in town.

"That's a drag," she said. "Maybe we can make it sometime this weekend."

"I'm determined to get there tomorrow. Do you think you'll be there?"

"Tomorrow's Friday," she mused. "Yeah, I might be able to make it."

"That would be great," I said. "If it turns out you can't, we'll do it another time. Otherwise, I'll see you there around five."

After we hung up, I spent a full hour stretching out my muscles and limbering up. Ever since the bike accident I'd been feeling positively ancient with all my aches and pains. That had to stop.

I stuck with the warm-up stretches, but vowed that tomorrow afternoon at the gym I would start getting my legs and arms back into shape. I could always go for a walk later today, but I was a little wary of running into any of my neighbors. I knew they would try to bully me into spilling the details of Wendell Jarvick's murder. I was fairly certain I'd be able to withstand their doggedness, but, really, who could blame them? Everyone loved gossip, especially in a small town. It was our lifeblood. That was doubly true when something gruesome happened on your own street. You owed it to the rest of the town to get the scoop and share it with others.

The garage cleanup took me almost two hours. That fine black fingerprint powder was more difficult to clean than I thought it would be. On the outside windowsill I started off with a soapy sponge and learned right away that any moisture added to the powder residue would turn it into something resembling India ink. I got it all wiped off eventually, though, thanks to the glossy white paint on the surface, which was so thick there were no crevices for the black powder to sink into.

My work bench inside the garage was different. The wood there was simply whitewashed, not glossy and thick, so the minuscule powdery flecks had burrowed into the porous surface. I finally resorted to using my industrial Shop-Vac with the HEPA filter that was so effective on sweeping up drywall dust. Except for a few tiny spots, it worked. I could live with the spots until it was time to paint the darn thing.

I put away all my cleaning stuff and turned to my tools. I'd amassed a pretty large collection over the years, but I had always been diligent about keeping them in order. I didn't find anything missing from the large rolling tool cabinet—yes, it was pink—I always kept at home. Likewise, nothing was gone from the two smaller toolboxes I used on job sites. I organized everything, culling some of the items I rarely used and rearranging the drawers to be more accessible. Then I locked up the boxes and went out to my truck to get my third tool chest, the one I'd brought home from the Boyers' place. The police had gone through the entire contents, and Eric had asked me to look through it, too, in case something else was missing. I had assured him that other than my pink wrench and the screwdriver used as murder weapons, nothing else was gone.

Before I locked it up, I decided to double-check that everything was where it should be. It looked to be in good order, until I shifted the big wooden claw hammer and realized that I had been storing three different hammers in this chest for the Boyers' job. My claw hammer and my framing hammer with the lightweight titanium head were both in their proper places. But to my horror, my pink-handled ball-peen hammer wasn't there. I went back through all of my tool chests to make sure I hadn't overlooked it. I couldn't find it anywhere.

I had no choice but to call Eric and give him the bad news.

The guilt was overwhelming. To distract myself, I spent the rest of the afternoon in my garden. It was October, harvesttime, and since our weather was relatively mild most of the year, I was looking forward to prepping the garden for a new crop of winter vegetables. It would be a few more weeks before I could do it, though, because all six of my good-sized vegetable beds were still producing veggies from the planting I'd done last spring. And that didn't even count all the pots of tomatoes and edible herbs I had lined up along the side fence.

All summer I'd been harvesting what I liked to call my salad veggies—lettuces, tomatoes, cucumbers, green onions—almost daily. Now I was eyeing my fall crop of

zucchini, spinach, beets, peas, carrots, peppers, and various root vegetables that I planned to roast or turn into
cold-weather soups and stews. At one end of the squash
bed were a dozen small pumpkins and two massive ones
that I hoped would grow even larger for the annual Harvest Festival and Parade at the end of the month.

I had already filled up one large basket with vegetables for soup and was starting to weed the beds when I
heard someone call out my name. Glancing up, I saw
Mac Sullivan looking over the fence.

"Hi, Mac." I stood and brushed the soil off my jeans.

"Hey, Irish. You look good in the garden."

"Thank you." I smiled as I unlatched the gate. The man
said the nicest things. "What's up?"

"I was hoping you'd show me one of those rooms you
rent out."

I was puzzled. "Are you doing research?"

"No," he said, laughing. "I'm looking for a place to
live."

"But you just bought a big new house."

"Can't live in it until it's refurbished. Thought I'd look
into renting for a while."

I stared at him. Not that it was a hardship, but I had to
wonder if he was pulling my leg. MacKintyre Sullivan
could afford the biggest deluxe suite anywhere in the
world, so why bother with my little rental? He looked serious, though, so I pulled off my gardening gloves and set
them on the side of the raised bed. "I'll go get the key."

I came back outside a minute later and led him upstairs to the apartments.

I stopped in front of Wendell's place and took in the
streams of yellow tape strewn across the door.

"Did they say how long they'll keep it a crime scene?" he asked.

"Eric said his guys will need a few more days to sift through Wendell's belongings. I didn't get a chance to look inside, so I have no idea what condition it's in."

Mac considered the yellow tape. "I can be like a rabid dog when it comes to doing research, but if it's all the same to you, I'd rather not stay in the murder victim's room."

"I'm glad to hear it." I walked a few more steps and unlocked the door to the second apartment. "This one's clean and ready for a new tenant."

He walked inside and glanced around. "This place is great. Lots of good light. Bigger than I thought it would be."

"It's basically one big room, but I tried to section it off so it feels like you've got several separate areas."

"I like it," he said, running his fingers down the matchstick screen that, together with a willowy ficus tree, created a partition between the bedroom and the living room space. "Hey, there's a desk."

I shrugged. "A lot of people travel with their computers."

As I'd done for Wendell over a week ago, I walked across the suite and pulled the blinds open. The view from this room was slightly better than Wendell's—at least I thought so. There was more to see of the green hills and redwood trees to the south, and the ocean was still in plain sight above the rooftops, too.

"Really nice view," he said. Pointing, he asked, "Is that an empty lot behind you?"

"Not for long." I gave him the quick explanation of

how I'd bought the property behind my house two years ago. The house had been what we called a cracker box, a run-down little beach shack that was rented out to tourists year after year. Even though cracker-box houses were small, they often sat on lots as big as my own.

In recent years, a buyer would snag one of those houses, tear it down and build a much grander house, an updated Victorian or a Craftsman to match the style and feeling of the town.

I had razed the old house, salvaging as much of the good wood and chimney bricks as I could, and filled the lot with mustard seed to treat the soil until I was ready to plant next year. I envisioned a row of trees along the edges of the property, grass and flower beds in the center, benches and walkways here and there. I wanted to turn it into a small park. I had already conducted a casual survey of my neighbors, who approved of the plan wholeheartedly.

"That's cool," he said.

"I like the idea of having a neighborhood park."

He nodded, glanced around the room again. "Did you do all the work in here?"

"Me and a couple of my guys."

He ran his finger along the beveled grooves of the decorative wood panel above the small fireplace mantel. "Who did this woodwork?"

"I did."

"It's exceptional." His gaze held on mine. "So you're also a carpenter."

"Yes."

Mac strolled around the room, checked out the kitchenette sink, mini fridge, two-burner electric stove, and microwave oven. He slid the closet door open and closed, popped into the bathroom, and then glanced out the window one more time. "So, how much to rent the place?"

I was still mystified by his interest, but decided to play along. "By the day or by the week?"

"By the month."

"Oh." I mentally calculated the price, took off fifteen percent for the long-term rate, and gave him the bottom line.

"Not bad. I'll take it."

Later that afternoon, Jane arrived to spend another night with me. She was bursting with excitement and danced around the kitchen as she told me all about her meeting with the landscaper and their plans for her garden.

"It sounds beautiful," I said. "I love the idea of having a little bridge across the koi pond. And the ferns planted around the bases of the trees will give the space a real magical quality."

"I know," she said, and provided more details as I poured two glasses of wine. When I handed her a glass, she asked, "What did you do today?"

"My day wasn't quite as exciting as yours, but let's see." I tried to think of all the positive things while avoiding the missing-hammer news. "I cleaned out the garage, worked in the garden for a while, and rented one of my apartments to a new tenant."

"You have a new tenant already?" she said, taken aback. "But you just got rid of Wendell— I mean, oh, dear. You know what I mean."

I tried not to laugh, since the subject was morbid. And she looked so utterly mortified that I knew it would be cruel to tease her. "I know what you meant. And it's not like I rented out Wendell's place. I can't. It's still a crime scene."

Her shoulders hunched up and she rubbed her arms. "Just thinking about it gives me goose bumps."

"Yeah, me too. Anyway, I rented the other apartment."

She considered it for a moment. "I would've thought you might want some privacy for a while."

"I thought I did, too, but then this guy came around asking if the place was available and I changed my mind."

"What guy?"

I bit my lip, unsure why I was so hesitant to tell her. Maybe to keep the toasty little secret to myself for a while? But that didn't make sense. Jane was my oldest and dearest friend and we had no secrets between us. "Mac Sullivan."

"Oh." She drew the word out for several syllables.

"Yeah." Hoping the subject was closed, I walked to the freezer. "I thought we could have chicken for dinner. Do you mind making a salad?"

"I'll be happy to. But let's just circle back around to Mac Sullivan for a minute."

"I figured you might say that." I pulled out a package of cut-up chicken pieces. I had planned to be sensible and grill them, but now I decided to fry them in a thick cornflake batter. I rarely ate such fattening meals, preferring healthier fruits and vegetables, lean meats, and fish, but lately I'd been going for high fat and calories. Clearly, murder wasn't good for my diet.

"Don't get me wrong," Jane said as she swirled her wine-glass. "Mac Sullivan is very cute and hunky and interesting, and he's a famous author, so it would be awesome to have him living nearby. But don't you wonder why he would want to live in a small apartment over your garage?"

"I did wonder. But he explained that he needs a place to stay until the restoration of his new home is completed."

"Has it even started yet?"

"No, and it probably won't begin for another month. And, yes, I'm bidding to do the work."

"Why doesn't he just hire you?"

"Actually, he did. But I insisted that he look at some other companies."

She shook her head at me. "Of course you did. He'll hire you, anyway, if he's smart. You're the best contractor in town. No, the county. Maybe even the whole state."

"That might be laying it on a little thick, but thank you." I smiled at her. "I love you, too."

She frowned. "Nobody's lived in the old lighthouse mansion for thirty years or more. Restoring it could take months or even a year."

"You're right." I began to wash the chicken pieces. "At least six to eight months. I'll know more once I see the inside."

"So he might be living here all that time."

"Maybe."

"Are you sure you want someone staying here for that length of time?"

I glanced over at her. "Um, we're talking about MacKintyre Sullivan, right? The author? Have you met him?"

"Of course I've met him. Oh, you mean because he's so adorable? Hmm." She found a head of fresh lettuce in the fridge and set it down near the small sink on the kitchen island. "Okay, I can see how having someone like him nearby would be nice."

"Nice?" I shot her a look as I patted the chicken dry.

"Sorry. I can't seem to come up with the right words to describe him."

"That's okay," I said, chuckling as I prepped the coating mixture. "I can."

"You like him."

"I do." I stopped working and turned to her. "He rescued me when I fell off my bike. He stayed with me, drove me back home, carried me up the stairs. It was sweet. And then he talked to the police and I really think he's responsible for Chief Jensen's change of heart about me. Mac is funny and kind and gorgeous. And now he's going to live right up there." I pointed out the window toward the garage apartment. "Yippee."

"Chief Jensen is gorgeous, too," she said softly.

"He is indeed." I met her gaze. "How lucky are we that two such handsome unattached men have moved to town so recently?"

"Pretty darn lucky," she said, and we both grinned.

As we talked, I dipped a piece of chicken into the egg mixture, then tossed it into the ziplock bag filled with crushed cornflakes and seasoned flour. Once I had half of the chicken pieces in the baggie, I zipped it closed and shook it until each piece of chicken was completely coated.

"I just hope Mac doesn't hurt you," Jane said, pulling a bright red tomato out of the vegetable basket.

"Hurt me? Why do you think he would hurt me?"

"Oh, I don't know." She turned away from me and fiddled nervously with the utensils next to the chopping block built into the island in my kitchen. "It's probably stupid."

"Maybe. But now I'm curious, so please tell me what you're thinking."

She didn't make eye contact with me as she took a quick sip of wine. "Lizzie and I were talking about Mac."

My lips twisted into a disgruntled pout. "Why do I get the feeling I'm not going to like this?"

"Just listen." She moved closer so she could speak in a low voice, as though someone might be eavesdropping. "Don't you think it's weird that he writes murder mysteries and he just moved here and already there are two murders?"

I stared at her, truly stunned. "I don't even know what to say to that."

"You're right." She walked back to the sink, shaking her head. "It's a ludicrous theory."

"You're damn right it is." Exasperated, I tossed the stuffed baggie down on the counter. "Where in the world does Lizzie come up with this stuff? I thought she loved Mac. Why would she ever believe he was capable of murder?"

Before Jane could speak, I held up both my hands to cut her off. "And don't try to pretend this was your idea. Lizzie is the original conspiracy theorist and this is right up her alley. I'll talk to her tomorrow, because I want to know why she would say something so crazy. And I don't want her spreading it around town, either. What's the deal with her? Is she jealous that I met Mac first?" I held up my hands again. "Okay, that was a stupid thing to say and I didn't mean it. I love Lizzie, but I'm mystified as to why she would ever say something like that."

It was Jane's turn to shut me up. "Wait. To be fair, it wasn't Lizzie who said it. It was Mac."

I scowled at her.

"It's true," she insisted.

"I need more wine." I grabbed the wine bottle and refilled my glass, then Jane's. I took a sip, then waved her on. "Okay, go ahead and tell me what you heard."

"Mac came into Paper Moon yesterday and right away he hit it off with Lizzie and Hal. He stuck around talking to them for an hour. So finally Hal tells him about the two murders that happened recently, and according to Lizzie, Mac laughed and said something like, 'Don't you think it's an interesting coincidence that I just happened to move here and murders started happening?'"

I sipped my wine while I considered Mac's words. "Okay, I can see how that would freak Lizzie out a little. But it was obviously just Mac's sense of humor."

"I think so, too," Jane said, "even though I don't know him as well as you do. But, Shannon, listen. Once Lizzie told me what he said, I thought about it. And the more I thought about it, the more I realized that you can't trust anyone right now. Not a soul."

"Why not?"

"For all the reasons we've already talked about. Someone in town is using your tools to kill people. They're trying to make you look guilty. Why? I keep asking myself what their motive is, but I can't figure it out. And who? I haven't got a clue." Jane shook her head and gave a complete body shiver. "It's crazy and frightening to consider that somebody around here has it in for you, but they do. That's why I don't think you should trust anyone right now."

"Not even you?"

"Well, of course you can trust me."

"Really? You were pretty angry about Jerry Saxton attacking me. You're a loyal friend to me, so what was to stop you from tracking him down and bashing him over the head, just to let him know he couldn't go around assaulting your friends and get away with it?"

She stared at me with her mouth open. After a long moment, I smiled. And so did she. And then we started to laugh.

"Oh, my God, what a ridiculous conversation," she said, leaning against the island counter.

"You started it," I claimed, and that made her giggle all over again.

After we sobered up, she faced me. "You're right, you know. I may have been angry enough to kill those two jerks on your behalf. But I would never turn around and try to make you look like the guilty one."

I smiled at her fondly. "I appreciate that."

We both went back to work on dinner, but after a minute I stopped and looked at her. "Jane, I trust Mac. He's smart and he makes me laugh. I'm happy he's going to be living on my property for as long as he wants to stay. I don't expect him to take care of me or anything, but having him around might discourage this horrible killer from coming after me."

"Nobody's coming after you," she said, and I noticed her face turning pale. "For God's sake, Shannon." She grabbed the wine bottle. "I need more wine. How about you?"

"I just poured you more wine."

She glanced at her full glass. "Oh."

I chuckled. "What's wrong with you?"

"Damn it, I'm scared to death for you!"

I grabbed a dish towel and wiped my hands clean. Then I walked over and enveloped her in a big hug. *We all seem to need more hugs lately,* I thought. "Thank you. I'm scared, too, okay? If I told you everything that Chief Jensen said to me after we found Wendell's body, you'd be even more afraid for me than you are now. But I'm going to get through all this. And I really appreciate you staying here with me for a few nights."

"I don't mind staying with you. We're having fun, right?"

"Well, mostly," I said, drowning the last piece of chicken in the egg mixture. "Except when I go into major conniptions thinking Lizzie believes Mac is a cold-blooded killer."

"Oh, what's a major conniption between friends?" Jane said lightly.

"Damn straight," I said, forcing myself to match her breezy tone.

As she pulled out more ingredients for the salad, she began to whistle her grandma's favorite song, "Put on a Happy Face."

Fake it till you make it, I thought, and determinedly hummed along with her. It wasn't easy because Jane was truly tone-deaf, but after a few minutes, I was surprised to find myself putting on a happy face.

*   *   *

The next morning, Mac brought me a check for the full amount of rent. By noon, he had moved his belongings into the garage apartment.

I still couldn't believe that the great MacKintyre Sullivan wanted to live in one of my little guest suites over the garage, but I wasn't about to complain. In fact, I was thrilled. Not only did I have a reliable tenant paying rent for at least a month and maybe longer, but I also had someone living on the premises who made me feel completely safe. The fact that he was crazy gorgeous was a big bonus.

After lunch, I walked up to the town square and grabbed Lizzie for a quick discussion. We walked out the back door of the shop and stood in the small parking lot.

"What is it?" she asked. "Something's wrong."

I had to take a deep breath or two before I could blurt out the question. "You don't honestly think that Mac Sullivan had anything to do with the murders, do you?"

"What? Of course not," she said, gawking at me like I was the nutball instead of her. "Who in the world would think that . . . ? Oh." She blew out her cheeks. "Jane. Oh, boy."

"Yeah. Jane. What's the deal?"

"Well, see, I was sort of gushing about Mac coming into the store and I told her what he said. I guess I didn't make it clear that it was a joke."

"No, you didn't. She thought it might be a joke, but she was still a little worried."

"I'm sorry, Shannon." She hung her head and stared

at the ground. "I'd better call and let her know I was only kidding about Mac."

"I know that would make her feel better."

"Of course."

"She's scared to death that someone's trying to set me up for the crimes and that they're coming after me."

"I'm scared, too," Lizzie said. "Nothing like this has ever happened here."

"I know," I said, and forcefully changed the subject. "So, you and Mac are new best friends, I guess."

She patted her heart. "OMG, Shannon. Hal and I had the best time with him. He's wonderful."

I smiled. "I agree." I gave her a quick update on Mac renting the garage apartment, and we commiserated over her daughter Marisa's crush on a new boy at school. Lizzie was sure the crush signaled the beginning of the end of her little girl's sweet disposition. I hoped she was wrong, but Marisa had just become a teenager, so anything was possible.

After Lizzie went back inside, I walked home in a much better mood. My friends might be a little crazy, but at least they were my kind of crazy.

Later that afternoon, Jane returned to my house. Even though I had a rugged new tenant, she was determined to stay with me until my father came home from his fishing trip. For dinner, we drank more wine and made linguini with grilled sausages, onions, and peppers.

She left again early Friday morning, and ten minutes later, Chief Jensen called to tell me about my bike.

"Good morning," he said, his voice deep and assured.

"The sheriff's team has finished going over the bike, so you'll have it back within a few hours."

"Did they find anything helpful?" I asked.

"A few prints that didn't match yours. They've sent them to IAFIS along with some prints and fibers from Wendell's car. It'll be a while before any results come through."

"Okay, thanks," I said, then had to ask, "I don't suppose someone turned in my hammer."

"Not yet," he said. "Try not to worry. That's our job."

"I'll try." I thanked him again and hung up the phone, feeling guilty despite his nice words. I made calls to Carla and Wade to let them know I would swing by their job sites that afternoon to check in and see what was happening. It felt like ages since I'd been on the job.

I took a few minutes to clean up the kitchen and vacuum downstairs before taking a shower and heading out to visit my crews around town. It was a long day and I was tired, but at five o'clock that afternoon, I walked into the Flex-Time gym and greeted the friendly employees at the front desk. As I slid my membership card through their electronic reader, I spotted Penny in the warehouse-sized workout room, running on the treadmill.

Just watching her work out made my muscles groan a little, but I was determined to get myself back into shape again.

After stowing my gear and my purse in a locker, I went out to the floor just as she was cooling down.

"Glad you made it," she said, breathless.

"I need a few minutes to warm up on the treadmill and then I'll catch up with you."

"Perfect." She flipped her towel around her neck and walked off, so I took over her treadmill.

As I got up to speed, I glanced around the large workout room. Mirrors lined all the walls so it was easy to see everyone else from where I stood on the treadmill. There was a good crowd this afternoon, but not so many that there were traffic jams at any of the machines. I thought about taking a leisurely swim after my workout, but then realized I'd forgotten my bathing suit. Maybe I'd do that next time to decompress after working out.

Two women walked into the room and I almost groaned out loud. They were Jennifer Bailey and Whitney Reid. It was odd to realize that even though Whitney had been married to Tommy Gallagher for more than twelve years now, I still called her by her maiden name. In my mind, she would always be the high school girl who made my life hell.

Jennifer saw me first and quickly whispered in Whitney's ear. The two of them seemed to have been frozen in that gossipy high school mode. And maybe I had, too, because my first concern was whether my outfit was cute enough. I checked the mirror in front of me and decided I looked good in a sleeveless lime green top with a jazzy pair of black-and-lime cropped tights.

Unfortunately, Jennifer was wearing the exact same outfit. And wasn't that just my luck? Maybe it was my imagination, but I was pretty sure I was rocking the lime green look, while the same color made Jennifer's skin appear sallow.

Of course, Whitney noticed our clothes right away. "Oh, look. Twins."

Jennifer scowled. "Shut up, Whitney."

"You shut up," Whitney said.

It was interesting that the mean girls could be just as mean to each other as to outsiders.

They walked to the other side of the room to use the big Pilates balls, so I ignored the two of them and continued my run. Five minutes later, I slowed down and then came to a stop. After wiping off the machine, I slung my towel around my neck and walked across the spacious gym floor to the free-weight area to find Penny.

She was working out on the bench press and I had to admit, I was a little intimidated. There were way too many weights on the barbell she was lifting.

I had used the bench press a few times when I first joined the gym and was able to work with a personal trainer, but, in general, I preferred to use the machines because I felt more in control of both the weight and my own movements. Penny was way beyond my level, at least when it came to the bench press. I was grateful she'd agreed to work out with me.

"There you are," she said, straining to lift the weight over her head. "Do you mind spotting me?"

"Not at all," I said, moving closer to the weight stand to lend her any support she needed. "How much weight are you lifting?"

"Hundred twenty-five," she gasped, as her biceps bulged from the effort.

"Holy mother," I muttered. "Those sedate little banker's suits you wear every day are hiding some amazing muscles."

She grinned and managed to slide the barbell onto the pins of the rack before letting her head drop back and exhaling loudly. She laid her hands on her chest, trying to catch her breath. When she finally was able to sit up, she glared at me. "Rule number one: you're not supposed to make me laugh on the bench press."

I could tell she wasn't really angry, but I apologized, anyway. "I'm sorry, but you really shocked me. You're so strong."

"For my weight and experience, it's pretty standard." She grabbed her water bottle and took a long gulp. Once she was standing, she wiped off the bench with her towel and said, "Okay, let me spot you."

"I'm going to be a severe disappointment to you." But I went ahead and stretched out on the bench. "I injured my shoulder the other day, so I'd better take it easy. Let's start with twenty pounds."

She laughed. "Oh, come on. Even with an injury, you can do better than that."

"Okay, thirty."

Shaking her head, she said, "We'll start with fifty."

"No way. I'll go forty." I was basically in good shape, thanks to my occupation, but I was a novice on the bench press.

"All right, but that's nothing. A ten-year-old could lift that much."

I laughed. "I'm okay with that."

"So am I, because the barbell weighs ten pounds on its own. So you'll be lifting fifty after all."

"Diabolical," I muttered.

She chuckled as she reset the weights on each side and then gave me the thumbs-up sign.

I grabbed hold of the bar with both hands and lifted it carefully off the sturdy pins that were screwed into the rack. "Oh, God."

"Bring it down first, easy, easy," she said softly. "That's it. Now lift."

"I'm so out of shape," I said on a rush of breath. I thought my aches and pains from the bicycle accident had faded, but they now came roaring back with a vengeance.

"No, you're not," she insisted. "You look good. You should be lifting at least ninety pounds, by the way. That's just according to your size."

"No way."

"I'm serious. Now on the next lift, focus on your pecs. Feel those muscles working. Can you feel them?"

"Are you kidding?" I could feel them screaming.

"Isn't that the best feeling there is?" she asked.

"Hey, Penny."

From the corner of my eye, I saw Jennifer Bailey catch Penny's attention.

"Jennifer! Hi!" Penny sounded happy to see her. Go figure. As they started chitchatting, my interest in bonding with Penny wavered. It got worse with every second that Jennifer hung around.

Ignoring me, Jennifer grabbed hold of the rack and swayed coyly. "Whitney had to go home."

"But you stayed," Penny said, her tone demure, not sounding like herself.

"Yeah. Did you think about what I asked you?"

"Sure did." Penny giggled. "I say let's do it."

It was odd to hear Penny giggle after watching her kick ass on the bench press, but I wasn't in a position to judge, having giggled myself a time or two. But never when talking to Jennifer Bailey. She was a vile, angry person. How could anyone possibly giggle around her?

Since Penny was new in town, though, I decided to cut her some slack.

` "You're doing great, Shannon," Penny said, her voice perkier than it had been a minute ago. "Keep it up. I'll just be a second."

I was a little miffed when they walked away, but I decided to keep lifting because I figured the stronger I got, the easier it would be to kick Jennifer's butt. Not that I ever wanted to get close enough to kick any part of her, but the visual worked. I was able to lift the barbell another six times before I was ready to collapse and die. I managed to slide the monster weight back onto the pins and after that my arms fell limply to my sides.

I closed my eyes and listened to myself wheezing. I knew I shouldn't have lifted that much weight, but I wanted to get back into fighting shape and make Penny proud. It was probably stupid, but I liked her and hoped we would become good friends. Or I had, until I saw her being so chummy with Jennifer.

The one thing I refused to do was compete with Jennifer for Penny's friendship.

I opened my eyes and stared at the ceiling. *You don't have to compete with anyone,* I thought, hating that any time I was around the mean girls, I felt like I was back in high school again.

I was about to sit up when I heard a sudden pop and a loud screech. I looked up and saw that one of the pins had cracked. The front of the pin launched into the room while the back screw dangled from the rack.

And fifty pounds of barbells were about to drop on my head!

Chapter Eleven

My scream came out more like a gasp. My arms shot up to catch the heavy weight, but I wasn't strong enough to catch the bar midfall. I did manage to slow it down, though, and changed its trajectory enough so that instead of landing on my neck and strangling me, it struck my already tender shoulder.

That was definitely going to leave a bruise.

I still had both hands gripping the bar, but I'd exhausted my muscles and couldn't budge it. I was trapped beneath the weight, but at least I wasn't dead.

"Help!" I shouted weakly.

Penny was already racing across the room. She grabbed the barbell with one hand and dropped it on the floor. "Oh, my God, Shannon! Are you all right? I'm so sorry I left you. You were doing so well, I thought you'd be okay for a minute, but I . . . Oh, my God. I'll go get the manager."

She ran off and I struggled to sit up. It wasn't easy to do without shrieking and crying in pain. I had to roll over on my good shoulder and push up from the bench.

My injured shoulder was throbbing so badly, I wondered if I would ever use a nail gun again.

That might've sounded crazy, but my nail gun was a big part of my life.

Penny was back in less than a minute with an instant ice pack. "Here, use this." I took it and pressed it against my shoulder. The cold seeped in immediately and I shivered.

"On your way out," Penny continued, "you need to stop and see Becky, the manager. Tell her what happened and fill out an insurance form."

"She should probably come over here and check out the rack," I said, pointing at the broken pin. "See how it snapped off?"

"Oh, crap." She wiped away a thin stream of sweat from her temple. "I'm just so sorry, Shannon."

"I'll be okay," I said, smiling weakly. "I'm still catching my breath."

A guy sitting on the incline bench across from me spared me a look of disgust. "Chicks should stay away from this place if they don't know how to use the equipment."

I kept my mean-spirited response to myself and instead muttered, "Yeah, thanks for your help."

But Penny whipped around and said, "Hey, pal, the rack broke. This place better have plenty of insurance, because otherwise, Shannon will own it by the time she gets finished suing their sorry asses."

Go, Penny, I thought, as I held the ice pack against my shoulder and tried not to whimper.

She turned her back on the guy and squatted down next to me. "What can I do?"

"Don't worry." I reached for my water bottle and took a sip. "You got here just in time. Probably saved my life."

"I wouldn't have had to if I'd been paying attention. There's no excuse."

"Let's forget it," I said, trying for a casual smile. "I'm going to go take a shower and then stop for a bite to eat at the pub on the way home. Do you have other plans tonight or would you like to join me?"

"I'd love to join you."

"Okay, good. Let's meet in the lobby in about forty-five minutes."

"Perfect."

I walked into the locker room, still irritated at Jennifer for distracting Penny in the first place. Maybe I should've been annoyed with Penny, too, but she was new enough to town that she hadn't quite figured out the good guys from the bad guys. And Jennifer was definitely bad. If she hadn't come over and started flirting with Penny . . . Wait. *Flirting?* But, yeah, Jennifer had been acting so coy, swaying around and twisting her hair like a ten-year-old talking to her first crush. It was embarrassing. And so out of character that I was instantly suspicious.

Maybe she needed a bank loan. Maybe she was desperate. Maybe her credit was lousy. It would be just like Jennifer to fake a friendship to get what she wanted.

In the locker room, I stripped and wrapped a towel around me and walked into the steam room, hoping some wet heat would help my shoulder. I'd have to remember to grab another ice pack on the way out.

I sat in the damp, sizzling heat for ten minutes and

then escaped to the showers. Thirty minutes later, I went to find Becky, the manager.

"Penny told me about the incident," Becky said. "I'm really sorry about it. We check the machines and equipment every morning and those pins were fine a few hours ago."

"I believe you," I said, and meant it. "It was just weird how it happened the way it did. I hate to admit it, but I'm still kind of shaken up."

"Let's have you fill out an accident report so we can get the insurance company involved."

As I filled out the form, she assured me that if I needed to see a doctor, their insurance would cover it. I didn't think it would come to that, but I appreciated her concern.

I didn't write it down on the form, but I'd been thinking about that moment when Jennifer came over to giggle with Penny. She had grabbed hold of the rack and was swaying around as she talked. I'd stopped paying attention because she was such a twit, but now I wondered if she had deliberately done something to the pin to break it while I was working out.

It was a far-fetched theory, but having known Jennifer for all these years, I wouldn't put it past her to try to sabotage me like that.

Becky gave me another instant ice pack for later and I walked back to the lobby. Penny was waiting for me, so we left the gym together.

"My car's right here," I said. "I'll see you at the pub."

"Great," she said. "And dinner's on me."

"That's not necessary."

"Yes, it is. I owe you." She glanced over my shoulder. "Oh, there's Jennifer. Should we invite her?"

"Uh . . ." Before I could answer, Penny skipped over and gave Jennifer a warm hug. I could hear her chirpy voice and knew she was asking Jennifer to join us. I also knew that Jennifer would be happy to join us—as soon as hell froze over.

Penny laughed at something Jennifer said and gave her arm a quick squeeze. She didn't seem to notice the mean girl glaring at me with stone-cold eyes that made me shiver.

"She can't make it," Penny said when Jennifer walked away. "So I'll see you in a couple of minutes at the pub."

"Okay." I waved at Penny, but kept my eye on Jennifer until she got into her spiffy little black BMW, gunned the engine for my benefit, and tore out of the parking lot.

I called Jane on the way to the pub to invite her to join Penny and me for dinner. I thought she might like to get to know Penny, since it was always good to be friends with a banker. Jane passed on dinner, but said she'd meet me at my house later on to spend the night.

The pub was lively on a Friday night. One table in the bar was overflowing with my crew members, so I stopped to talk with them for a minute. I'd seen a few of the guys earlier that afternoon, but I'd been missing out on regular visits to the job sites and wanted to catch up. That would have to wait, though, because I saw Penny walk in a minute later.

We found a table in the dining area and both of us

ordered a beer and the fish and chips. We ended up staying for almost two hours and found out we had a lot of common interests. If only she would tell Jennifer to buzz off, we might manage to be good friends.

"Hello."

I looked up and found Police Chief Eric Jensen's compelling blue eyes staring right at me. He was out of uniform in a casual jacket, a denim shirt, and blue jeans that looked alarmingly good on him.

"Oh, hello," I said, sounding foolishly breathless. "Are you on duty tonight?"

He grinned. "No. I've got the night off. Thought I'd come in for a beer."

"That's nice." I was about to invite him to join us when I glanced at Penny, who looked positively terrified.

I gave him a regretful smile. "I would invite you to join us, but we're just about to go."

"No worries. I've got some friends waiting for me at the bar. I just wanted to stop and say hi."

"Thank you. It's good to see you."

"You, too." He lifted his hand in a wave and walked off toward the bar.

I turned to Penny. "Are you okay?"

"Thanks for making up an excuse," she said with relief as the waitress brought the bill. "I didn't want him to sit down."

"What's wrong? He's actually pretty nice." *Easy for me to say,* I thought. I hadn't always thought of him as *nice*.

Still on edge, Penny reached for the beer bottle and took a sip. "I hate feeling this way, but I just get so nervous around the police. W-we had a robbery at the bank where I used to work. When the police arrived, they accidentally shot one of our own tellers instead of the bank robber. Ever since then, I can't help it. I feel really anxious around the police. It's their guns, I guess."

"I understand." I leaned in and whispered, "It probably didn't help that we were all under suspicion for a while."

"So true." She signed the check and finished the last of her beer.

"Are you ready to go?" I absently rubbed my shoulder, feeling achy again and way past tired.

"Yes," she said, smiling with pleasure. "This was so much fun. Let's do it again soon."

"I'd love to," I said, and meant it. At least, as long as she didn't invite Jennifer.

I slept in fits and starts that night. Not only was my shoulder killing me, but I also suffered another nightmare. This one featured Jennifer and Whitney chasing me on bicycles around the curves of the Old Cove Highway. Cars would swerve and screech their brakes, barely missing me. My bike kept finding gopher holes and ejecting me. I would fly through the air but never hit the ground. Instead, I would wind up back on my bike, racing down the highway with the mean girls in pursuit.

Saturday morning, I was still in pain. I felt drained and stiff all over again. But on a positive note, at least I hadn't dreamed of barbells strangling me.

Another happy note was that when I hobbled downstairs to make coffee, I found Jane already there, fixing breakfast.

"Good morning," she said, sounding way too cheerful at this hour of the morning. "Coffee's ready and breakfast is minutes away."

Recently, Jane had begun testing recipes to use for breakfasts once Hennessey House opened for business. Today she was making her famous apple, bacon, and French toast casserole. I could smell the syrupy topping bubbling in the oven.

It was as delicious as it sounded and went a long way toward making me feel better about life in general again.

After breakfast, Jane went home to take care of some chores and run errands. I washed the dishes and cleaned up the kitchen.

As I was finishing, the phone rang and I grabbed it.

"Hello?"

"Hi, it's me." I recognized my sister Chloe's voice instantly.

"Hey, superstar, how are you?" I poured myself another cup of coffee and sat down at the kitchen table to talk.

After years of office and production work in Hollywood, Chloe had climbed up the food chain and had recently become the host of her very own home-improvement show on the DIY Network.

So all those years of hanging out on construction sites with our dad had finally paid off for both of us.

These days, Chloe rarely came back home to visit except on holidays. She had made a good life for herself in Hollywood and had a number of close friends who had also moved there from everywhere else in the country. Last year, Dad had helped her buy an adorable cottage in the Silver Lake hills. She'd been with her steady boyfriend for a few years now and his parents loved her.

After we touched on all the important stuff—health and happiness and new clothes—I said, "Tell me about the show. What are you working on?"

"We just filmed a segment on earthquake damage to concrete patios."

"Ooh. Fascinating stuff."

We both laughed. As long as she was happy, that's all I cared about. Chloe had a warm, caring soul that somehow, for no lack of effort on Dad's part or mine, had never fit in here in Lighthouse Cove. During her freshman year in high school, her best friend had died of cancer. Some of the new rich kids in her class thought it was funny that Chloe was so distraught about it, so they liked to make fun of her. Chloe kicked the crap out of a few of the girls and even one boy. After she was threatened with expulsion from school, she resisted making friends again or even getting close to anyone from around here.

She loathed the whole class structure that some newer, wealthier residents had tried to impose on those of us who'd been born and raised here. The *townies*.

Maybe it helped that in Hollywood, everyone she knew was from somewhere else, so they all started out on an even playing field. For whatever reason, she had found it easier to make friends there and be happy again. Dad and I missed her, but we both knew she was better off where she was. Besides, I talked to her on the phone every other week or so.

I shared all the stories about the murders and she was fascinated, especially with my major role in the macabre scenarios. When I revealed that the murder weapons were actually my own tools, she was horrified.

"Yeah, it's been pretty awful," I confessed, "especially when our new police chief thought I should be his number-one suspect."

"No way," she said. "You wouldn't hurt a flea."

"You're wrong. I kill fleas all the time. I take great pleasure in doing so."

"Well, no wonder he suspects you. You're a brazen flea killer."

And after I told her about my bicycle crash and the severed brake line, she accused me of going to a lot of trouble just to meet the delectable new author. We laughed awhile longer, talked about our holiday plans, and promised we would send photos and e-mail more often before we finally ended the call.

Once I hung up the phone, I felt restless and unsure of what to do next. After talking to my sister for almost an hour, I missed my dad. But since he wouldn't be home for a few more days, I was stuck with this antsy feeling.

Whenever I felt this way, the best thing to do was bury myself in work. But, sadly, I was still in too much pain to actually show up at one of my job sites and pound nails. Instead, I decided to do some gardening and then figure out where to go from there.

For the next hour I clipped fragrant herbs and tied them in bundles to dry. Later this winter I would stir the savory bundles into soups and stews. Some of the herbs I dried were pretty enough to use for decorating and aromatic enough to add to sachets and potpourri. So rather than aimlessly running out the clock, I could chalk up this extra time toward making Christmas goodies for my friends.

Although the air was cool, the sun had grown warm, so I took off my sweater and stared up to see if there were any clouds in the sky. That's when I noticed that the window of Mac's apartment was halfway open. I took that to mean that he was in there, even though I hadn't seen him since he'd moved in. His big black SUV was parked in front of my house, another sign of his presence. As I continued to wrap twine around stalks of herbs, I began to fantasize about his lifestyle.

Was he hunkered down writing a new book? Did he work all night and sleep all day? I wondered if he knew many people in town, the best places to eat and shop, and whom to call for deliveries. Did he realize that our town was a magnet for New Age foodies and health nuts? Did he care? Was he a vegan? I hoped not, although it was none of my business. But, really, what was wrong with a little red meat, anyway, as long as the animal was raised humanely?

He hadn't said so, but maybe Mac had moved here to join our well-known and very active Zen Buddhism society. They had a lovely retreat, the Sanctuary of the Four Winds, north of town up near the redwood forest. There the Zen acolytes trained and meditated under the guidance of Kikisho—he had the one-word name because he was said to be as famous in his world as Cher was in hers—and prepared themselves for the next phase. Whatever that was.

Many of the tourists who came to the sanctuary were into all sorts of other disciplines, including transcendental meditation and multiple-life regression. And if those didn't float your boat, there were spas on Main Street dedicated to aura-color enhancement, chakra cleansings, and sacred-stone healing.

And then there were a few space cadets who showed up wearing backpacks in anticipation of the mother ship carrying them off to the astral plane.

Not that I was judging, but Mac didn't seem like the type to hook up with a spirit guide for a quick trek out to planet Flerb.

Okay, maybe I was judging a little.

Whatever Mac's reasons for moving here, he would certainly enjoy some fresh produce—wouldn't he? I found a small basket and gathered up some lettuce, tomatoes, onions, broccoli, and an artichoke, and tossed in a bundle of herbs. Getting into my mission, I went inside and found a box of tasty crackers and a small round of cheese I hadn't opened yet. I added a chocolate bar for fun and then climbed the stairs to his apartment.

I knocked on the door and waited. It was a full minute before Mac opened the door and I sort of wished he hadn't. His eyes were bloodshot and his hair was sticking straight out from his head as if he had been pulling on it for hours. He wore a faded, out-of-shape T-shirt and a pair of plaid shorts that hung loosely on his hips. The outfit might've been sexy if the rest of him was a little more pulled together. But again, I wasn't judging.

"What?" he said, looking startled. "What happened?"

"Nothing. Are you all right?"

"Fine." He glanced out the door to see if there was someone else with me. "Working. What do you want?"

I held out the basket. "I thought I'd bring you some fresh—"

"Hey, thanks," he said, grabbed the basket, and shut the door in my face.

"You're welcome," I said to the door. So much for rattling the beast's cage. At least he'd said thanks. And now he would eat well—if he even remembered he had food.

*   *   *

A few days later, I was making a salad for dinner when I happened to glance out my kitchen window and noticed three very big, extremely muscular men walking up the stairs to the guest apartments. Were they from the police department, coming to clean up the rest of Wendell's apartment? Were they friends of Mac's? Or maybe enemies? They were awfully big and potentially fearsome.

I dried my hands quickly and jogged out to the garden. "Hi, guys. Can I help you?"

The biggest one, who was leading the pack, leaned over the railing and smiled politely. "No, ma'am, but thank you. We're here to see Mac."

Don't hurt him, I wanted to say, but didn't dare, for fear of him turning on me. The guy was huge and bald and wore a skintight black T-shirt with the sleeves cut off. He could've been a world wrestling champion for all I knew. Or a paid assassin. He pounded on Mac's door and stood back to wait.

The other two men weren't quite as large, but they were still intimidating. One wore a black bomber jacket and looked like he might've been part of a motorcycle gang. The third was dressed sedately in a pressed shirt tucked into blue jeans. He didn't look particularly mean, but you never knew. Maybe he was the brains behind the muscle.

I worked up my courage and called out to them, "I don't know if he'll answer the door. He's been very busy lately."

Just then, Mac swept the door open and the three men greeted him with hoots and howls. There were manly hugs with a lot of backslapping and arm punching. But the truly surprising thing was Mac himself. He looked wonderful. His beautiful thick hair was brushed back neatly. He looked rested and clean and handsome, and completely straight-arrow in a navy pullover sweater and khakis. This was no longer the eccentric writer yanking his hair out for the sake of his art.

"Dude, what is this place?" the motorcycle guy said, glancing around.

"It's a little piece of heaven," Mac said, then noticed me watching them and grinned. "See? There's an angel."

I shook my head and walked back into the house.

A few minutes later while I was finishing up my salad, I saw Eric Jensen walk up the stairs to Mac's place.

I'd heard some loud laughter and raucous voices coming from his apartment, but I couldn't believe that one of my neighbors would've called the police so soon. I didn't expect a confrontation, but I watched from the safety of my kitchen, anyway, and pushed open the casement window a few inches in order to hear the conversation as Eric knocked on the door.

Mac opened the door and grinned. "Hey, glad you could make it, Chief. Guys, this is Eric Jensen. You'll all want to watch yourselves since he's the chief of police of this fine village and won't take crap from any of y'all."

"At least he won't cheat," one of the guys shouted from inside the apartment.

"That's what you think," Eric said, chuckling.

Mac closed the door behind Eric, leaving me mystified.

But a minute later, I saw Hal bounding up the stairs. What the hell? I ran out to the garden and waved at him. "Hal!"

He glanced down. "Hey, Shannon. What's up?"

"What are you doing here? Where's Lizzie?"

"She's at home with the kids. I'm going to Mac's."

"But why?"

"It's his monthly poker game." He rubbed his hands together in excitement. "See you later, kiddo."

The poker game broke up around two in the morning— *not* that I'd stayed up watching and waiting to make sure everyone left at a decent hour. I didn't care. I was a little surprised that Jane and I hadn't been rudely awakened by any shouting or drunken laughter in the middle of the night. No, I just happened to wake up to get a glass of water and saw Mac walking with the other guys down the stairs and out to their cars. They were talking in low tones and I must say I appreciated their courtesy.

I had grown up playing card games with my dad and Uncle Pete, so I'd never considered poker some sort of esoteric ritual among men. But some of my girlfriends did and they were always peeved when they weren't included. I had joined in plenty of poker games with my crew guys, and while I liked to play, I didn't like to lose.

The one time I had put up a quiet stink about not being allowed to play in a big poker game was when a new builder came to town from Mendocino. He invited all the local contractors except me and another woman, a friend who was co-owner of a local plumbing company. I found out later that I had also not been invited to bid on a job he was about to start. That pissed me off and I let people know it. Not that I was all that powerful, but I was a firm believer in fair dealing, so suffice to say it never happened again.

In the case of Mac's poker party, though, I was just

happy he was making new friends in Lighthouse Cove and also inviting his old friends to be a part of our town.

And didn't I sound like Little Miss Sunshine working overtime for the Chamber of Commerce? I finished drinking my water and went back to bed.

Jane had made coffee and was gone by the time I woke up the next morning. I walked outside with my coffee mug in hand to pick up the mail I'd forgotten to get the day before. As I strolled back to the kitchen door, I saw Mac waiting at the gate.

"Hello."

"Morning, Irish," he said, pushing the gate open. "I hope we didn't keep you up last night."

"Not at all," I said. "You guys were pretty quiet. Did you have a good time?"

"Sure did."

"Who was the big winner?"

"Hal." He shook his head in disgust. "The guy's got a computer inside his head."

"I hope you didn't lose too badly."

"I never do," he assured me. He grabbed something off the picnic table and handed it to me. "I wanted to return this to you."

"My basket."

"Yeah. Thanks for putting all that stuff together for me. You saved my life."

I laughed. "I doubt that, but I'm glad you were able to use it."

"No, I'm serious, you saved my life. The chocolate, the vegetables—everything. It was really thoughtful of you.

Sometimes I get into a zone and forget to eat, forget to sleep, barely remember to breathe."

"I'm not very creative, but I can see how that could happen when you're really into the story."

"Yeah, it happens." He took a step closer and touched my arm with the tips of his fingers. "But you're wrong. When I look around here, I see creativity in everything you do."

"Oh." Self-conscious now, I glanced around at the garden, the house; tried to see it through his eyes. "I guess you could look at it that way, but it's nothing like what you do."

He laughed softly. "You have no idea."

I smiled. "Anyway, if you'd ever like to take something from the garden, you're more than welcome to—"

"I'm dazzled by you, Shannon Hammer."

"You are?"

"Yeah," he said, moving closer. His fingers skimmed up and down my arm and brushed my hair back off my shoulders. "I forgot to eat and sleep and breathe because of you. I dreamed of your green eyes."

"Oh, dear."

"It's all good," he said, smiling as he leaned in and kissed me. It was such a surprise that I held my breath for a few seconds. But then I relaxed and gave in to the sweet excitement of having a man's lips on mine. Something stirred inside me. Attraction, of course, but more than that. Electricity. Happiness. *Wow*.

When he stepped back, he was still smiling.

"Well. Um." Apparently I had forgotten how to speak.

He chuckled. "I know what you mean."

I shook my head. "It's just . . . well, that was unexpected."

"But kind of awesome, right?"

I laughed, charmed by him. "Definitely awesome."

"Good." He grabbed my hand companionably and walked me up the steps to my kitchen door. "I'm going back to work. I've got a great new character in this book. Jake Slater has finally met a woman who befuddles him completely."

"Really? That sounds like fun."

"It is," he said, sounding gleeful. "They've just met because her bicycle brakes failed."

"Oh," I said, baffled that he would use the story of how the two of us met in one of his books. "Isn't that sort of a low-tech complication for Jake Slater?"

"Yeah." He laughed. "But it's such a refreshing twist on the tired cliché of car brakes failing, I couldn't resist."

"Well, I hope he solves the mystery."

He opened the kitchen door, caught me in a quick embrace, and kissed me again. While my head was still spinning, he said, "I'll keep you posted."

Chapter Twelve

Thursday morning I finally felt good enough to get back to work on the Boyers' job site. My shoulder was still a little iffy, so I didn't plan to go crazy with a sledgehammer or carry a bag of cement around. But I was perfectly capable of stripping old wallpaper or soaking balusters in paint-remover solution if the situation called for it.

I told myself that even if Joyce Boyer showed up today, I could handle her. I was stronger now, and surely enough time had passed that she had calmed down about Jerry Saxton and all of his women. At least, I hoped so.

"Hey, boss," Wade said when I walked up the new front stairs to greet him on the porch. "What do you think?"

"Stairs look good and feel solid," I said. "And I love that siding."

"Better than the lattice, I think."

"Much better." I walked back down the stairs and, from the walkway, studied the new base of the house. "I'm glad it worked. The Boyers will love it, too, don't you think?"

"Since it was your idea, I completely agree."

I smiled. Many Victorian porches were built high above ground level and a common way to hide the underbelly was with latticework panels. We had gone a different route using thin vertical siding reminiscent of traditional wainscoting. When it was painted glossy white to match the front porch banister and railings, it would give a look of upscale elegance to the house.

He leaned against the post. "So, what's up?"

"What needs to be done, Wade?" I asked. "I'm here to work. Nothing too strenuous because my shoulder's still a little screwed up. But I had to get out of the house and I want to stay busy. I promise I won't slow you down."

"I'm not worried about that and, besides, it's your call, boss. You can work on anything you want."

I glanced at the front door, already stripped of six old coats of paint. "It's a miracle we're close to being on schedule after all that's happened. I'd like to try to keep it that way."

"Okay. I've got Todd and Billy starting on the foyer today, so let's stick to that area. How about if you go to work on the newel post?"

"Sounds good." He pushed the door open and we walked into the foyer. The thick carved post at the bottom of the main staircase was one of the highlights of the entryway.

"Most of the ornamentation is in good shape," he said, "but a few of the carved pieces closest to the base are damaged. And there are so many coats of old paint, you can barely see the detail."

"Okay." I studied the newel post. While much of the damage to the wood was due to the normal wear and tear of aging, I also noticed some tiny termite holes and some shredding near the base, just as Wade had said. We'd already tented the house, so I wasn't worried about termites anymore. The shredding could've been caused by a sharp-clawed family pet or a rambunctious child who liked to kick things. Either way, it would have to be fixed.

"I'll remove the ornamental medallions first, strip off the paint layers, and get them cleaned up. Then I'll deal with the post itself."

He nodded. "I'll leave you to it."

It was a small but time-consuming job. It would have to be done by someone eventually, so given my current disability, it made sense for me to do it. That way, I wouldn't be taking one of the guys away from a job requiring heavy lifting.

I went back to my truck to pull some tools out of the small chest I'd brought with me.

"Well, well, she finally shows her face."

Joyce Boyer. My back straightened at the sound of her voice. She didn't sound happy, but I knew I'd have to run into her eventually. I turned and said, "Hello, Joyce. Good to see you." It was a lie, but a necessary one. She was my client, so it was past time I made nice with her. If I kept the conversation centered on the job, we would get along fine. "Things are looking good, don't you think? And we're right on schedule."

"No thanks to you."

I smiled, despite wanting to smack her. "True enough. I was on the disabled list for a while there, but Wade and the guys did a great job while I was gone. I'm back now and feeling a lot better."

"Well, la-dee-dah," she said nonsensically.

My smile was a tight line. I ignored her to rifle through my tool kit for a thin putty knife and a small hammer. So I guess Joyce knew how to hold a grudge. I just wasn't sure why I was the focus of her rage. If she was so angry about Jerry cheating on her, she should've been relieved not to have to deal with him ever again.

I found the putty knife and also grabbed my favorite pink work gloves. I decided to take a utility knife, too, just in case the old paint was so thick that it might take off some of the wood when I pried the ornamental pieces away from the post. I could slide the utility knife in between the post and the ornamental piece and cut the paint without damaging either.

I pushed the tailgate closed and turned. Joyce was still there, standing right in my path.

"I'm not finished with you, Pinkie," she said, exaggerating the nickname.

Pinkie. Because of my gloves? What. Ever. I couldn't work with a client who hated me, though, so I decided to nip her attitude in the bud here and now.

"Look, Joyce, if you're angry at me because of Jerry Saxton, you should know that—"

"Aha. So you admit you were trying to steal him."

Steal him? "Are you kidding? I didn't even know him. I definitely didn't like him. I was set up on a blind date and you probably heard what a success it was."

"I heard you kicked him."

"Yeah, because he attacked me."

"No way."

"Oh, guess you didn't hear that part." I looked at her quizzically. "I'm not even sure why you care about him.

He was a creep and a womanizer, and while I'm sorry he's dead, I'm not sorry he won't be around to attack another woman."

Her hands fisted in frustration. "He didn't attack women."

"If that's what you think, you're deluding yourself."

"You didn't understand him like I did."

"Really? You understood him? So you knew that he was dating numerous women at the same time and making promises he had no intention of keeping? And despite your claims, he did hurt women. He threatened them. I guess you're lucky you weren't one of them. But you didn't understand him quite as well as you think you did."

"You don't know anything. Jerry was fun. He was a good listener. And he was a wild animal in the sack."

"Stop." My stomach pitched and I held up my hand. "Too much information."

"You're just jealous."

"Trust me, I'm not. Besides, you've been telling everyone in town that you hated him, so why are you suddenly defending him to me?"

"Because he cheated on me, the jerk! I could've lived with it, but thanks to you, everybody in town found out."

They found out because Joyce had blabbered it all over the place, but she wouldn't appreciate my pointing out the obvious. Instead, I said, "I truly didn't know you were involved with him and, besides, I had no intention of ever seeing him again after that night." Since her brain didn't seem to be functioning, I added slowly, "He would've been all yours."

"Except somebody killed him," she said sullenly. "It was probably you."

"It wasn't." There was no reason to continue this conversation. Joyce was unhappy and confused and I couldn't convince her of the truth. "I've got to get to work. Despite your personal feelings toward me—which are unfounded, by the way—I still want to do the best job possible on your house."

"I should fire you."

I stopped and stared at her. "Why?"

She scowled. "Because I'm mad at you."

"Please don't be. I didn't mean to hurt you."

"I suppose not." Her shoulders slumped. "I'm just so bummed."

"Why?"

She sighed. "You've met Stan, right? Well, Jerry was a Greek god compared to Wham-Bam-Thank-You-Stan."

"I've really got to get to work." I rushed back to the house and ran inside before she could give me one more appalling fact about Jerry's prowess or Stan's lack thereof.

Inside, I shook off the vibes from the confrontation and concentrated on the job. Folding a couple of old towels on the floor to protect my knees, I went to work on removing the newel post ornamentation. I was left blessedly alone for two whole hours, plenty of time to pry away the twelve carved wood medallions that had graced the four sides of the thick post for as long as the house had been standing.

I stood and stretched for a long minute to ease the stiffness in my legs from kneeling for that much time. Stacking the medallions on a sturdy piece of discarded drywall, I carried them out to the front porch, where a large plywood table and a couple of folding chairs were set up to do any of the detail work we occasionally had.

The table also held the stack of blueprints Wade and I referred to whenever there was a question of taking down a wall or ripping up a floor. The architect I worked with always redrew an updated, clean version of the blueprints whenever I started a new job, but I kept the old sheets as well, for reference.

Laying out the medallions, I took a closer look with a magnifying glass and decided that, yes, I could save them all. They would have to be soaked in solvent and stripped completely so that no layer of paint remained. When they were cleaned up, I would use wood filler to patch any damaged areas and then sand them until smooth. After that, the newel post itself would get the same basic treatment and then the medallions would be reattached to the post. Once the entire staircase was stripped down, we would stain and varnish everything to a high-gloss finish.

"Well, hello there."

I looked up to find Stan Boyer grinning at me. "Hi, Stan. Good to see you."

"House is coming along."

"The guys are doing a great job," I said, and brought him up-to-date on the work they'd done that he might not have noticed.

"I'm real pleased with everything, Shannon."

"I'm glad. You've got the bones of a beautiful home here."

He leaned his hip against the table. "I saw Joyce corner you earlier. What were you two talking about?"

"Oh." I thought fast. "I was just telling her that we're right on schedule. How are you doing? I saw you at the pub the other night but didn't get a chance to say hello."

"I've been around." His eyes twinkled. "You're the one who's been missing."

I smiled ruefully. "True. I've been nursing a shoulder injury, but I'm better now and happy to be back at work."

He scuffed his shoes on the ground a few times. "Listen, I want to apologize for the last time we talked. I sent you on a wild-goose chase that turned ugly."

"I'll say it did," I said lightly, trying to match his casual tone. But *ugly* was putting it mildly. Because of Stan's phone call last week, I had come over here to do him a favor and found Jerry Saxton's dead body instead. Both Mac and Eric had suggested that maybe I'd been lured to the basement to find Jerry's body. If that were true, then Stan would've played a part in luring me.

"I heard you got called down to the police station," he said.

"Sure did," I said mildly. "They hauled me down there and asked me a lot of questions."

He grimaced. "Yeah, they asked me a bunch, too."

Since he seemed to be in a talkative mood, I went ahead and brought up the one thing I'd been dying to know the answer to. "What happened that afternoon, Stan? You told me on the phone that your neighbor telephoned you, but the police said later that none of them would admit that they called you."

Frustrated, he raked his fingers through his sparse patch of gray hair. "I didn't lie to you. I did talk to my neighbor's daughter. Daphne said she was out walking the dog and passed my house on the way to the beach. The dog took off running and ended up sniffing around the side." He pointed toward the back of the house. "Over there. He started barking and wouldn't stop. When Daphne caught up with him, she could hear water running, so she called me on my cell."

"Didn't the police interview her?"

"Well, here's the thing." He looked embarrassed again. "She took off that night for San Francisco to catch a red-eye for her semester abroad in Spain. It was hell getting in touch with her right away because she was going to go hiking around the country for a week or so before starting classes. But they finally got hold of her and she told her story just like I said. So that let me off the hook."

"I'm glad to hear it."

"You and me both, girlie." He gave a cursory glance at the medallions I was working on. "I'll let you get back to whatever you're doing."

"Okay."

Stan walked away and I went to work stripping the medallions. I placed them neatly at the bottom of a big plastic bucket and carefully poured the solvent over them. I estimated that they would need a few hours of soaking to get rid of the paint and varnish they'd been coated with. I tucked the bucket under a window on the porch and taped a piece of paper to the side that said, CAUSTIC SOLVENT AT WORK. DO NOT DISTURB.

I thought about my conversation with Stan. I hadn't learned anything except that he hadn't been lying about the reason he'd called me that day. I still didn't know why he'd told me he was in San Francisco, but decided I didn't want to know. I'd already heard way too much about his and Joyce's personal relationship. I didn't need to know more.

As I was stowing my tools back in my truck, my cell phone rang. I checked the number and groaned out loud. I didn't dare let it go to voice mail, though, because that would exact a worse punishment than if I just faced the music and took the call. "Hello?"

"My family room ceiling is leaking. I'm having a very important dinner party tomorrow night and this has to be fixed."

Gracious as always, I thought. "Hello, Whitney," I said.

"I'll expect you to be here in fifteen minutes." She hung up the phone.

What a charmer. Here was the thing about Whitney Reid Gallagher. She and Tommy and their three children lived in a gorgeous, modern Victorian-style home near the Alisal Cliffs. Their beautiful, trendy housing development was called Cliffside. My father had built many of the Cliffside homes over the past twenty years, including Whitney's. So in her little mind, this made it okay for her to call me whenever anything went wrong in her house.

The reason I always responded was not because I was the nicest contractor in town—which I was—but because I knew that if I didn't repair the damage immediately, she would bad-mouth my father's beautiful work to all her snooty friends.

She was just that kind of a bitch.

I looked around for Wade and found him clinging to the side of the house like a determined spider as he worked to replace several rows of cedar shingles underneath the second-floor gable. I checked to make sure he was securely belted to the scaffolding before yelling his name.

"Hey, Shan." He waved. "Come on up."

I laughed. "I would love to, but I've got to take off for a little while. The Gallaghers' ceiling is leaking."

"Oh, great." I could see his eyes rolling from here.

"I might need to pull a couple of guys to help me patch it up, but I'll let you know."

"Whatever the princess wants. See you later."

I jogged to my truck, stashed my tools in the toolbox, and took off for Whitney's house a few miles away. It was still hard to believe that she and Tommy had stayed together all these years. The man had to have the patience of a saint, or maybe he just ignored her most of the time.

I realized that I would much rather deal with Joyce Boyer's angry snark than Whitney's cold bitchiness any day of the week.

I pulled to a stop in front of Whitney's place and shoved my pink work gloves into my purse.

Before I could ring the doorbell, she whipped open the door. She wore a sheer black lace top with black skinny jeans and black high heels. Just a casual little something to wear around the house.

She scanned me, as well, from my worn denim shirt down to my scuffed work boots. "Took you long enough to get here."

"Oh, shut up," I said, and walked inside.

She laughed. It was a genuine shock to hear the sound of her laughter. I hated to admit it out loud, but once in a blue moon we actually managed to get along. Even crazier, we occasionally had the same taste in home styles and interior decor. I knew this because she had managed to get herself a wholesale license a few years ago and had convinced people around town that she was an interior designer. Consequently, I was forced to work with her every so often. Because we both wanted the work and wanted to do a good job, we feigned cooperation when the clients were around. Invariably, they were happy with our results. That's what mattered most.

As soon as the clients would leave the vicinity or one of Whitney's friends, especially Jennifer, would come around, Whitney would turn back into the Wicked Witch of the West.

"Where's the leak?" I asked.

"In here." Her stiletto heels *click-clack*ed on the smooth oak floor as she led the way to the great room off the kitchen. As I walked through the house, I took a moment to admire my father's work. The kitchen and large family room featured high ceilings with contemporary industrial lights that hung down over the bar. The kitchen was ultramodern, with stainless-steel appliances, mission-style cabinetry, and French doors leading to a small kitchen garden. There was a larger backyard off the family room, as well.

Whitney stood by the bar and pointed up. I stared at the ceiling until I finally found the minuscule water spot she was referring to. "I don't see any water actually dripping. Are you sure it's leaking?"

"It was earlier and it left that stain. I don't want it to start up again."

"Did you leave the bathtub running?"

"Of course not."

"I'm going upstairs to see what's causing it." An hour later, I had tracked down the leak to the kids' playroom on the third floor. The youngest little darling had spent all day pouring small buckets of water down the laundry chute. Some of it had leaked into the space between the first and second floors and had pooled, which had caused the tiny water spot to appear on the ceiling downstairs.

I called two of my guys to bring over our heavy-duty wet vac to suck up any remaining moisture, along with a few strong fans to help dry out the laundry chute. The guys would work here for the rest of the afternoon, until everything was dry.

I found Whitney in the kitchen and told her what the problem was and how we planned to fix it. "Todd and Johnny will be here for another couple of hours. Then Todd will come by first thing in the morning and touch up the spot on the ceiling. Will you be home?"

"I have to take the kids to school, but I'll be home by nine."

"Okay. He'll meet you here at nine."

"You swear the spot will be gone by the time my guests arrive?"

"Yes."

Her eyes narrowed in thought. "What about the paint fumes?"

"That's why I want him to get an early start. You'll have to leave some doors open, but the smell should be gone within an hour or two."

"It had better be," she warned.

"You're welcome," I said dryly. I packed up my tools and headed for the front door. Whitney followed me to the door, just as her friend Jennifer was about to press the doorbell.

"Well, well," Jennifer said, casting an accusing look at me and Whitney. "Isn't this cozy?"

"*Cozy*? As in *warm and friendly*?" I snorted. "Hardly."

I passed her on the front step and heard her mutter, "Nice hair."

"Get over yourself," I said wearily, and kept going. How many more years would I have to put up with her giving me grief about my wavy red hair? There were plenty of people around who liked my hair. And she needed to get a life.

Meanwhile, I wanted to shove a pry bar up her nose.

"God, Whitney," Jennifer said loudly. "How could you let her walk into your house in those hideous dirty boots?"

I glanced back and saw Whitney shake her head. "It wasn't easy. But you know how these townies are."

"I'll bet Penny likes those boots, though," Jennifer continued snidely. "The two of them were pretty tight at the gym the other night. I even saw them hugging." She gave Whitney a knowing look. "I think Shannon might like girls better than boys."

I should've kept walking, but she was so infuriating, I had to stop and turn around. "Not that there's anything wrong with that, but isn't it time you learned to shut your mouth?"

"Ooh, defensive," Jennifer said.

"You think she likes girls?" Whitney asked, egging her on.

"It makes sense," Jennifer reasoned. "The only man she's dated since Tommy dumped her back in high school is Jerry Saxton, and we all know what happened to him."

I cocked my head to study her. "Will you ever grow up?"

"I don't know," Jennifer taunted. "Will you ever go to jail for killing Jerry?"

My eyes went wide. Where had that come from? I didn't know how to respond, it was so offensive.

Whitney snorted with laughter.

I found my tongue and said in an innocent voice, "But gosh, Jennifer. I saw you hugging Penny, too. Maybe what I'm hearing from you is a little bit of . . . jealousy?"

Whitney roared with laughter and elbowed her friend. "Snap! She got you there."

Jennifer's eyes were narrow slits of fury as she jabbed her finger at me. "Everyone knows you killed Jerry because you were jealous of him sleeping with Penny."

I was taken aback. "Jerry was sleeping with Penny?" I thought about the conversations I'd had with Penny. "I don't believe it."

"Shows you what you know." Jennifer's laughter sounded forced, but she didn't back down. "It's all true."

"No, it's not." I met Whitney's gaze and caught her aiming a look of pure contempt at her so-called friend. Wow. Things weren't exactly perfect between Whitney and Jennifer.

Finished here, I turned and walked to my truck, leaving them to face off with each other.

But as I drove away, I was more confused than ever. Was Jennifer telling the truth? Had Penny slept with that jerk Jerry Saxton? It was impossible. Penny despised him as much as I did. Jennifer was lying just to annoy me. Or was she? Who knew what was going on in her spiteful little mind?

At this point I was certain of only one thing: I really couldn't stand Jennifer Bailey.

*   *   *

Ten minutes later, I was driving home. But as I approached the turnoff for the Boyers' house, I decided on a whim to go back to the job site instead. It was a little after four o'clock and I figured I could squeeze in another hour of work before going home.

After dealing with Jennifer and Whitney, I needed a distraction. I was still fuming over our bizarre confrontation and figured it would be better for me to work on something tangible and practical at the job site than to have to face my own four walls in this rotten mood.

I parked the truck in the Boyer's treelined driveway, grabbed my bag and toolbox, and walked up to the house. The guys had all gone home for the day. I decided to continue Todd's work of lining up the newly painted balusters for the porch railing. He had dropped everything when I called him to come to Whitney's house, so the least I could do was pick up where he'd left off. It was easy but time-consuming, a matter of fitting the new decorative baluster into the groove in the bottom railing that the guys had built last week.

The best part of the job was that it was mindless. I had already finished a third of one side of the porch when my cell phone rang.

This time I answered it eagerly. "Dad! Where are you?"

"I'm heading home. Wanted to give you a heads-up."

"I'm so glad."

I told him I was still at the Boyers' house and asked how his fishing trip had gone. We made plans to walk down to the pub for dinner later. After I ended the call, my mood was completely lifted. I would finish this portion of the railing and then pack up and go home.

The sun was just starting to slide below the horizon

when I trudged back to my truck to pack up my tools. Despite feeling good about my father's return, I realized that the earlier confrontation with Jennifer had exhausted me. There was nothing I could do about the woman, so I would have to learn to let go of the frustration and negativity I walked away with every time I had to deal with her.

I turned and gazed out at the horizon and took a moment to appreciate the deep blue ocean and the vivid colors of the crisp fall sky. I could smell leaves burning somewhere nearby. I waited until the last bit of sun disappeared into the ocean before I turned and pulled the tailgate down to slide my toolbox into the truck bed. It took a minute to secure it to the side of the truck and then I slammed the tailgate closed.

The soft snap of a tree branch behind me was my only warning. Something brutally heavy slammed into my temple and everything went bright before it all turned to darkness.

I awoke slowly. My vision was splintered; my head throbbed in pain. I couldn't quite swim out of the blackness. I had to remind myself to keep breathing, but even the act of sucking in air was difficult. Every little movement was like a power drill boring a hole into the side of my head. I had to ignore the pain, try to revive myself in order to track down whoever had done this to me.

I was wasting precious time while that person was getting away, but I couldn't be too impatient with myself, since I was incapable of sitting up. I blinked again and realized I couldn't see. *Am I blind now? Oh, my God.* I started to panic.

It was a few long seconds before it occurred to me that it had grown dark while I was unconscious. *Idiot!* I must've been hit even harder than I thought. Stretched out on the cold concrete driveway, I moved my head back and forth, looking around, concentrating on my vision, trying to pick out shapes and objects. My truck. A neighbor's house. The moon rising.

I heard a vehicle approach and tried again to sit up. The bright headlights blinded me and I moaned and rolled over onto my side. I was a mess.

A door slammed and footsteps ran toward me.

"Shannon! You here?"

I'd never been so happy to hear my father's voice.

"Dad," I uttered.

"Baby, what are you doing on the ground? What happened?"

I touched the side of my head. "Somebody hit me."

"Oh, my God. My baby." He fell onto his knees, pulled me close, and rocked me in his arms. "Who did this? Who was it?"

"I don't know," I whispered. "My head."

"Hell, I'm hurting you."

"Not you," I insisted. "Someone hit me. Not you."

"I'm taking you to the hospital."

"No." I couldn't face answering questions from nurses and doctors and, no doubt, the police. My head pounded, my stomach was iffy, and I was just miserable enough to crave my comfy couch. "Please, Dad, let's go home."

He picked me up and carried me in his arms to the Winnebago. By the time I was sitting in the front seat of the huge RV, I was a little more lucid.

"Will you go back and find my purse and car keys, Dad?"

"Sure, honey." He was gone for less than a minute and came back with my purse. "I locked up your truck. It'll be fine here overnight."

"Hey, Dad," I murmured a minute later. "Do you remember passing any cars on your way here?"

He thought for a moment. "There was one black car driving pretty fast toward the highway. It looked like a little foreign job. Sporty."

Great. Everyone I knew had a black car. But one of them stood out in my mind more than the others: Jennifer Bailey's BMW.

I couldn't think of anyone more likely to want to hurt me than her. And nobody was more capable of murder, in my opinion. But why?

I had to admit, Dad's little black-car clue was weak at best because didn't Whitney drive a groovy little black Jaguar? *Her parents must've bought her that car,* I thought, *because there is no way Tommy could've afforded it on a cop's salary.* And wasn't Penny's little Miata black? Or was it blue? Heck, even Lizzie's SUV was black. So was Mac's car. And Emily drove a black Mini Cooper. Did anyone in this town drive a car that wasn't black?

The pounding in my head was getting worse and I couldn't think straight. There were plenty of people in town who had hated Jerry enough to kill him. And the same went for Wendell Jarvick. But who hated those two men—and *me*? And which of them drove a black car?

I had been enemies with Whitney most of my life. But if I died, who would fix her water leaks? Who would she call to unclog her toilets? No, I couldn't believe Whitney would bother trying to kill me. But Jennifer? Definitely.

My head was spinning painfully with clues and possibilities and too many dead ends. As my father drove his unwieldy monstrosity slowly toward town, I finally slipped back into blessed unconsciousness.

Chapter Thirteen

"I can't believe you betrayed me like this," I muttered when I woke up and found myself laid out on a gurney. I was surrounded by a flimsy curtain in some cubicle at the urgent-care center.

"You were hit hard, honey," Dad said, clutching my hand. "There was a lot of blood. You needed a doctor to check you out, make sure everything's okay."

I hadn't seen him look this pale and anxious in years, and that frightened me almost as much as being hit in the head had.

"Okay, I get it," I whispered, squeezing his hand as I closed my eyes. "Thanks, Dad. You're right."

"You know how much I love to hear those words," he said, chuckling softly.

I smiled weakly. I hadn't mentioned that I still felt dizzy in both my head and stomach and my eyesight was a touch blurry. So, yeah, probably a good thing he'd brought me here.

I raised my hand to my head, but I couldn't feel a thing. "What did they do to me?"

Dad pulled my hand away gently. "They wrapped

your head in a bandage. I think they gave you a shot of something, too."

"Ah." I sighed, then slipped under. I must've dozed off for a few minutes, because when I opened my eyes again, my father was gone and the person holding my hand was Police Chief Eric Jensen.

"Oh. Hi." I slipped my hand away.

"Hi," he said.

"Is my dad gone?"

"No, he's waiting outside with your uncle. I wanted to try to catch you when you woke up. Do you think you can talk for a minute?"

"Yeah," I said, my voice a little croaky. "I'm sorry I didn't see who did it. I heard something like a branch snap or a leaf crackle behind me. That was my only warning that someone else was there. And then he hit me and I blacked out."

"Okay." He pulled a chair over to the gurney and sat so that his blue eyes were focused right on me. He reached for my hand again and I didn't protest because his hand was big and warm and callused enough to feel safe and real.

"Let me try to jog your memory a little," he said. "And if your head starts to hurt or you feel sick or anything, I'll stop. Deal?"

"Yeah."

"When did it happen?"

"Not sure of the exact time, but the sun was setting. I watched it disappear behind the ocean."

"That's a nice time of evening," he said. "So it was dusk, not quite dark yet."

"Yes."

"You didn't hear anything but the sound of a branch snapping or a leaf crackling. Did you smell anything? Was there a scent in the air?"

"Someone in the neighborhood was burning leaves. It smelled like fall."

He smiled. "That's a good one."

"I thought so, too."

"A few seconds ago, you said, 'Then he hit me.' So you think it was a man who did this to you?"

I thought for a moment. "I have no idea. I said that because . . . I don't know. It had to be someone strong. I just assumed it was a man."

"Did you hear him take a breath?" He shifted forward in his chair. "You know how sometimes if you're about to hit something, like a baseball, you take a quick breath before you swing the bat? Did you hear anything like that? A gasp or an intake of breath?"

I tried to remember. "No. Sorry. Whoever it was was very quiet."

"Did you smell anything else besides the burning leaves?"

"Like what?"

"Like perfume," he said. "Or cigarettes. Coffee. Sweat. People sometimes smell like their work. Sawdust. Gasoline. Anything."

I closed my eyes and put myself back at the spot. I breathed in and out, then opened my eyes and stared into his. "Not anything related to another person. I smelled the salt air, of course. And there was a slight whiff of paint remover, but that probably came from the equipment in my truck."

He nodded reflectively. "Your father said that when

he was driving to your job site, he passed what he thought was a sporty black car. It was going pretty fast in the opposite direction. It's a sketchy clue, but I'm willing to check it out. Do you know anyone who drives a car like that?"

"Whitney Gallagher drives a black Jaguar," I said a little too quickly.

"Tommy's wife?"

"Yes. You know her."

"Sure. Nice lady."

It figured she would be nice to Tommy's boss. And Eric was such a handsome guy, what woman wouldn't play nice around him?

"Anyone else?" he asked.

"So many." I rattled off names. "Jennifer Bailey drives a black BMW. Emily Rose drives a black Mini Cooper. Liz Logan drives a black SUV. So does Mac Sullivan, but neither of those are small or sporty. Oh. Buddy Capello. Do you know him?"

"Capello. Yeah, we talked to him a week or so ago."

"He drives a navy blue Porsche. He's Luisa Capello's brother."

"Yes, I know."

"I don't know what kind of car Luisa drives. Or her brother Marco, either."

"I can get that information," he said.

"Of course." I'd never been so happy to be driving a gunmetal gray truck. Nothing about it was small and it wasn't black, either. Not that it mattered. I wasn't a suspect anymore. *Unless, of course,* I thought wryly, *the police decided that I'd bonked myself in the head to clear suspicion.* Oh, that was depressing.

"That's it?"

"I almost forgot Penny. She drives a dark-colored Miata. And Jane Hennessey has a dark gray Lexus."

"Is there anyone whose car you don't know?"

"It's my town," I muttered, and closed my eyes.

A few seconds later I felt Eric let go of my hand and I opened my eyes. "Are you leaving?"

"I've worn you out," he said, standing. "Besides, I want to check in with a couple of officers who are combing the area around your truck for any evidence. They'll be talking to the neighbors, too, in case anyone saw anything. The black car is a long shot, but we'll make sure we check every one we can find."

"Can I ask you something?" I rubbed at the wide strip of gauze that was wrapped around my head to hold the thick bandage in place over my ear. "What did they hit me with?"

He paused. Taking hold of my hand again, he said, "They used a hammer."

I shuddered. A hammer? Damn, I really was lucky to be alive. And then it hit me, so to speak. "How clever of them."

He scowled. "I figured they saved that one just for you."

Because my name was Hammer, of course. It would've been silly if it weren't so frightening. "You found it?"

"They dropped it right next to your truck."

"Was it . . . ?"

His jaw tightened visibly. "Yeah, it was pink."

I groaned softly. My missing hammer. The killer had taken it from the same toolbox from which he stole the wrench and screwdriver used to murder Jerry Saxton and Wendell Jarvick.

The only good thing about being attacked with the pink ball-peen hammer was that it was lightweight, not big at all. Still, it could've killed me for sure if my assailant had hit me in the right spot.

Damn, I was glad he hadn't taken my sledgehammer or my heavy-duty framing hammer. Those would've caused me a lot more damage and I probably wouldn't be here to whine about it.

I watched Chief Jensen's teeth clench, felt his grip tighten around my hand. His reaction made me uneasy. "You look angry."

"Of course I'm angry. I'm furious." He pulled his hand away, paced a few feet back and forth. "I'm determined to catch this son of bitch, Shannon."

"I appreciate it," I whispered.

"I'm also determined to keep you alive."

"That would be nice." I was starting to fade a little and wondered if anyone would notice if I just drifted off to sleep.

He stopped pacing and stared down at me. "Why didn't you tell me what happened at the gym the other night?"

I was puzzled and had to think for a minute, which made my head start pounding. "You mean with the bench press? How did you find out about it?"

"From Jane. She called me a while ago to make sure I knew."

"That was just an accident."

He sat down again and grabbed my hand in such a natural move that I wondered if he was trying to comfort me or himself. "Shannon, I can buy that the bench-press mishap and even your bicycle brake line might have been accidents. But tonight someone smashed your head with a hammer and knocked you out. My guess is that he was trying to kill you. That was no accident."

I was shivering now. "Nope."

"Right. So now I've got to go back over all these little coincidences and determine if they're all connected or not."

"Okay." It should've been obvious to me that he would have to go back over everything that had happened to find a pattern or a time line that fit a particular suspect, but I hadn't been thinking too clearly. I had to pause and breathe for a moment to help myself think. "While I was working out on the bench press, Penny was spotting me and Jennifer Bailey came over. She was holding on to the rack and sort of swinging back and forth. It bugged me. It was rude, you know? Penny was trying to help me and Jennifer was a distraction."

"Penelope Wells, from the bank," he said.

"Right. We saw you later at the pub."

"Yes." He smiled.

My eyelids drooped until they closed completely. I was losing steam, but I had one more thing to tell him. "I was going to ask you to sit with us that night, but Penny didn't want to. She's afraid of cops ever since one of them shot a bank teller where she used to work."

"I can't hold that against her," he said easily. "A lot of people are afraid of cops."

"I'm going to sleep now."

"You do that," he whispered.

The doctors moved me to a hospital room and forced me to spend the night. Nurses kept coming in and waking me up every two hours to make sure I wasn't dead, I guess. When I got cranky and whined about it, the nurse in charge said, "You have a concussion."

"I know."

"In other words," she continued, "you were hit hard enough that it injured your brain. We know this because you complained of dizziness and blurred vision. You're having a hard time thinking and making decisions. So, now it's our job to make sure you don't stroke out while you're on our watch."

"Okay, thanks." I sighed. "That's a really good explanation."

"That's how we roll."

"I appreciate it. No more whining."

I made it through to the next morning and then called my dad to have him come and get me.

That night, Jane insisted on sleeping over, even though my father planned to spend the night in the guest bedroom right down the hall from mine.

"I'm glad he's home," Jane said, "but I'm staying right here in your room with you. I'm not letting you out of my sight until I'm sure you're fully recovered."

She showed me pages of information she'd printed out, every little fact about concussions that she could find on the Internet. And she followed to the minutest detail the care they suggested.

She fed me a light dinner, refused to pour me any wine, woke me up every few hours to ask me my name and to check if I was slurring my words.

She checked for fever and interrogated me on my every ache and pain, and wrote it all down on the calendar in my kitchen office.

The next day was Friday and I moved myself downstairs to the living room couch, where at least I had a view of the outside world through the big picture window. Jane stacked a few books and magazines on the coffee table to keep me occupied for a while. I wasn't about to mention that I couldn't read anything. My vision was still too blurry.

"I appreciate your diligence," I said, when Jane handed me a glass of diluted apple juice instead of soda or chocolate milk. "You'll make a really mean mom someday."

She laughed. "My pleasure. You've still got a headache, don't you?"

It wasn't a question. She could tell by the way I groaned at the least little noise and squinted at the light coming from the lamp on the side table. The woman was watching me like a mama hawk. She clicked off the lamp and lowered the other lights in the room, too.

"Thanks," I said, although I hated that my eyes were still so sensitive to the light.

"You're welcome. What else can I do?"

"I'm sorry I'm so miserable," I said. "I should feel better tomorrow."

"You will. I guarantee it, because if you're feeling better, I'll make you chocolate-cheesecake crepes from a new recipe I found."

"I love you the best," I said. "And it has nothing to do with your fantastic cooking skills."

She smiled. "I'm staying tonight and tomorrow morning, and then I've got to go home to get ready for that conference I'm going to. So Lizzie will be coming by to stay with you."

"Wait," I said, struggling to sit up straighter. "I would

love to have her here, but it really isn't necessary. Dad plans to be here for as long as I need him."

She just gazed at me. "Your father is a wonderful man, Shannon, but . . ."

My shoulders slumped. "You're right. I can wrap him around my finger and get him to do whatever I want."

"Exactly. Lizzie won't put up with your crap for one minute."

"Remind me again why I'm friends with you people."

"Because we love you." She patted my shoulder lightly and walked back to the kitchen.

As soon as she left the room, my mind drifted back to trying to solve the mystery of the person who had assaulted me. More and more, I was wondering if Jennifer Bailey could be that person. That would mean, of course, that she had also killed Jerry Saxton and Wendell Jarvick. I knew she was capable of horrible acts, so I wouldn't put it past her. But one question remained: *Why?* Did she really hate me enough to try to implicate me in the murder of Jerry and Wendell? And then once she'd killed them, why did she decide to come after me, too? Had I made her so angry when I told Whitney that I saw her hugging Penny?

Ridiculous. So I had to go back to the question, *Why?*

And if not Jennifer, then who?

I finally pulled a lined notepad and pen out from the drawer in the side table. I forced myself to go step by step through each attack and incident from the very beginning. My penmanship wasn't the best because I couldn't always focus on the words I was writing.

I had gone out with Jerry on a Thursday night three weeks ago. We had a nice dinner and then went walking on the beach. He attacked me, ripped my clothes, and I kicked him in the general vicinity of his family jewels to make him stop.

An audience had gathered on the pier to watch the action. Had Jennifer been part of the crowd? Or, worse, had Jennifer been dating him secretly?

The only person I could ask was Whitney, but would she tell me? Of course not. I supposed I could ask Tommy to ask her, or even Eric, but would the chief yell at me again for running my own little side investigation?

I was hoping we might be past all that, but he seemed to be a stickler for keeping nosy people away from police business. But, really, how could he blame me for trying to figure out who had bopped me over the head?

Turning back to my step-by-step process, I wrote down that according to the coroner's report, Jerry was killed sometime Friday night, the night after our date. I didn't find his body until late Sunday afternoon at the Boyers' house.

Stan Boyer's neighbor Daphne had been walking her dog by their house, and when the dog began to bark she went to investigate and heard water running. She had called Stan to let him know. And then she left for Europe.

The following day, Monday, was when Wendell Jarvick arrived in town. I tangled with him almost instantly, first over whether I would carry his suitcases upstairs and then, a while later, I told him to move his car out of my driveway and he refused. My two neighbors had overheard my argument, but was there someone else in the vicinity who heard it, too?

Around that time, my closest friends and I decided to

find out what had really happened, mainly to draw suspicion away from me. They began to talk to people around town, asking questions, gathering information. Did one of them spark someone's indignation? Did someone object to my friends asking too many questions?

The next night, I was in the pub with Jane and Emily and saw Wendell attack Whitney with the ketchup. Joyce and Stan had been there that night, too, and Penny and her friends. Eric and Tommy were there, and Jennifer, as well. She might've gone after Wendell in retribution for humiliating her best friend.

The following Sunday, my truck battery died. I had never considered it a part of the bigger picture, but now I had to wonder if the dead battery was another "coincidence" connected to my other so-called accidents.

That same afternoon, I'd had a late lunch by myself at the Cozy Cove Diner and witnessed Wendell treating Cindy the waitress very badly. I could still hear that coffee mug shattering against the wall and wondered how traumatized Cindy was. She might have been angry enough to kill Wendell in that moment. But, then, what did she have against Jerry? Or me?

I almost crossed Cindy's name off my list. I felt ridiculous for suspecting her and had no doubt that she was completely innocent in all of this.

I tried to remember who else was eating in the diner that afternoon when Wendell pulled his juvenile stunt. I visualized the booths; saw Penny and her bank friends in one, Stan and Joyce Boyer huddled together at another against the back wall.

There were plenty of other townspeople dining there,

too, because of the Sunday prime-rib special. I wouldn't be surprised to find out that Wendell had had run-ins with every single one of those people. I wished I could recall who else was sitting at the front counter, but all I had seen were their backs.

And that was the same afternoon I had met Luisa Capello and her brother Buddy, practically right outside the diner. Maybe they'd had a run-in with Wendell earlier, but that was admittedly a long shot.

The following day, on my bicycle ride out to the lighthouse, my brakes had stopped working and I'd crashed into a field. That's when I met Mac Sullivan fortuitously.

If my bicycle brakes had been tampered with, would it automatically have been done by the same person who killed Jerry? When would he have done it? And how would he have known I would be forced to ride my bike for the next few days?

Had he screwed around with my truck battery? Or had he merely seen me riding around town on Sunday? Maybe he had seen my truck being towed to the auto shop. It was either one of those possibilities—or it was all one big coincidence.

The next night, I picked up my truck and parked it in my driveway. The following morning, Wendell was found dead in his car. Two days after that, the bench-press rack broke—or was tampered with—and I was almost strangled by the heavy barbell. If the gym incident was deliberate and connected with the other attacks, then Penny and Jennifer were the ones to watch. Whitney had been there, too, but had left early. Or so Jennifer claimed. Had another suspect been at the gym that evening? Someone

I hadn't noticed? Stan or Joyce? What about Luisa? Or her brothers, Buddy and Marco?

Three days after the gym accident, I was bashed over the head with my own hammer, less than two hours after a nasty run-in with Jennifer and Whitney.

And that was it.

No wonder I was exhausted. And dizzy. I stared at my list of occurrences and couldn't quite believe I had been through all that grief and trauma in just a few short weeks. I wasn't the only one, of course. Two people were dead and the entire population of Lighthouse Cove was awash in fear and suspicion and guilt.

I stared at my notes and tried to see a pattern somewhere. Sadly, though, my brain had turned to mush. I couldn't begin to make any connections to anything with my head spinning and my vision fogging up. I would have to think about it later. For now, I popped two headache pills, grabbed the soft throw, and pulled it over me and tucked myself into the couch for a nap.

I woke up to eat a little dinner and then went back to bed and slept for twelve hours straight. When I arose the next morning, I felt better than I had in days.

The first thing I noticed when I stared at myself in the bathroom mirror was that my eyesight was no longer as impaired as it had been. My face wasn't as blurry. I was so happy I almost cried, except I knew the tears would screw up my vision, so I stopped myself.

A part of me was sorry my vision was so good again, because now I could see that I looked like crap. My hair was a tangled mess because I'd done nothing but sleep and avoid showers for the past three days. I had been warned not to get the bandage wet, so while I'd soaked in the bathtub yesterday morning, I hadn't been able to wash my hair. I now looked like a red-haired, washed-out zombie.

I went downstairs to grab some coffee and call my doctor. I needed to remove the damn bandage and finally wash my yucky hair.

"You're looking a little more lively today," Dad said when I walked into the kitchen. He was eating cereal and reading the *Lighthouse Standard*, our local newspaper. Dad always said it gave him all the news he needed.

"I feel pretty lively, except for this hair."

He raised one eyebrow. "I don't know. I'd say it's looking pretty lively, too."

"But not in a good way, right?" I chuckled as I poured the coffee and glanced around. "Did Lizzie take off?"

"She's got something with the kids this morning. She said she'd be back later this afternoon."

"Okay, although I really don't think she needs to stay with me. I'm feeling so much better."

"Glad to hear it." He flipped a page of the newspaper. "Your new tenant came by to see how you were doing."

"You met Mac?"

"Yeah. Nice guy." He flipped through the newspaper to find the sports section.

"Dad, didn't you recognize him?" I sat down at the table. "That's MacKintyre Sullivan."

"Who?" He gave me a puzzled look; then his eyes went wide. "Wait. You kidding me? That's the Jake Slater guy?"

I grinned. "The very same."

"What in hell is he doing here?"

"He bought the old lighthouse mansion and he's going to have it restored. While that's going on, he's renting the apartment upstairs."

"Whoa," he whispered.

I grinned. "I know."

"MacKintyre Sullivan," he whispered reverently, and shook his head. "I love that guy." He tried to go back to reading an article on the World Series, but he was too distracted. He finally gave up, folded the newspaper, and stuck it in the recycle bin. Setting his cereal bowl in the sink, he headed for the back door. "I gotta go call Pete. This is the biggest news in years."

I shook my head as I watched him jog down the kitchen stairs. Great. Two grisly murders, one deadly assault on his own daughter, not to mention any number of other weird accidents lately. But Jake Slater was the biggest news in years. What else could I do but laugh?

Two nights later, Lizzie picked up a pizza before coming over to spend the night.

"Hooray for pizza," I said, reaching for my first piece. "I'm feeling so much better. I didn't want to tell anyone how dizzy I was for a while, but that's all cleared up."

"I'm really glad." She poured herself a glass of wine and handed me a small bottle of apple juice. Wine was still forbidden, and that was getting old, too.

"Of course, we still have no idea who did it."

"And it's driving everyone in town crazy," she said as she sat down and placed a slice of pizza on her plate. "This kind of stuff has never happened here."

"I know. I'm as mystified as anyone."

Lizzie swallowed a small bite of pizza. "But now everybody goes around eyeing strangers and friends alike. Nobody trusts anyone. That's the worst part."

"I hate hearing that."

"Luisa Capello was taken in for questioning," she said.

"What? No way. Really?"

"She was dating Jerry Saxton. Did you know that?"

"Yeah. I heard." I'd included Luisa's name on my personal suspect list right after Jerry Saxton was found. But how could she have had anything to do with Wendell's death? Or my attack? Unless the police knew something I didn't know.

I suppose that's possible, I thought, and chuckled at myself.

"Things have really gone squirrelly, as Taz would say." Lizzie grabbed her wineglass and took a healthy sip. "And what must be going through Mac's mind? He just moved here. He must think we're a town full of bloodthirsty pirates."

"I wouldn't know what he's thinking because he's been holed up in his room writing all week." I was beginning to feel some pressure behind my eyes and grabbed two headache pills to ward off the pain. "Let's talk about something pleasant. How's the store doing?"

"Business is booming. It's probably because I'm your friend. Everyone comes in to talk—well, gossip, really—about you, of course. And then they feel so guilty for trying to suck information out of me that they end up buying something. And I'm perfectly happy to guilt them into it."

I laughed. "Good to know I'm helping to drive commerce."

"You are, believe me." She put her wineglass down and fiddled with her rings, so I knew she was nervous about something.

"What's going on?" I asked.

"Well, don't get bent out of shape, but I've met a really nice man. He's in sales. He came into the store the other day and we hit it off."

"What does Hal have to say about this?"

"Very funny," she said, brushing off my question. "Look, since I haven't seen you going out with either Mac or with Eric, I figured nothing was happening there, so I thought I would ask you if you wanted to meet Frank."

Was my jaw on the floor? I couldn't believe it. "You're joking, right? You're honestly asking me to go on another blind date?"

"No," she said bluntly. "Look, I want you to be happy and settled. You live a good life and you're a wonderful friend, but I don't think you've been really happy for a long time. And I haven't noticed Mac making any moves in your direction. And as far as Eric is concerned, well, does he still think you're guilty of something? Because he's not coming around, either. So I say it's time to look elsewhere."

"Like with *Jerry*?"

Lizzie winced. "Okay, granted, Jerry was a mistake. This guy Frank, though, is a gem. I really think the two of you could hit it off together."

Rather than blow a fuse, I actually smiled at Lizzie's latest attempt to set me up.

It made me realize that I hadn't told any of my friends about Mac kissing me or about Eric's sweet words of determination in the hospital. I knew why I'd kept mum. I just wanted to keep a few little secrets close to my heart for as long as possible, because I knew that as soon as I mentioned them to anyone, they would cease to be mine and become breaking news on the Lighthouse Cove gossip wire.

And though I wanted to keep a few things to myself, I had to convince Lizzie to quit the matchmaking already. I tried for a gentle smile. "Thank you for thinking of me, but no. I'm sure Frank is a nice guy, but I refuse any more setups."

"Come on, it wasn't that bad."

"Jerry ended up dead, remember?"

"Yes, but it wasn't *your* fault."

"Thanks for that," I said, and patted her hand. "But seriously, Lizzie, let it go, okay?"

"Fine. I'm officially retiring as your date Yoda."

"Thank you, O wise one." I gave her half a bow.

"Very funny," Lizzie muttered, and sank back into the couch. Then she perked right up. "You could always try dating a woman for a nice change of pace."

I gawped at this person I'd known since I was in first grade. I had shared countless secrets with her over the years because she had been my babysitter and an older woman by five years. She had life experience. Naturally I had looked up to her. But somehow, just recently when I wasn't looking, she had gone bat-crazy insane.

"Are you high?" I asked.

"Of course not," Lizzie said, and leaned forward across the table. "Shannon, men haven't been working out for you, so . . ."

"Lizzie, listen carefully." I grabbed both of her hands.

"I like guys. Men. And when I'm ready, I'll get one on my own, okay?"

"Fine."

"I know a bunch of nice men." I grabbed another slice of pizza and took a big bite. "I just meant I never want to go on a blind date again. So the next time you get a bug up your butt to set me up on a date with anyone—I mean, *anyone*—I want you to remember these two words: *Jerry Saxton*."

"I will," she said, sighing. "But I can't help wishing those two words were *Mac Sullivan*."

I shrugged. "We'll see."

It was such a wrong thing to say. I knew it the second the words left my mouth. I watched her ears literally perk up and she almost bounced in her chair. "Exactly what does *we'll see* mean?"

I shook my head. "You're incorrigible."

"That's right, so if you don't want me hounding you forever, I suggest you spill your guts right now."

I hesitated, then said, "There might've been a kiss."

She froze. Then she started to shake with excitement.

"Stop it," I said, laughing. "You nutball. It was just a kiss."

"It was a MacKintyre Sullivan kiss." She leaned both elbows on the table. "Tell me more."

"There's nothing more to tell. I brought him a basket of vegetables and a few days later he returned the basket and told me I . . . I dazzled him."

"You dazzled him?" She pressed her hands to her heart. "That's so sweet."

"And then he kissed me."

"Oh, my." She fanned herself. "Then what?"

"And then . . . nothing," I said. "I got conked on the head and I've been housebound ever since."

"So Eric is out and Mac is in?" she wondered.

"Eric held my hand at the hospital," I said.

She gasped. "Two men want you."

"Not exactly," I said, laughing. "He was giving comfort to the injured, that's all."

"He could've done that from across the room. No, he held your hand. It means something."

"You're a lunatic. But I love you." I rubbed my forehead, pushed back my chair. "I need to lie down. I just hit the wall, energywise."

She jumped up from the table, her mission suddenly clear. "We've got to get you feeling better. Pizza won't do it." She took our plates over to the kitchen counter. "Tomorrow I'm making you a big pot of healthy vegetable soup. Did you talk to the doctor? When can you take off that bandage?"

"Tomorrow morning."

"Okay, I'll stay in the morning and help you remove it. Then you'll take a shower and do something with that giant Texas hairdo you've got going on. What is with that hair of yours, anyway?"

"It's thick."

"I know. I'm jealous."

"Don't be. Look." I pointed to my head of hair and she nodded in sad agreement.

"Oh yeah," she said. "That's quite a do. Never mind—it'll be pretty again tomorrow. And those two men won't know what hit 'em."

Chapter Fourteen

Lizzie's vegetable soup helped. Washing my hair helped. It also helped when Mac showed up at my door to say how happy he was that I was feeling better. He didn't stay; he was deep into the book and it was working for him, so he had to get back to it. I gave him a container of Lizzie's soup and, in return, he kissed my cheek and then jogged back upstairs.

So that was kind of nice. Not earth-shattering, but nice. The kiss didn't, however, bring normalcy back to my life. Nothing would truly get me back to normal until I finally made up my mind to take direct action. And now that I was feeling better, I was ready to do it, ready to find the person who had tried to kill me.

The police had sent Luisa Capello home after briefly questioning her, so I knew she wasn't guilty of murder. No, I was convinced that Jennifer Bailey was that person.

I could've reported my feelings to the police chief or even to Tommy. But I didn't want to throw accusations around and then find out I was wrong. Instead, I wanted to talk to the one person who would know the truth.

And that meant I had to go and face the evil Queen of Mean herself, Whitney.

I was hesitant, and who could blame me? But Whitney was the only person around who would know what was going on with Jennifer.

I didn't want to do it. The thought of facing Whitney made me feel physically uncomfortable and spiritually weak. And, no, I didn't think I was being overly dramatic. The woman didn't play by the same set of rules that I or any of my friends played by. The few times I had ever been forced to talk to her sincerely or honestly—in other words, *openly*—it had sucked my soul dry.

But I had to do it. Because for all her faults, Whitney would tell me the truth. And if she didn't, I would threaten to go straight to the police with my theories. And I would be sure to let them know that Whitney had known all along what was going on, but chose not to tell the police—not to mention her own *husband*. Yes, it was blackmail. But it was *good* blackmail.

The whole confrontation would be unpleasant, but considering the alternative, what else could I do? I couldn't talk to Jennifer, for God's sake, because while Whitney was manipulative, judgmental, and cold, Jennifer was biting, spiteful, and vindictive.

Anyone could see the difference.

I dressed carefully, pulling on my best black jeans, attractive boots, a flattering red sweater Lizzie had given me last year, and my black leather jacket—the one with no holes.

Instead of letting my hair dry naturally, I had actually used a hair dryer and brush to straighten it enough that it didn't tumble around my shoulders in a tangle of curls.

And alert the media: I even applied a bit more makeup than usual. Into this kind of battle, I had to go armed.

I figured I needed to do whatever I could to keep Whitney from focusing on everything she criticized about me—namely my looks, my clothing, my very existence—rather than focusing on the fact that her best buddy might be going around killing people.

As I drove out to Whitney's, I thought a lot about the conversation I'd had with Lizzie the other night. Not just because it had made me realize that my dear friend was a certifiable crazy person, but also because of what she had pretended to infer about my lifestyle preferences. *It would be easy—and wrong—of someone to* infer *that sort of thing about a lot of people,* I thought. Just as Jennifer Bailey had *inferred* that I might prefer women to men.

Not that it mattered what my preferences were, but I hated what she'd been trying to do to me. She was a bully, had been one for as long as I'd known her, and I didn't like it. And I didn't much like *inferences*, either.

I pulled up in front of the Gallaghers' house and gazed at the place that had been Tommy and Whitney's since they were married. At one time, I had loathed them for buying one of my father's designs, but now I didn't care.

My father had always preferred the Queen Anne style of Victorian home and he had done a beautiful job with this one. The elegant millwork and thick columns of the front porch and balconies gave it a much more graceful, almost feminine look than some of the other Victorians built by his contemporaries.

And I was stalling for time.

Out of excuses, I climbed down from the truck and walked to the front steps. The closer I got, the more I regretted my decision to talk to Whitney. I knew that it wouldn't go well, of course. But what else could I do? I kept walking, determined to follow through on my plan, no matter what. I knocked on the door and waited. After almost a minute passed, I thought of leaving, but Whitney's car was parked in the driveway, so I knew she had to be home.

Maybe she was avoiding me. I couldn't really blame her, since I would consider doing the same thing if I saw her standing on my doorstep.

But suddenly Whitney whipped open the door, her eyes wild with panic.

"Get out of my way!" she screamed, slammed the door behind her, and almost knocked me down trying to get out of the house and down the steps.

"What's wrong? What is it?" I shouted, staring at her as she raced around to the driver's side of her convertible black Jaguar. I almost laughed at her outfit. Baggy plaid flannel pajama bottoms and a sweatshirt for a top. And sneakers? Her hair wasn't even combed. I liked the look, but what could she possibly be . . .

Had she seen me coming up the walkway? Was she trying to get away? Was it possible that Whitney was the killer? There was no way she could've known the reason why I was there. And I wasn't about to let her escape if she was responsible for two deaths and one attempted murder—of *me*.

I heard the engine start up.

"Stop!" I went running after her, and before she

could throw the car into reverse I grabbed the driver's door and yanked it open. "Where do you think you're going?"

"Get back!" she yelled, trying to grab the door handle to shut it. "What's your problem?"

"You are," I said. "Why are you running away?"

"Shut the damn door! I'm trying to get to the hospital."

"Why? What happened?"

"Somebody tried to kill Jennifer!"

So that didn't go quite the way I thought it would.

I sat at a table in the back room of Emily's tea shop, sipping decaffeinated tea and taking small bites of the beautiful cookies she'd brought me. Not that I was worthy. I felt like a complete idiot.

"Tell me what happened," she said, rubbing my shoulder before sitting down next to me and folding her hands on the table. "You look miserable."

"I'm so stupid." I spilled the story in halting, unfinished sentences. When I was finished, she grabbed the teapot and filled my cup.

"You're not stupid," she insisted in her lilting Scottish brogue. "Seems perfectly logical to think that those horrible girls were the ones who were killing men and setting you up to take the blame."

I smiled at her. "Thanks, but clearly I was wrong. The one person I thought was the culprit is now struggling for her life in the hospital. She might be dead by now. I feel like hell for even thinking it might've been her."

"Oh, now, cut yourself a bit of slack." She grabbed a cookie and broke off a piece. "Have you checked on her condition?"

"Not yet."

"Let's do it right now," she said gently. "It always helps to have as much information as possible at all times, don't you think?"

"I guess so."

"Do you want to use my phone?"

"No, I've got mine." I pulled out my phone, took a deep breath, and called Eric's cell.

He answered immediately. "Shannon, where are you?"

"I'm at the tea shop on the town square."

"Stay put. I'll be there in ten minutes."

"Are these yours?" Eric asked, holding up a clear plastic bag containing a pair of thin leather workmen's gloves.

Pink ones.

"Oh, God." I buried my head in my hands. "Of course they're mine. Where did you find them?"

"Near the latest crime scene."

I gazed up at him. Somehow he looked even bigger and more masculine surrounded by the soft pink and pale green walls of the tea shop. "The crime scene. Naturally."

"Did you realize they were missing?"

"No. I was using them just the other day." My eyes widened in realization. "It was the day I was attacked. I had shoved them into my purse on the way to Whitney's house. Later, I remember setting my purse on the tailgate while I stowed the toolbox in the back of the truck. The person who hit me must have gone through my purse."

And that pissed me off as much as anything did.

"What else can you tell me?"

I stared blankly at the wrinkled gloves. "I like them because they're thinner than the usual work gloves. Even the ones made for women. They stretch with your hand movements. You can wear them all day for all sorts of jobs and they don't chafe." I pressed my fingers against my eyes. "And I'm blathering. Sorry. What else did you want to know?"

"We'll hold on to these," he said, placing the bag on the table. "We might be able to capture some prints off them."

"That would be great, but they'll probably just find my prints."

"Someone else wore them after you did, Shannon. We'll see what we can get."

I pressed my lips together, hesitant to ask the next question. But I really needed to know. "What happened to Jennifer?"

"She was strangled, left for dead."

"She's dead?"

"No, but she's in bad shape."

"Someone strangled her while wearing my gloves?" I tried to swallow around the giant lump in my throat. I felt sick to my stomach and it wasn't from cookies. The thought of a person slipping their hands into my gloves and using them to choke someone to death was hideous.

"She's not dead," I said, my voice barely above a whisper.

"No. She'll survive." He rested one arm on the table. "How well do you know her?"

"Well enough to hate her." *Crap.* I couldn't believe I'd said it out loud.

Eric sat back in his chair and observed me. "That's honest, anyway."

"You'll find out if you ask the right people, so I might as well be the one to tell you. We really don't like each other. She's spiteful and calculating and just plain awful. We went to high school together and never managed to hit it off, to say the least. She pretty much tries to make my life a living hell as often as possible."

"She was at the gym the night your equipment broke."

"Yeah," I said darkly. "And up until an hour ago, I was certain that she was the one who'd attacked me."

"It seems unlikely now," he said without humor.

"I suppose," I said, resigned to the fact that I was dead wrong. Again. "Anyway, I don't like her, but I don't wish her harm, either."

"Fair enough," he said.

I stared at my pink gloves, dismayed that another one of my belongings had been used in such a destructive, evil way. I huffed out a breath. "So, how's she doing?"

"She's in a coma," he said flatly.

I stared across the table, met his determined gaze with my own. "We really need to find this guy soon."

He leaned toward me. "I did not just hear you say *we*. There is no *we*, Red. You're going home and locking your doors until this creep is behind bars. Get it?"

I frowned. "Okay."

"Because on the off chance that you missed it," he whispered angrily, "this is another case where the killer went after a person that you don't like. See the pattern coming back?"

My eyes widened. "Oh no."

"Yeah, and they're still using your own tools to try to frame you. So while someone is out there continuing to play games with your life, I would prefer that you not make yourself a target. They already tried to kill you once. Maybe more than once, considering all those so-called coincidences. I don't want them trying it again. You got that?"

I nodded. "I got it."

"Good."

Even though I believed Eric was right, I still couldn't stay home all day. I called him to let him know I had to go to work. I told him I'd be careful to stay where I could be seen by one of my crew at all times and I would always go home before dark.

The first day back on the job, I noticed a police cruiser driving by and slowing down. It happened five times in total that day. I was grateful, really, but it didn't help that my guys were starting to tease me about being a fugitive from justice.

I was also a little irked when I found out that the chief had talked to Mac. So now he stood outside by the back gate every afternoon and waited for me to get home, then watched me walk into the house and lock the door behind me. The second day he did it, I turned around and watched him jog up the garage stairs and disappear into his apartment. Okay. So this routine was not exactly conducive to any sort of male-female bonding, the kind that would set Lizzie's tender heart a-pounding. Basically, I felt like he was babysitting me.

And that made me more single-minded than ever in my quest to find the damn killer. Because until he was caught, my love life, such as it was, was going nowhere.

I spent a few sleepless nights worrying about my gloves and the killer who'd used them. One night I sat up in bed, turned on the light, and stared at my hands. *They're not bad-looking,* I thought. Small, feminine, despite the kind of work I did.

But the point was, I had small hands. Whoever had used my gloves to throttle Jennifer had to have small hands, too. My mind kept returning to Whitney, but it wasn't a viable theory. She was a bitch and I think she wore that title proudly, but she wouldn't have committed murder. It would ruin her manicure.

"Meow," I muttered, and smiled when Tiger hopped onto the bed and settled down next to me. I checked that Robbie had tucked himself into his doggie bed and all was right with his world. Then I fluffed my pillow, turned out the light, and fell back asleep.

Two days later, Jennifer was still in a coma and I was reaching the end of my rope. I ran into Tommy, who, despite my gentle requests, wouldn't spill a damn word about the case. I was still losing sleep, the police wouldn't talk to me, and I needed answers.

I had tried to picture Penny wearing my gloves and wielding my tools, but I couldn't see it. She was too nice and too new to town to want to kill anyone.

I knew what I had to do. I had to go forward with my original plan to talk to Whitney. For a different reason than before, of course. Now I wondered if she knew why Jennifer had become a target all of a sudden. Did Jennifer know something about the killer? Had she shared it with Whitney? Jennifer and Whitney were best friends and confided in each other their deepest, bitchiest secrets. If anyone knew who had hurt Jennifer, it was Whitney.

And since I didn't believe that Whitney had anything to do with the murders, I was safe talking to her—at least physically. Psychologically, I could be damaged for life. We were still talking about the evil Queen of Mean, after all.

But a positive way to look at it was that between Whitney and me, we knew everyone in Lighthouse Cove. I was close to the townies, while Whitney had her finger on the pulse of everything going on with the wealthy homeowners and rich tourists.

Once again, I prepared for the confrontation by making myself look really good. Hair, makeup, pretty clothes—the works. But when I pulled to the curb across the street and a few houses down from her place, I had second thoughts. Who could blame me? Maybe they were even third thoughts. I asked myself again: *Am I absolutely certain Whitney isn't the killer?*

"You're being ridiculous," I muttered. I reached for the door handle, then stopped. Was I doing the right thing? Maybe it was time to call Eric and ask him to join me.

"Oh, right." After all of his admonitions, he would sooner send a patrol car to arrest me than join me here at the Gallagher home to grill Tommy's wife about her best friend.

As I was sitting in my car, arguing with myself, Whitney's garage door opened. I froze. Was she going somewhere? The door took its sweet time before it opened all the way and Whitney drove out in her shiny black Jaguar. My gray truck was innocuous enough that she didn't seem to notice it was parked in front of her neighbor's house. The Jaguar's windows were tinted, but I could see someone sitting next to her in the passenger's seat.

Curious, I waited until they got to the end of the block and then I made a U-turn and followed them out to the Old Cove Highway, where they turned south. It was a beautiful if narrow and winding drive along the Alisal Cliffs. To the west, perched atop the cliffs, were more of the grand Victorians that made our little town famous. They overlooked the stretch of sandy beach below, and the rocky outcroppings and choppy blue ocean beyond.

Skirting the east side of the highway was a steeply wooded ravine. At the bottom was a pretty creek that overflowed every winter with clean, icy water, thanks to a tributary of the Eel River that got its start up in the snowy Mendocino National Forest, northeast of Potter Valley.

I followed behind Whitney at a good distance, catching sight of her every now and then along the winding road. She traveled another four miles, and if I had blinked I would've missed seeing her swerve to the right onto a pitted gravel road that led to the ocean.

I recognized this spot. Barnacle Beach. Back in high school, we used to drive out here every summer to go to the beach. It was more private than our local beaches in town and therefore more attractive to teenagers for parties and dates. It had been rumored that smoking and drinking occurred out here. Or so I'd heard. I certainly had never taken part in any of those activities. No more than five or six times, anyway.

Wood stairs had been built into the side of the cliff

that led down to the beach. There were caves here, too. I had been inside a few of them and had spent one memorable day exploring one of the deepest, darkest caves with Tommy.

At high tide, ocean water would fill them completely within minutes. Over the years, a few people had been drowned and washed out to sea. Parents always warned their children never to set foot inside the Alisal Caves, but what kid ever listened to advice like that?

Whitney came to a stop on the rutted gravel road a few yards from the edge of the cliff. I parked my truck behind a thicket of pine trees about a hundred yards back from where the Jaguar stopped and waited to see what would happen next.

Whitney and her passenger both got out of the car and faced each other. From where I stood, it looked like they were yelling. Her passenger was a woman, but I had to focus hard to see her face. Unfortunately, my vision wasn't quite back to normal, thanks to that thump on my head. I didn't notice the problem too much anymore unless I really had to work at it, like now. It didn't help that I was staring into the setting sun, either.

After a long moment of squinting, I suddenly realized who I was looking at. And that person was now pointing a *gun* directly at Whitney. *A gun?*

"Oh, my God."

The person holding the gun was Penny.

Chapter Fifteen

Penny.

My new friend. My new *client*. I had been to her house, wandered around in her attic. We had chatted and laughed at her kitchen table while she picked out colors and patterns for her remodel. We had gone to dinner together. Worked out together. She was the one who'd saved me from being choked by the weights on the bench press.

"No," I muttered, still dumbfounded. She hadn't saved me. She had sabotaged the rack, causing the weights to fall on me while she'd wandered off, looking innocent. She was no savior. She was a callous, vicious killer.

She was wearing a small backpack, I noticed as I watched her shove Whitney closer to the cliff. Was she going to push her over? I couldn't let that happen, no matter how ambivalent my feelings were for Whitney.

I grabbed my phone, pushed speed dial, and in seconds Eric answered. I told him where I was and what I was seeing.

"She's got a gun," I said, watching as Penny waved the weapon again. "I thought she was going to push her off the cliff, but now they're walking toward the steps that lead down to the beach. There's nothing down there but sand and water and caves. I'll bet she'll try to trap her inside one of the caves."

It was the only possibility I could come up with. I just didn't know why Penny had suddenly decided to target Whitney.

"Get out of there," Eric shouted. "I'm on my way."

"I'll stay until you get here."

"No, you won't. Drive away now."

"But you don't know where you're going."

"I'll find it," he insisted.

"Tell Tommy it's Barnacle Beach," I said, ignoring his demands. "You'll be able to see my truck from the highway and that's where you'll turn off."

"Damn it, Shannon."

"Hurry." I had to hold the phone away from my ear to keep from going deaf. For a soft-spoken man, he could really raise his voice when he wanted to.

I hung up, got out of the truck, and tiptoed around the trees to get a closer look, just in time to see Penny shove Whitney again. In her silly high heels, she stumbled along the grassy edge until she reached the top of the rickety old stairs that led down to the beach.

They disappeared down the steps. I was shaking now from fear as well as the cold breeze off the ocean, but I had to see what they were doing. I crept over to the edge of the cliff and saw them step onto the beach. Penny pushed Whitney toward the nearest cave as the tide rolled in.

Whitney suddenly let loose a scream and Penny smacked the back of her head. "Shut up!"

I could hear them all the way up the side of the cliff,

despite the roar of the ocean waves as they crashed a hundred feet offshore.

The two of them entered the cave and vanished from my sight.

I was tempted to scramble down the stairs and try to help, but I had no defense against a gun in the hands of a violent woman who had killed two people and attacked two—now *three*—others.

So I waited.

My mind envisioned the insides of the old caves. It had been fourteen years since I'd seen one, but I could still recall the moist darkness, the heavy, low walls, the rocks and sand, the clumps of seaweed strewn along the edges.

The caves were also home to the old, rusted trestles that had once been used as mooring for the ships that traveled along the coast from San Francisco up to British Columbia and back. This place had come to be called Barnacle Beach because of all the barnacles clinging to those old ship hulls.

A trestle would be good for tying someone up, I thought, and then shuddered at the possibility. I wouldn't put it past Penny to come up with that plan. All she had to do was tie Whitney to an old trestle post and let the incoming tide finish her off. It wasn't just evil; it was premeditated and downright diabolical.

The sun was starting to set and the sky was splashed in corals and pinks as Penny tramped out of the cave and crossed the sandy beach toward the stairs. I ran back to the tree line to watch and see what she would do. Was she actually going to leave Whitney to drown and then blithely drive off in her Jaguar? That was cold.

When Penny reached the top of the stairs, I could see

she was breathing a little heavier. It was a long, steep climb and she was probably moving on pure adrenaline by now. She must've stowed the gun in her backpack, because she wasn't holding it anymore. She stopped at the driver's side of the car, slipped off her backpack, and stood there, seeming to ponder her next move.

A piercing scream split the dusky air. It was Whitney crying for help, and the sound of it caused the hair on my arms to stand up on end.

Penny turned and stared out at the cliff's edge. She knew Whitney was going to die, but what else was she thinking? Did ice water flow through her veins? Did she really believe she would get away with this? God only knew what was going through her head.

In that moment, I didn't stop to think about it. I began to run toward her. My boots didn't make much noise on the grassy surface as I got closer. My only plan was to rush her, pin her down, and hold her there until Eric arrived with his cavalry. I just hoped they would make it in time to save Whitney.

Penny was still watching the ocean when I rushed up behind her and shoved her hard. She fell facedown on the ground.

"What the—?"

She scrambled to get up, but I jumped on top of her and straddled her back to keep her down. "You're not going anywhere."

"You." She laughed harshly. "You really think you can stop me, you wimp?"

"I'm not a wimp," I sputtered. Probably wasn't a good idea to argue with her, especially considering how strong she was. But that pissed me off. What had I ever done to her? Why did she want to kill me? "I thought we were getting to be friends."

Okay, it was a wimpy thing to say, but I couldn't think straight.

"You were asking too many questions," she snapped. "Then you brought that cop around."

"I didn't bring him . . . Wait." Why was I even talking to her? But I wanted answers. "I was the one he suspected, not you."

"He kept coming around to the bank," she griped. "And as soon as he saw me with you at the pub, he knew."

"That's ridiculous."

"I can read a cop's face."

"Oh, bull." If Eric had known that Penny killed those men, she would've been in jail.

"Shut up and get off me."

"Did you screw with my bike?"

"Of course," she derided. "There you were, riding around town like the Pink Princess everyone thinks you are. I thought it would be fun to shove a stick through the spokes, so to speak."

"So besides being a murderer, you're just a bitch."

"I'm a survivor," she snarled, and, without warning, she bucked and bounced me off her back. It took her a few seconds to get enough traction to run away, and in that moment I grabbed hold of her foot. She kicked my hand away and raced over to the car. Grabbing the backpack, she pulled out the gun. But I was already right behind her. I yanked on her arm and she bobbled the gun. I managed to slap it away with my other hand.

With a guttural growl, she smacked my face and I fell

backward, but caught myself before I hit the ground. She went running for the gun and I plowed into her. We both fell on the damp grass, but I was on top of her again and able to hold her down.

I could see the gun lying in the grass barely ten feet away.

Where the hell were the cops?

My cheek was stinging where she'd smacked me, and I wanted so much to start beating her head into the ground. I'd never been a violent person before but she was turning me into one.

"Tell me why you killed Jerry Saxton," I demanded.

She tried to buck me off again. I grabbed her hair and pulled it hard, causing her to shriek.

"You scream like a girl," I said, sneering. I hated to be petty, but it felt good to say that.

"Up yours," she snarled.

"Why did you kill him?"

"I did the world a favor," she blurted.

While that may have been true, I wanted to know what drove her to murder him. I asked her again and she grudgingly told me what had happened.

"He threatened to tell the entire town that I was in love with Jennifer."

I almost felt my jaw hit the ground. She must have sensed my confusion, because she tried to throw me off her again. I was ready this time, though, and held her down more forcefully.

"Okay, first of all," I said, "why would you fall for Jennifer? And second, how did Jerry find out? And third, who cares if you and Jennifer were an item? You can love whoever you want. Although that brings me back to my first question. How the hell could you ever like Jennifer? She's a horrible person, in case you couldn't tell."

And clinging to life right now, I remembered. "Oh yeah, and if you loved her so much, why did you try to kill her?"

"If you'll shut up for a minute, I'll tell you."

I grabbed hold of her jacket more tightly, just to let her know who was still on top. "Go ahead and talk."

She rambled on about first meeting Jennifer when she came into the bank to fill out some loan papers. And she added that she ended up telling Jerry all about it because he was just so darn easy to talk to.

I knew in an instant that Jennifer had only sweet-talked Penny for some ulterior motive. I almost felt sorry for this silly woman who'd bought into Jennifer's scheme. My pity for her was short-lived, though, since she'd tried to kill me more than once.

She was right about one thing: Jerry really had been very easy to talk to. I remembered that much from our blind date. Still, Penny was holding something back.

"Jerry may have been easy to talk to," I said, "but why would you tell him something so personal? Were you two honestly friends?"

"We worked on some loans together, got to know each other." I could hear the evasion in her voice.

It dawned on me what she was leaving out of the story. "You were the one who worked with him to scam those home buyers."

"I didn't mean to do it," she said, her voice whiny, "but it was easy money. Homeowners these days don't pay enough attention to their loan documents."

I let that sink in. Apparently it was easy to justify going from fraud to murder when you had no moral compass to start with.

"How did you get Jerry over to the Boyers' house?" I asked.

She shook her head in disgust, apparently realizing that I wasn't going to stop asking questions. "We had worked together on the Boyers' bank loan, so I told Jerry to meet me there to discuss an issue that came up over the closing costs. So we're standing in the kitchen and he starts coming on to me."

"What a jerk," I muttered, realizing that their confrontation must've taken place the night after our blind date. He really was something else.

"Yeah, so, needless to say, I refused his advances and that's when he started taunting me. He threatened to tell my boss that I was in love with a woman. I was furious. He was throwing back in my face something I'd told him in complete confidence. I guess I went a little crazy."

"So, you were in the kitchen, but he died in the basement."

"I was just waiting for the right moment. I'd seen your big pink toolbox in the corner of the kitchen and was looking through it. Meanwhile, Jerry's thinking everything's going his way. He opens the basement door and says we should go down and check out the work that you guys were doing. Like he really thought I was going to go down into the basement for some kind of romantic interlude with him."

"He seemed pretty clueless that way."

"Exactly. So I grabbed that big wrench and followed him downstairs. He was chatting like we were best friends as he wandered around the basement. I waited until he turned away from me and smashed the wrench down on his head. When I realized that he was dead, I wrapped up the wrench and tossed it into the sump pump. Then I got the hell out of there. Oh, but first I stopped and grabbed a bunch more of your tools. Because you never know. It's always good to be prepared."

I let that go. "Why did you kill Wendell?"

"Oh, come on. That guy deserved to die."

Her words gave me chills. There had been a point when I'd hated Wendell enough to be tempted to toss him over a cliff. But I wasn't about to act on it. Apparently Penny didn't have that same braking action on her emotions. No, for her it was *Get mad. Take him out.*

"But why did you kill him?" I asked again.

She didn't answer. Instead she twisted and tugged under me, but I continued to hold her down. Finally, panting heavily, she admitted, "I needed to deflect attention away from me."

"So you picked him out and just . . . killed him."

"He was an easy target. I met him at a bar on the pier one night. He was such a prissy thing, I was amused. So a few nights later I ran into him on the street and walked back to your place with him. I praised him and pretended to take his side on everything he complained about. He was bitching about your truck in the driveway and that's when I figured out what to do with him.

"I complimented him on his beautiful car and asked if we could take a ride. He drove around the block, but that was it. He didn't want to waste any gas. He was another jerk. Anyway. We sat inside the car, talking, while I waited for my moment. When he wasn't looking I pulled that screwdriver out of my purse and nailed him in the neck. I knew nobody in town would mourn his loss."

I had to force myself not to shiver at her cold words. She was a sociopath. Pure evil. And the fact that no one had noticed was chilling as well. I wondered if the people she'd killed here in my town were her first victims. I doubted it. This had all been too easy for her. I just had to keep her talking until Eric showed up. *Where is Eric?*

"Didn't you get blood all over you?"

She snickered. "I wore a plastic poncho over my clothes. I told him I thought it might rain."

I sighed. "So, once Wendell was dead, the police stopped coming around, asking you questions."

"Yeah. Pretty smart, huh?"

"Except that they turned their attention directly onto me."

"Oops. Sorry," she chirped in a mocking tone. She jerked her shoulder to pull her jacket away, but I grabbed it again. She jolted, trying to bounce me off, but that didn't work, either.

"Even if you do try to run," I said, "Jennifer will identify you once she recovers."

"You think so?" she said through clenched teeth. "Well, maybe I'll just sneak into the hospital and finish the job."

I was certain that she planned to do it, anyway, and the thought of her sauntering down the hospital hall in a fake nurse's uniform made my stomach turn again. I switched the subject back to her main issue.

"I still don't get what the big deal is about you liking women. Just because Jerry knew didn't mean he could hurt you with the information."

"You're really nosy."

I couldn't dispute that. "Well?"

"Fine. In case you never noticed, Jerry liked to research the people he was dealing with. After I told him about Jennifer, he delved into my past. It didn't take him long to find out what really happened at my former job."

"What a scumbag."

"Yeah. And by the way, Jerry seemed to know a lot of dirty little secrets around town. He enjoyed using the information to get what he wanted."

"I'm glad I kicked him," I muttered. "Still, that was no reason to kill him. Nobody here cares that you're gay."

"You don't know what you're talking about," she chided angrily. "A year ago I lost my job because the homophobic old bat who ran the bank didn't want *my kind* working in her family-owned bank. I wasn't about to let that happen again."

"You should've sued those people."

"Easy for you to say."

"Did you drain my truck battery?"

She cocked her head and gave me a puzzled look. "Why would I do that?"

"Did you rig the bench-press rack to break while I was on it?"

She smiled. "That was almost too easy. And it was so sweet of you to think I saved your life."

"Stupid of me."

Whitney's shrieks echoed from down below. I knew how fast the tide could come in. I estimated that it had been fifteen minutes since I'd called, so where were the damn cops?

The sounds of Whitney's cries must have spurred

Penny on to try to escape my hold. Without warning, her entire body quaked and kicked until she succeeded in throwing me off. I fell backward and she was able to push herself up and dash off.

"You're not getting away," I shouted.

She headed straight for the gun, but I dove at her, wrapped my arms around her waist, and pulled her back. She tossed me off again and ran blindly toward the cliff's edge.

"Look out!" I screamed, and took a flying leap to tackle her sideways. It stopped her from going over the ledge, but she was furious now. She slapped me again and we grappled with each other, rolling and tumbling closer to the precipice.

Penny shoved my face away and I futilely punched her shoulders. I wasn't much of a fighter, but I refused to let her get away. I also refused to fall off the side of the damn cliff, so I grabbed her jacket and yanked as hard as I could. It stopped our momentum just inches from the cliff's edge. I don't know how I did it, but I pulled her a few feet and flipped her over onto her back. Then I leaped on top of her again and straddled her, holding her shoulders down.

"Why did you use my tools?" I shouted. "Why did you try to frame me? And then you turned around and tried to kill me. Why?"

"I told you," she said through clenched teeth. "You were getting too close. I saw that look you gave me that night at the gym. I could tell you suspected me. The only reason I went to dinner with you was to keep an eye on you. When you invited the cop to sit with us, that's when I knew you couldn't be trusted."

I choked on a laugh. "I looked at you suspiciously because you were giggling with Jennifer. I couldn't believe you had the bad taste to like her. I thought I wanted to be your friend, but that wasn't going to happen if you were friends with her."

She sniffed. "You can't choose the people you fall in love with."

"Oh, spare me," I said. "She was just using you to get a bank loan."

She froze. "That's not true."

"I've known her a long time," I said. "She doesn't do anything without an ulterior motive. Usually a self-serving or malicious one."

Penny took a long, deep breath in and let it out slowly as she seemed to ponder that possibility.

I almost felt sorry for her in that moment, but knew the feeling would pass. "Okay, okay, you loved her. So why did you try to kill her?"

"She was starting to hound me about the loan," she admitted. "She wanted more money. I'd already taken a chance by approving the original loan, even though her credit was too lousy to get one. Then I found out she told Whitney about me. They decided to have a little fun and blackmail me. I decided that both of them would have to die."

As if on cue, Whitney's screams grew even more shrill and earsplitting.

I must've looked alarmed, because Penny chuckled. "Oh, don't pretend you wouldn't love to see the end of that loudmouthed bitch."

"I'm not saying I care for her, but you don't get to go around killing people you don't like!"

"Don't see why not," Penny argued. "At least it's honest."

Honest? I shook my head in revulsion. *Try* psychopathic.

"You tried to kill me, too. Remember?"

"Nothing personal."

When Whitney shrieked again, it grated on my soul. I knew that even if Penny escaped me, she couldn't hide from the police forever. Meanwhile, Whitney was probably close to drowning. I considered my options. There were only two: let Penny go and rescue Whitney, or stay with Penny until the police arrived. And Whitney could die in the interim.

Sensing my hesitation, Penny took advantage. She jerked her arm loose and swung at my head, clipping me above my ear, right where she'd pounded me with the hammer a few days ago.

I groaned and fell sideways. She pushed me off her and started to run, but her feet slipped on the wet grass and in the next instant she slid right off the edge of the cliff.

I screamed and scrambled to grab her.

She managed to clutch a thick tuft of the elephant grass that grew along the edge. Now she was hanging on precariously.

"Take my hand," I shouted.

"Go screw yourself," she yelled.

"I'll pull you up."

I could hear sirens now, growing louder and more urgent. Several cars screeched to a stop near my truck, and within seconds Eric was out of his car and running across the ground to my side.

"She's going to fall," I shouted. "Can you pull her up?"

As Eric sprawled by the cliff's edge, Tommy came sprinting over, frantic. "Where's Whitney?"

I pointed toward the steps. "She's tied up in one of the caves. The tide is coming in. Hurry!"

He took off on a run just as Whitney's shrill scream filled the air again.

Eric reached his hand down over the edge. "Grab my hand."

"Penny, take his hand," I begged her.

"Let me go," she cried. "I'd rather die than go to prison."

"Don't be an idiot!" I yelled.

She glared right at me. "No way am I going to live the rest of my life in a ten-foot cell with someone called Big Beulah."

I could see her point, but she didn't have to die to prove it. Her hand slid down the long blades of thick grass.

"She's letting go," I screamed.

"Oh no, she isn't," Eric muttered tightly.

Just as Penny released her grip on the elephant grass, he snagged her wrist and hauled her up the cliff in one smooth motion.

"Wow," I said. He'd lifted her as if she were a child. Now, those were some serious muscles.

Eric scowled. "No way am I having another dead body on my hands." He turned to a waiting officer. "Cuff her."

It was poetic justice that Penny would have to suck it up and play nice with Big Beulah after all.

A few minutes later, Tommy arrived at the top of the stairs holding his terrified, wet, and exhausted wife in his arms.

"Is she all right?" Eric asked.

"She will be," Tommy said grimly.

"Ambulance is right behind us."

"Thanks." Tommy walked away, clutching Whitney for dear life.

"Are you all right?" Eric asked me.

I pushed back my hair. "Yeah. A little shaken up and smacked around, but I'll be fine."

"You look different. Your hair is straight."

I'd forgotten. "Yeah."

He touched the neckline of my wrinkled, grass-stained red sweater. "That's a pretty color on you."

"Thanks. I always like to dress for these outdoor events."

He choked on a laugh, then shook his head. "You scared me—you know that?"

"I scared myself."

"I'm glad to hear it." He pulled me close and held on. "Don't do it again."

It took me a few seconds to get over my surprise, but then I wrapped my arms around his waist, feeling warm and comfy in his embrace.

"I'm going to give it another minute or five," he murmured in my ear. "And then I'm going to start yelling at you for disregarding my orders."

I smiled and breathed him in. "I can live with that."

Chapter Sixteen

Two weeks later, things in Lighthouse Cove were settling back to normal.

Conversations no longer ceased when I walked into a room. People didn't stop to stare at me as I strolled down the sidewalk. My bike was repaired and tidied up and ready to ride again. I wasn't having nightmares about people chasing me with oversized pink tools anymore.

There had been a few surprises, like when Tommy and Whitney came to my house to personally thank me for following Whitney's car out to Barnacle Beach. Tommy raved on and on about my foresight and courage. I was about to suggest a group hug when Whitney put things into perspective for me.

"You probably think I owe you my life," she said evenly, "but don't hold your breath waiting for me to do your laundry or something."

Yeah, I would've told her the same thing.

I never heard a word of thanks from Jennifer Bailey, and that was fine with me. But just to set things right, I let Whitney know that Penny had threatened to sneak into the hospital and put Jennifer out of her misery forever. If I hadn't stopped her on the cliff's edge, she might've carried it off. So Jennifer knew she owed me big-time. And that was satisfying enough for now.

Eric told me that as soon as Jennifer came out of the coma, she pointed the finger at Penny as the person who tried to strangle her.

Eric also let me know that before I'd called him from Barnacle Beach, he had already narrowed his search down to Penny and was on his way to take her in for questioning when he got my phone call.

He came by my house a few days after Penny was carted off to jail. It was a sunny afternoon so I poured iced tea for us both and we sat in the wicker chairs on my front porch.

"I realized that Penny was lying," he said, "after I checked out what she told you about her fear of cops."

"Oh, right. The night I had dinner with her at the pub."

"Yes. She completely fabricated that story about the cop shooting one of the tellers at her old bank."

"I'll bet she made it up on the spot to keep me from guessing the real reason why she didn't want you to sit with us." I shook my head in disgust. "She must've had a hard time keeping all of those lies straight."

"That's how a lot of criminals get caught," Eric said.

We talked for a while longer and I realized I was growing more comfortable around him every day. It was nice. Such a difference from the first time we'd met at a crime scene and he'd taken me in for questioning.

I smiled and sat back in the cushioned chair, studying his muscular arms and big strong hands as he sipped his iced tea. And that's when he informed me in no uncertain terms that if I ever pulled something like I did at

Barnacle Beach again, he would toss me into a jail cell for my own protection.

"Believe it," he said, reaching over to give my hand a friendly squeeze.

So, that was sweet.

Mac, meanwhile, was still living in my garage apartment and planned to stay there through the restoration of the old lighthouse mansion. He was still insisting on hiring me and my crew for the work and I couldn't be happier about that. He also insisted that he liked the view from his apartment of the garden and especially the gardener. Me. I liked when he said cute stuff like that, even though my face would turn red. I was just as glad that he was sticking around, because I liked having him nearby. He made me laugh, among other things.

When I finally returned home from Barnacle Beach that day, Mac had been waiting by the gate.

"Irish," he said.

"Mac," I said, breathing a sigh of relief. Seeing him made me so happy, I thought I might cry.

"I hear you've just escaped from the clutches of a psychopathic killer." He said it as casually as he might've commented on the weather. "You lead the most interesting life."

"I could go for a little less excitement," I said.

"That's too bad. I was hoping to hear you rehash all the grisly details."

We had a good laugh, and while I thought I'd never want to relive those moments fighting Penny on the cliff, he made it easy for me to talk about it. After an hour of conversation and a glass of wine, I felt better and Mac went back to work on his book.

A week later, Mac announced that he had finished his latest story in record time. He asked me to read the manuscript and give him my honest opinion. I was thrilled and honored and touched, but also deeply afraid that if I didn't love it, I wouldn't know what to say.

Thankfully, I loved it. But I still didn't know what to say to him except that I'd finished it.

He decided we should celebrate, so he invited himself over for dinner. He grilled steaks and I made garlic mashed potatoes and a salad. We had moved to the living room couch to finish the last of our wine before I finally told him my feelings. "I really enjoyed your new book."

He grinned boyishly. "Don't hold back. Tell me everything you loved about it."

"Okay," I said, laughing. "Well, first of all, Jake Slater is awesome."

He nodded intently. "That part is autobiographical."

I laughed again, something I seemed to do a lot when I was with Mac. "I really loved the climax where he was tied up in the cave and the tide was coming in. It was amazing to see how he untied his ropes underwater."

"That's his Navy SEAL training."

"I know. I loved it."

"Good." He shifted on the couch until he was looking right at me. "How'd you like his evil twin?"

"Fantastic. Frightening. Truly evil. I believed him completely." I took a sip of my wine.

"Don't stop there," he said, amused.

I hesitated. "Well, I thought this book was more romantic than the others you've written."

"You think so? But I always have a woman or two in the story."

"But Jake actually falls in love this time. With Shana."

"What man wouldn't fall in love with her?" he wondered.

"And she's still alive at the end. That was a surprise. Any woman Jake gets close to usually dies."

"Yeah, that's getting old." He gave a casual shrug. "But beyond that, there was no way I could kill Shana."

"I'm glad you didn't."

"Tell me what you thought of her."

"She was wonderful." I bit back a smile. "Courageous and smart. Their banter was hilarious. But I particularly liked her tangled red hair and wide green eyes the color of sea grass."

"I particularly liked that about her, too," he said as he reached out to play with a thick strand of my hair. "I must admit I was inspired."

"Jake definitely seems smitten by her," I said, staring at my wineglass.

"I know the feeling," he murmured.

I met his gaze. "What will your readers think of her?"

He set down his wineglass and took my hand in his. "My editor once told me that if I ever wanted Jake to settle down with one woman, I would have to make sure she was completely worthy of him. Shana is worthy of Jake. My readers are going to love her."

"I hope so."

"Oh yeah. Especially when she saves Jake's life by blasting his evil twin with her nail gun."

"She kicked his ass," I said heartily.

Mac laughed as he leaned over and kissed me. "At the risk of repeating myself, I know the feeling."

My girlfriends took me out to dinner at Uncle Pete's wine bar to quietly celebrate the end of Penny Wells's horrific killing spree.

As we all shared the large antipasto salad appetizer, Marigold studied me. "You've changed over the past few weeks, Shannon."

"I'm wearing glasses," I said. Apparently, getting my head bonked had weakened my eyesight ever so slightly. The ophthalmologist thought I would completely recover my full vision eventually, but for the time being, I was more comfortable wearing my new glasses at night, when my eyes tended to get tired.

"They're really cute, but that's not it," she said, shaking her head.

"So how do you mean?" I wondered.

"You're happier," Lizzie said thoughtfully.

Jane smiled knowingly. "I think you've found your niche."

"Oh, definitely," Emily said, and glanced around the table. "Wait. Did she lose it somewhere along the way?"

I laughed. A few years back, I had told Jane and Lizzie that I wanted to rediscover that happy niche I felt I'd lost when Tommy broke up with me back in high school.

Had I really not found happiness in all the years since then? That sounded a little pathetic—and not true at all. I loved my life, my work, and my friends. My house and my garden. My town. The beach. Beautiful sunsets. Ocean breezes. I had been content for a long time. Still . . . I thought about it now and concluded that I did feel happier these days. I let it go at that.

Jane swirled her wineglass. "It probably helps that you've vanquished the enemy and have two gorgeous men besotted by your charms."

"Vanquished," Marigold murmured, clearly impressed. "That's a good word."

Emily leaned over to look at Jane. *"Besotted,* really?"

"Don't mind Jane," Lizzie said, shaking her head. "She's back on a Regency romance kick."

"Whatever you want to call it," Emily said wisely, "that's quite a lovely niche to fall into."

I couldn't have agreed more.

Keep reading for an excerpt from
Kate Carlisle's next Fixer-Upper Mystery . . .

This Old Homicide

Available in paperback!

"It's a monstrosity, isn't it?"

I gazed at the behemoth structure before us and hid my dismay with a bland smile. "No, not at all. It's . . . beautiful. In its own way."

"You're a terrible liar, Shannon," my friend Emily said. Her soft Scottish accent was thicker than usual, probably due to the stress of deciding to buy a house and then doing so in less than two days. "But I appreciate your attempt to make me feel better."

She frowned at the three-story, multigabled, over-spindled, gingerbread-laden . . . *monstrosity*—there was no better word for it—she'd just purchased. The old Victorian house was shrouded in shadows, making it appear even more foreboding than it might've been if even a smidgen of sunlight had been allowed to peep through the thick copse of soaring eucalyptus and redwood trees that surrounded the place on three sides. This wasn't the time to mention it, but I planned to suggest a good tree trimming once Emily closed the deal.

To be honest, the place was magnificent—if you overlooked the obvious: peeling paint, broken shutters, slumping roof. All of that was cosmetic and could be magically transformed by a good contractor. Luckily for Emily, that was me. I'm Shannon Hammer, a building contractor specializing in Victorian-home renovation and repair. I took over Hammer Construction five years ago when my dad suffered a mild heart attack and decided to retire. I had grown up working on the grand Victorian homes that proliferated along this part of the Northern California coastline, so I couldn't wait to get started on Emily's.

For many years, Emily had been living in the small but pretty apartment above her adorable tea shop on the town square. In the last few years, though, the square, with its multitude of fabulous restaurants and charming shops, had become such a popular destination spot that she'd decided it was time to find a quieter place to live. When an uncle back in Scotland died and left her some money, Emily decided that with property values being what they were, it was a good time to buy her first home.

She had announced her major purchase earlier today, after gathering together our small circle of friends in the back room of her tea shop.

"Champagne?" I said when I walked in and saw the yummy spread and the expensive open bottle in her hand. "What's going on?"

My friend Lizzie shook her head. "I don't know. Did somebody die?"

Jane, my oldest friend, laughed. "I don't think we'd be drinking champagne if somebody died."

"Are you sure?" Lizzie whispered. "Maybe that's how they do it in Scotland."

Emily, clearly excited, shushed everyone and held up

her glass. "I want to propose a toast to the town's newest homeowner. Me."

"You bought a house?" I said, a little stunned that I hadn't heard. I liked to think I had my finger on the pulse of the housing market in Lighthouse Cove.

"Cheers!" Marigold cried.

Lizzie gave Emily a quick hug. "That's wonderful, Emily."

Emily took another sip of champagne before placing her glass on the table. "I figured it was about time I set down roots in Lighthouse Cove."

"You think so?" Marigold said, laughing. "You've only lived here for ten years."

She grinned. "I'm a thrifty Scotswoman. It takes me a while to part with money."

Emily had moved from Scotland all those years ago with her boyfriend, who was going into business with one of our local fishermen. Sadly, a year later, the boyfriend was lost at sea. Emily was devastated, but decided to stay in Lighthouse Cove. She had only recently opened her tea shop and she had her good close friends who saw her through the tragedy.

"Where's the house?" I asked.

"It's over on Emerald Way," she said. "Overlooking North Bay."

I pictured the neighborhood with its glorious pine trees and amazing view of the coast. I'd worked on a number of homes in that area, and as far as I could remember, there was only one available house and it was . . . whoa. "You bought the old Rawley mansion?"

"Yes," Emily said, and paused to pat her chest. "I get

a little breathless when I think about it. I can't wait for you all to see it."

I exchanged a look of concern with Jane, but quickly covered my unease with a happy smile. "If you need any help with renovation or with the move itself, I'm available."

"We'll all help," Jane said.

"Thank you. That means so much." Emily blinked, overcome with emotion. "And, yes, Shannon, I would love your help with the rehab. It needs a lot of work," she admitted, "but I had to have this house. I can't explain it, but it spoke to me. It's going to look like a fairy castle when it's all spiffed-up. I can't wait to move in."

"When do you close escrow?" Lizzie asked.

"Since nobody's living there, I was able to get a fifteen-day escrow."

"Good grief, that's fast," Marigold murmured.

Lizzie nodded. "The faster she closes the deal, the faster Shannon can get started on the rehab."

"Well, then." Jane raised her glass again. "Here's to Emily's castle."

"May all your dreams come true," Lizzie said fondly, and we drank down the rest of the sparkly champagne.

Now, as I gazed up at the old house, I knew Emily *really* needed help. Still, the place had good bones and that's what counted. Right?

At the thought of good bones, I shivered. I wondered if Emily had heard the tales of old Grandma Rawley's ghost still haunting the place. It didn't matter. All those scary stories were just silly urban legends, meant to frighten small children on Halloween. Weren't they?

I brushed those thoughts aside. Everything would be

fine. There was no such thing as ghosts. I repeated the mantra as I studied how the roof rolled and dipped in spots.

Emily frowned as the sun slipped behind a cloud and the house grew even darker. "Perhaps I exaggerated a bit, thinking you might be able to turn it into a fairy castle."

"Don't worry. I'll make it beautiful for you," I assured her, and I meant it. Making Victorian homes look beautiful was my business, after all.

Years ago, our town had been designated a National Historical Landmark District because of all the Victorian-era homes and buildings located here. The Rawley mansion had once been a gorgeous example of that nineteenth-century-Victorian style, until the last Rawley heir died and their gracious home was left to rot. But it didn't have to stay that way. Within a few months, my crew and I would restore it to its original luster, and this shadowy eyesore before us would be a vague memory.

"Thank you, Shannon." She slung her arm around my shoulders and gave me a quick squeeze. "If anyone can do it, you can."

"Never doubt it."

She laughed. "I did doubt it for a while, but now I must admit I'm starting to get excited."

"I don't blame you. The house is amazing."

She looked up at the imposing structure. "Or it soon will be."

It was true—the house really was amazing, if you had the vision to see past its dilapidated exterior.

It was a classic Queen Anne Victorian, but with one eclectic detail that must've suited the original owner's idiosyncratic style. The rounded, three-story tower on the front-left side of the house was topped by what they used to call a Hindustani roof. Instead of the typical tower roof that came to a point like a witch's hat, this one's undulating profile resembled a large bell. It sat atop a small, round balcony roomy enough for a table and two chairs. Emily thought it would be the perfect place to enjoy a cocktail and watch the sun set.

The rest of the home was more traditional, with a deep-shadowed entrance framed by elaborate ornamentation, asymmetrical rooflines, a wraparound porch, fish-scale shingles on the lower half of the house, and four chimneys.

On the downside, a number of the balusters were rotten or simply missing from the porch railing. The stained glass on the door was cracked and faded. Externally, the ravages of time, termites, overgrown plants, and stiff ocean breezes were obvious. Internally, anything was possible. A family of raccoons could've taken up residence. Wood floors could be rotted clean through. Pipes might be fractured. I just prayed I wouldn't have to rebuild the whole thing from scratch.

I dismissed those thoughts. Why invite trouble? Once escrow closed in a few weeks and Emily took possession of the house, she and I would conduct a sober walk-through to determine exactly what the rehab would entail. Depending on the amount of work, she would be able to move in within three to four months. I had a feeling that that would be cutting it close—like, by a year maybe—but for one of my dearest friends, I was determined to make the timing work. I was already mentally rearranging my crew members' schedules. Emily's monstrosity was now at the top of my long priority list.

I wanted her new home to be spiffed-up, as she put it, in record time.

"Looking on the bright side," she said with a cheerful grin, "at least there won't be any dead bodies in the basement. I checked."

I swallowed uneasily. "That's good to know." A few months ago, I had come across that very thing. A man had been murdered in the basement of a home I'd been refurbishing. I was the one who'd discovered the body and our new chief of police was not amused. For a short while, my name was at the top of his suspect list until the killer decided to focus on me. I never wanted to go through anything like that again.

"I'd better be getting back to the tea shop," Emily said with reluctance, and turned to walk to her car. "I really appreciate your coming out here to take a look with me."

"I'm glad I did. I can't wait to get started." But as I opened the car door, I took one more look at the old Rawley mansion and shivered.

I had a sinking feeling that raccoons would be the least of her problems.